FOUR CHILDREN and IT

Jacqueline Wilson

FOUR CHILDREN and IT

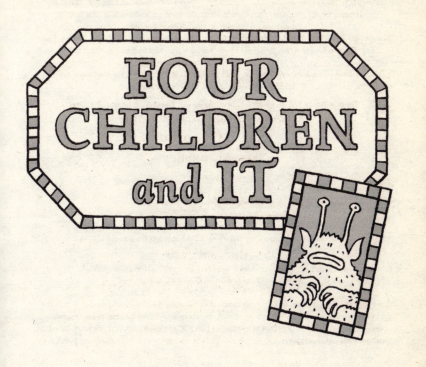

PUFFIN

PUFFIN BOOKS

Published by the Penguin Group

Penguin Books Ltd, 80 Strand, London WC2R 0RL, England

Penguin Group (USA) Inc., 375 Hudson Street, New York, New York 10014, USA

Penguin Group (Canada), 90 Eglinton Avenue East, Suite 700, Toronto, Ontario, Canada M4P 2Y3
(a division of Pearson Penguin Canada Inc.)

Penguin Ireland, 25 St Stephen's Green, Dublin 2, Ireland (a division of Penguin Books Ltd)

Penguin Group (Australia), 707 Collins Street, Melbourne, Victoria 3008, Australia
(a division of Pearson Australia Group Pty Ltd)

Penguin Books India Pvt Ltd, 11 Community Centre, Panchsheel Park, New Delhi – 110 017, India

Penguin Group (NZ), 67 Apollo Drive, Rosedale, Auckland 0632, New Zealand
(a division of Pearson New Zealand Ltd)

Penguin Books (South Africa) (Pty) Ltd, Block D, Rosebank Office Park, 181 Jan Smuts Avenue,
Parktown North, Gauteng 2193, South Africa

Penguin Books Ltd, Registered Offices: 80 Strand, London WC2R 0RL, England

puffinbooks.com

First published 2012
This edition published 2013

005

Text copyright © Jacqueline Wilson, 2012
Illustrations copyright © Nick Sharratt, 2012
All rights reserved

The moral right of the author and illustrator has been asserted

Set in Baskerville MT Std
Typeset by Palimpsest Book Production Limited, Falkirk, Stirlingshire
Printed in Great Britain by Clays Ltd, St Ives plc

British Library Cataloguing in Publication Data
A CIP catalogue record for this book is available from the British Library

ISBN: 978-0-141-34144-6

www.greenpenguin.co.uk

Penguin Books is committed to a sustainable
future for our business, our readers and our planet.
This book is made from Forest Stewardship
Council™ certified paper.

For Alex and Elv

'What's that you're reading?' said Smash, grabbing the book out of my hand.

'Hey, give it back,' I said, but she waved it out of my reach and poked me sharply with her elbow when I tried to retrieve it. She was always grabbing my things when she was bored. Her stupid nickname should have been Smash-and-Grab.

'*Five Children and It*,' Smash read in a silly voice. 'Well, that's a stupid title for a start. What's the *It*?'

'It's the Psammead,' I said.

'What's a Sammyadd?' asked Smash. She seemed mildly interested now. 'Is it a monster?'

The only books she ever read were Marvel O'Kaye horror stories, the gorier the better.

I

'No, it's a strange magic creature, a sand fairy,' I said.

'A *fairy*!' said Smash scornfully. 'I grew out of those silly fairy stories when I was *six*. You're such a baby, Rosalind.'

'It's not a *silly* fairy, it's a very pernickety creature like a monkey with eyes out on stalks and it grants wishes,' I said. 'It's a fabulous story.'

'You're such a sad little nerd – you think all books are fabulous,' said Smash.

She hitched herself up on the kitchen table and leafed through my book, waving her legs. My brother, Robbie, happened to be *under* the table, lying on his stomach, privately playing with his zoo animals. Smash's feet in their sparkly trainers were swinging dangerously near his head, so he wriggled back against the wall. He liked arguing with Smash even less than I did.

Smash paused at a picture.

'Why are they wearing these weird clothes? They look stupid,' she said.

I sighed. Robbie under the table sighed. Doubtless all his little plastic lions and tigers and elephants sighed too. It was Smash who was stupid, not the children in the illustration. She was seriously the worst stepsister in the world.

'It was written more than a hundred years ago,' I said. 'So the children are dressed in Edwardian clothes, pinafores and knickerbockers.'

'Knickerbockers to you too,' said Smash. 'I hate historical books.' She yawned and casually chucked my book on the floor. She was deliberately trying to pick a fight – and I knew who would win.

'Exactly how old are you?' I said, trying to sound lofty. 'Even Maudie behaves better than you.' I picked my book up. Some of the pages were crumpled now. I tried to smooth them, my fingers trembling. I didn't know how I was going to cope, being with Smash day after day. She was so hateful to everyone – especially Robbie and me. She was younger than me and yet I couldn't help feeling scared of her.

'Oh, diddums, did your boring little book get all bumped?' said Smash. She swung her legs harder and felled two elephants and a monkey. 'Whoops!' said Smash.

Robbie's hand shot out, trying to gather up his fallen beasts.

'Help, there's a wriggly, scrabbly thing under there. Perhaps it's a rat? Better stamp on it quick,' said Smash, sliding down from the table and stamping hard on Robbie's hand.

'Stop it! You leave my brother alone, you big bully,' I said, goaded into losing my temper at last.

Robbie didn't say anything because he was trying so hard not to cry, but he made his favourite lion bite Smash on the ankle. She laughed at this little plastic nibble, seized the lion and tossed it high in the air. It

3

landed on all four paws on the Jamie Oliver cookbook on the kitchen shelf.

'Hey, that lion should be in the circus doing tricks like that,' said Smash, jumping up and snatching it back. 'You know that trick where the trainer puts his head in the lion's mouth? Well, this lion would be rubbish at that – but maybe we could try the lion putting his head in the trainer's mouth? Yeah, nice one.' She put the little lion in her mouth and bit down heavily.

'*No!*' Robbie screamed.

I jumped up, seized hold of her and yanked hard at the lion's haunches. It came out glistening with Smash-saliva – and streaked with blood.

'Ow! You made my lip bleed, you pig!' said Smash, holding her mouth.

'Good! It's your own fault,' I said, though my heart was pounding. 'Why do you have to be so hateful all the time?'

'Because I can't stand you or your pathetic little wimpy brother and I wish you'd clear off,' said Smash.

'Hello, kids! What's all the shouting about?' said Dad, bursting into the kitchen. He stood there in his pyjamas, scratching his head. He looked at Smash. 'I don't think that sounded very friendly.'

'*They* weren't being friendly to me!' said Smash. 'Look!'

She stuck her chin up and pointed to her cut lip. Dad peered at the little smear of blood.

'How did you cut your lip, Smash?'

4

Smash looked pointedly in my direction.

'Rosalind?' said Dad, sounding astonished. 'Rosalind, you didn't *hit* your sister, did you?'

'She's not my real sister,' I mumbled stupidly.

'I can't believe you hit her!' said Dad.

'She was sticking up for me,' said Robbie, crawling out from under the table.

'Oh, so you let your sister fight your battles for you, do you, Robert?' Dad said coldly.

'Well, I'm not very good at fighting,' said Robbie, truthfully enough.

'What were you fighting *about*?' asked Dad.

We stared at our bare feet. I chased a couple of corn-flakes with my big toe. We'd been eating them straight out of the packet and some had got spilt.

Dad sighed heavily. 'Oh, never mind. But you watch that temper, Rosalind. Don't you ever hit anyone again! I'm not having that sort of behaviour in my house. Now come on, help me start breakfast, chop chop.'

Dad bustled to the crockery cupboard and trod heavily on one of Robbie's scattered animals.

'For God's sake!' He picked up the elephant and chucked it at Robbie. 'You're worse than Maudie for scattering your toys. Aren't you a bit old for this sort of thing anyway?'

Robbie hung his head. Didn't Dad *remember*? He gave Robbie his first three animals himself when he still came to see us every weekend and took us to the zoo.

5

'I don't know,' said Dad, shaking his head. 'I have a daughter who picks fights and a son who hides away with his toys under the table. You're the wrong way round, kids. I shall have to put you in a bag and shake you.' He was saying it as if it was part of a comedy routine, but Robbie and I burnt, not finding it the slightest bit funny.

Smash laughed at us, knowing Dad wouldn't pick on her. It wasn't fair. We knew Dad didn't like Smash any more than we did, but he didn't criticize her because she was Alice's child, not his.

Alice herself didn't appear until we'd all had breakfast and Dad was on his second cup of coffee.

'Hello, darlings,' she said, wafting around, smiling at us, like a famous actress onstage, expecting a round of applause. She was still in her filmy nightie that showed a little too much of her, but her long blonde hair was carefully brushed and she was wearing her glossy pink lipstick.

'It's so lovely to have you all here together,' she said, clasping her hands.

We stared at her. Who did she think she was kidding? She didn't want any of us, not even Smash, her own daughter. We usually came separately in the holidays, Robbie and me first, and then Smash. But this summer Smash's dad was off to the Seychelles on honeymoon with his new wife, and our mum had gone to her Open University Summer School. So we were all stuck here in Dad's house in Surrey, playing Happy Families.

I was missing Mum terribly, even though I'd seen her only yesterday. I was sure Mum must be missing us too. She'd cried when she hugged us goodbye. It was so awful never having Mum and Dad together any more, like a proper family. We'd wanted to see Dad this summer, of course – but we didn't want to see Alice. We especially didn't want to see Smash.

We didn't mind little Maudie, though.

'Hello, hello, hello!' said Maudie, right on cue, like a very tiny comic policeman. She shuffled precariously after Alice in her pyjama bottoms, a pink-and-cream bra slung round her neck, a pair of high-heeled sandals on her tiny feet.

'I'm a big grown-up lady,' she said.

She staggered across the room, smiling at us. This time we all smiled back, even Smash.

'Maudie!' I said, holding my arms out.

I loved my funny little half-sister *so* much. She seemed to love me too, and followed me around like a little shadow when we stayed with Dad and Alice. But now Smash was here as well. She leapt up, grabbed Maudie and spun her round and round. Maudie's high heels went flying and she shrieked with laughter.

'Careful, Smash. Don't be so rough with her,' said Alice.

Smash flushed. 'I wasn't being rough,' she said.

'She's only little. Put her down. She'll get dizzy,' said Alice.

Maudie wriggled free, still chuckling. She found Robbie's lion and put it in her own mouth experimentally.

'No, Maudie, *dirty*!' said Dad, squatting down beside her and putting his hand out. 'Give it to Daddy-Pop.'

Robbie and I looked at each other. *We'd* never called him Daddy-Pop.

Maudie took the lion out of her mouth, gave it a kiss on the end of its muzzle and handed it over. Dad wiped the lion on his pyjama sleeve, and then peered at it.

'Good lord, Maudie's left teeth marks!' said Dad.

'Maudie have lion back now?' said Maudie hopefully.

'Well, don't bite him so hard, darling. You'll hurt your little toothipegs,' said Dad, washing the lion thoroughly under the kitchen tap. He dried it with a clean tea towel and handed it over to Maudie with a flourish.

'There! Say tank-oo to Daddy-Pop,' said Dad, making Robbie and Smash and me squirm.

'Tank-oo,' said Maudie obligingly.

We were sure she could say 'thank you' perfectly, but Dad and Alice seemed to prefer her to speak baby talk.

'It's *my* lion, actually,' Robbie muttered.

He sat beside Maudie at the table while she ate her special yoghurt with chopped-up banana. He made the lion prowl up and down, roaring hungrily, while Maudie giggled.

'Why can't she have ordinary cornflakes and toast,

like us?' said Smash, helping herself to another slice of bread from the packet, and spreading it thickly with butter and strawberry jam.

'Well, we like her to have a healthy diet. We don't want her to get fat,' said Alice.

Smash flushed again. It was clear this was a dig at her. She wasn't *fat* fat, but she was podgier than she'd been last time we saw her.

'You're mad, Mum,' she said. 'Maudie will end up anorexic by the time she's ten if you keep fuss-fuss-fussing about her weight when she's still only a baby.'

Alice's mouth twitched, as if she might start saying all sorts of unkind things about Smash's weight. I edged towards the kitchen door, clutching my book, hoping to escape. I couldn't go up to my bedroom because I was sharing with Smash, while Robbie had a camp bed squashed into Maudie's room. There wasn't anywhere I could be totally private. Even if I locked myself in the loo someone would come banging on the door. I wished I had a torch and then I could hole up in the cupboard under the stairs.

'Where are you off to, Rosy-Posy?' said Dad.

I felt myself grow hot. I hadn't been called that since I was Maudie's age. Smash snorted with laughter.

I mumbled something about reading my book.

'Oh, for goodness' sake, sweetheart – you and your books! You can't just slope off by yourself and *read*. Let's make the most of our time. We'll have a real family day out, how about that?' Dad rubbed his hands together cheerily. 'Where shall we go then?'

'Chessington World of Adventures,' said Smash. 'They've got some really cool rides.'

'And I think they've got animals!' said Robbie, gathering up his own plastic zoo. He made a lion and tiger dance in front of Maudie. 'You'd like to see the animals, wouldn't you, Maudie?'

'Yes, animals, big doggies,' said Maudie, patting them happily.

'And we'll all go on amazing roller coasters,' said Smash, grabbing the lion and tiger, and making them swoop wildly up and down.

'Watch out, darling. You nearly poked poor Maudie in the eye,' said Alice. 'I think Maudie's much too small for roller coasters.'

'Really?' said Dad. 'I'm sure there are lots of little-kids' rides.'

'And it's going to cost a fortune for all six of us. Maybe we'll go later on in the holidays,' said Alice.

She meant without *us*.

'Well, let's go for a trip to the seaside then. A real bucket-and-spade day,' said Dad. 'You'd like that, wouldn't you, Maudie? Daddy-Pop take you for a paddle?'

Maudie grinned, but Alice sighed and rolled her eyes.

'Do *think*, David. How could we all fit in the car? You and me in the front, Maudie in her baby seat in the back. There're only two seats left – and three children,' she said.

'They can squash up small,' said Dad.

Robbie and I imagined being squashed up to Smash the entire journey.

'Robbie and I don't need to go. We'll be fine by ourselves, honestly,' I said quickly.

'Yes, I'm sure it's against the law or Health and Safety or something, three children in two seats,' said Robbie.

We had a vision of a glorious day by ourselves, me lying on the bed reading, Robbie exercising his animals up and down the stairs – endless hours of calm and peace.

'Don't be silly, you two,' said Dad. 'It's against the law to leave children in the house by themselves, Mr-Know-It-All.' He swatted at Robbie with the tea towel. He was only playing, but Robbie winced as if he had hit him.

'Cheer up, chum,' said Dad. He gazed into space for inspiration – and then his eyes lit up. '*I* know! We'll go on a lovely long tramp in the country. It would do the kids good to have a bit of exercise, and I'll give Maudie a piggyback if she gets tired. And we'll have a picnic. Yes, a picnic! I haven't had a proper picnic since I was a little kid myself. Sandwiches and hard-boiled eggs and cherry cake and lashings of lemonade,' said Dad.

'That's an Enid Blyton picnic – and it's lashings of ginger beer, not lemonade,' I said, but so quietly that only Robbie heard.

Alice didn't look very enthusiastic about the picnic idea.

'I've got eggs, but I don't have enough bread left for

sandwiches, let alone cherry cake or lemonade, and that sounds a very weird picnic anyway,' she said.

Dad sighed and looked as if he might lose his temper with her at last. He was always losing his temper when he lived at home with Mum and Robbie and me. But he managed to keep cheery – just.

'Nil problemo,' he said, in what he thought was a foreign language. 'I'll nip off to Sainsbury's and buy a few provisions, while you guys boil the eggs.'

Robbie and I hung around the kitchen obediently, and fetched and carried while Alice boiled eggs and fried some bacon and chopped lettuce and tomatoes. Maudie started moaning because she wanted to do some chopping too.

'Shall I take her to get washed and dressed?' I offered, holding out my hand to Maudie.

'No, *I'll* take her. Come and have a splash-splash with Smash-Smash, Maudie,' said Smash, grabbing her quickly by the other hand.

We were like two toddlers ourselves, fighting over a favourite doll.

'No, *I'll* see to her in just a minute,' Alice snapped. Then she saw our faces and took a deep breath. 'But thank you so much for offering, darlings. It was really sweet of you.'

Smash didn't look at *all* sweet now. She looked as sour as lemons. She stomped off and shut herself in our bedroom. I thought it wiser to stay out of her way. In fact I stayed out of everyone's way. Alice asked me to fetch the salt and pepper from the larder. I thought it was just a cupboard but it was a proper little walk-in room. Robbie was happy in the kitchen showing Alice how to make chocolate crispy cakes, his speciality. Robbie likes cooking a lot.

I hid in the larder with *Five Children and It*. It was almost too dark to read and the floor was very hard, but I managed an entire peaceful hour to myself, and finished my book. It didn't really matter. I had heaps more in my suitcase, one for every day of the holidays. That meant I'd had to leave quite a lot of tops and shorts and jeans and dresses at home, but I decided I'd just have to stay very, very clean in the clothes I was wearing.

I started the first chapter all over again, where the children find the strange Psammead buried in a sandpit. I heard Dad's voice in the kitchen and an awful lot of bustling about, but I stayed put. I'd felt too shy and lonely to eat very much at breakfast, and the different delicious smells of bacon and chocolate were making me feel hungry now, but I found a packet of sultanas in the larder and had a very satisfying secret snack.

Then Dad started calling for me and calling for Smash. I didn't hear Smash answer so I didn't either. Maybe I'd manage to stay hidden away all day long and they'd go off on their walk and have their picnic without me.

No such luck. Dad tracked me down like a

bloodhound. He flung the larder door open and discovered me in seconds.

'Rosalind, what are you *playing* at?' he demanded.

'Hide-and-seek?' I said.

'For goodness' *sake*. Can't you act your age? You're the oldest. You're meant to set an example,' Dad said.

I wished I wasn't the oldest. I wished I was the youngest, little and cute like Maudie, everybody's favourite.

It took Dad much longer to track down Smash. We looked all over the house but there was no sign of her. That was because she wasn't *in* the house. Dad and Alice started searching the garden. She wasn't technically in the garden either – she was *above* it, halfway up the big lime tree at the back.

Alice made a fuss, saying it was dangerous, and then she made a further fuss when she saw Smash had got her white T-shirt grimy. So it was quite a while before we were all rounded up and ready, practically lunchtime.

'We could just as well have the picnic here in the garden, without having to lump all this stuff about,' said Alice, juggling rucksacks and carrier bags.

'Nonsense! I know a perfect picnic place in Oxshott woods,' said Dad. 'I used to go on picnics there when I was a kid. We used to bike over from Kingston. It's wonderful there. I want the kids to see how lovely it is.'

Robbie and I exchanged glances. He'd never tried to take us there all the years he'd lived at home with Mum.

We set off for these woods. Dad had the big rucksack on his back, Alice had a bulging bag-for-life in one hand and held Maudie by the other. I carried a canvas bag full of fruit and Robbie clutched a bag of paper plates and cups and a bottle cooler of wine for Dad and Alice. Smash carried a string bag of Coke and fizzy lemonade. She swung it wildly round and round, obviously intent on making them explode.

We plodded along the pavement for a long time, past row after row of suburban semis just like Dad's.

'Funny-looking countryside,' Smash remarked.

'We're *nearly* in the country. Stride on,' said Dad. 'Breathe in all that healthy fresh air.'

'The country, the country, the country!' Maudie chanted, hanging on to Alice and Dad as they swung her along between them.

We walked on and on. The roads got busier and busier until there was such a roar of traffic we could hardly hear each other.

'Let's fill our lungs with all the healthy fresh petrol fumes,' said Smash.

The houses gradually grew bigger, and retreated down driveways. Alice gazed enviously at each large house, trying to decide which she liked the best. There were several for sale, which excited her. She even rang one estate agent on her mobile to find out the asking price.

'It's more than a million!' she said, round-eyed, switching off her phone.

'Of course it is,' Dad said irritably. 'Completely out of our price range.'

'Well, obviously. But I reckon we could just about afford to trade up a bit, especially if I work longer hours when Maudie starts school – and if you get another promotion. There'd be enough money coming in, if only we didn't have so many commitments.'

She wasn't looking at Robbie and me, but I knew she meant us. Dad paid Mum for our keep every month and I think Alice had to give Smash's dad money too. It wasn't *our* fault, but it somehow felt as if it was.

I slowed down to walk beside Robbie, who was lagging behind. He clutched his paper sack awkwardly, red in the face with effort.

'Here, give me that wine cooler. It must weigh a ton,' I said.

'No, I'm fine,' said Robbie, breathing heavily.

I grabbed his sack and felt for the wine cooler. My hands scrabbled over many manes and haunches and tails. I raised my eyebrows.

'I thought my animals might like to roam free in these woods,' said Robbie.

'I don't think we're ever going to *get* to these woods. They probably don't exist any more. All the trees round here got chopped down donkey's years ago so they could build all these big houses,' I said.

But after an endless trudge we crossed a main road and suddenly there we were, walking in woods at last.

'Right, let's have this picnic. I'm *starving*,' said Smash, sitting down cross-legged.

'No, not *here*, where we can still hear the traffic! We'll go further into the woods. When I was a boy we always had our picnics by the sandpit.'

'There's a sandpit in my book,' I said. 'That's where the children found the Psammead.'

But no one seemed remotely interested.

2

Maudie had long since started to droop, and
Dad was struggling to carry her as well as the
big rucksack – but she perked up when he
said the word *sandpit*.

'A sandpit!' she repeated enthusiastically, clapping her
hands.

'You didn't tell us there was a sandpit,' said Alice. 'She
loves playing in the sandpit at nursery, don't you, Maudie
love?'

'This is a great big natural sandpit in the middle of
the woods. I remember thinking it was just like the
seaside,' said Dad. 'We should have brought your little
bucket and spade, eh, Maudie?'

We tramped further and further into the woods,

struggling uphill now. There was no sign of this sand-pit.

'Who *cares* about the wretched sandpit,' said Smash. 'Let's have the picnic here.' She flung herself down on the grass and took off her fabulous trainers. They were obviously brand new, sparkling with emerald-green sequins. I had been eyeing them enviously until I saw the red marks on Smash's feet.

'I've got blisters, look! Really huge terrible blisters because you've made me walk miles and miles and miles,' she wailed.

'You should have worn socks. I told you back at home. It's your own fault,' said Alice. '*Do* stop making such a silly fuss. Come on, let's walk just a little further.'

'I *hate* walking,' said Smash.

'It's good exercise – and you really need it. Your father lets you slump around the house and drives you every-where in that fancy car. It's not good for you,' Alice fussed.

'It's not good for me being marched along through this dreary wood for hours when my feet are practically bleeding – *look*!' said Smash. 'I'm not going a step further.' She crossed her arms defiantly.

But then we heard Robbie shouting. He'd wandered on through the trees, but now he came running back.

'I've found the sandpit!' he called. 'I can see it, all golden, through the trees. Come on!'

So we all went to look, even Smash, swinging her

sparkly shoes by the laces and walking barefoot. Robbie had sounded excited, but the sandpit was rather a disappointment. Even Dad seemed a bit cast down.

'I'm sure there was *more* sand when I was a kid. And it was a real *pit*. You slid down into it. It was such fun.' He looked reproachfully at the sandy hollow under the pine trees as if it had shrunk itself on purpose. He put Maudie and the rucksack down and gave the sand a little kick with his canvas deck shoe. 'You can't really play in it now,' he said, mopping his forehead.

'It's still a lovely spot,' said Alice, sitting down gracefully. The skirt of her pink dress spread out around her, so that she looked like a flower. She arched her back, one hand on her tiny waist, the other combing her long blonde hair. 'It's so hot,' she said, though she looked completely cool and composed.

I didn't like her at all, because she had lured Dad away. I especially didn't like her being so pretty. I thought of our mum with a pang. She had messy mousy hair scragged back in a little ponytail, and ever since Robbie was born she kept saying she was going on a diet, but she never actually got round to it.

Dad sat down eagerly beside Alice, cheered up already.

'Picnic time!' he announced, delving in the rucksack.

It was a very good picnic. We had bacon, lettuce and tomato sandwiches and cheese and tuna ciabattas and hard-boiled eggs sprinkled with salt with crisp toast triangles. There was an asparagus quiche, and little chipolatas and a vegetable dip. We had a blackberry and apple pie for pudding with Greek yoghurt, and peaches and grapes and clementines. The Coke and lemonade fizzed spectacularly when Smash opened them, but there was still enough for us to drink, while Dad and Alice shared the wine.

We ate solidly for twenty minutes – and then the picnic was over.

'What do we do now?' said Smash, gobbling the last of the sausages.

'Smash, for goodness' sake, stop it! You'll burst!' said Alice.

'You go and play now, while Alice and I have a little nap,' said Dad, lying back, using the rucksack as a pillow.

'You have a little nap too, Maudie,' said Alice. She made her cuddle down beside her. Maudie lay still for a minute or two, and then wriggled free, deciding she'd have much more fun playing with us.

'Let's climb trees,' said Smash.

'But we're not allowed,' I said.

Smash rolled her eyes. She pointed to Dad and Alice who were fast asleep already.

'Come on, I dare you,' said Smash, running through the trees, away from the parents. I picked up Maudie, and Robbie and I trailed after her reluctantly. I didn't *want* to try climbing any of the tall spindly pine trees all around us, but it's very difficult when someone dares you – particularly someone like Smash.

'Come on, it's easy-peasy,' said Smash, starting to climb the nearest tree. 'Let's all climb this one.'

She was already way above our heads. Robbie looked up at her, his face white. Robbie isn't a very sporty kind of boy. He's also terrified of heights.

'You look after Maudie,' I said, transferring her to Robbie's arms. He clutched her like a shield.

'There. Right. I'll give it a go,' I said, reaching for the first branch.

I decided I'd show her. I pretended not to be scared. It seemed relatively easy at first. The branches were close together, sticking out at convenient angles, so it was just like going up a ladder. I climbed steadily. Maybe it really was easy-peasy.

'Come on, slowcoach!' Smash shouted, from way up high.

I looked up at her. She was right at the top, where the pine tree thinned out dramatically. The trunk was spindly and Smash seemed to be swaying in the wind. I felt my picnic stirring uneasily in my stomach.

'Come back down a bit!' I shouted, but she just laughed at me.

'Smash, it's dangerous!' I called.

'No, *this* is dangerous,' said Smash, and she let go of

the trunk with one hand and waved wildly down to Robbie and Maudie.

I looked down too, which was a big mistake. I felt sicker than ever. My brother and little half-sister looked like tiny toys.

'Come down, Rosalind!' Robbie called, and Maudie started wailing. Their voices sounded like little mouse squeaks.

I *wanted* to come down, but my arms and legs had started trembling and I didn't dare move in case I lost my grip altogether.

'Oh dear, is little diddums stuck?' Smash called down mockingly.

It was enough to goad me into action again.

'Of *course* I'm not stuck, stupid,' I lied. 'I'm just having a rest. Looking about. Surveying the world.'

'Come up here then!'

'There's not room for both of us. And – and you're too heavy. The tree will snap in half if we're both up there. You come down.' I paused, trying desperately to think of some other way to persuade her. 'You're frightening Maudie – she's crying.'

Smash stopped waving and held on to the trunk properly. She didn't like me. She certainly didn't like poor Robs. She didn't like our dad and she didn't seem to like her mum either. The only person she really seemed fond of was Maudie.

'It's okay, Maudie! I'm coming down now,' she called,

and she started swiftly descending, hand over hand, sliding sometimes. She passed me in a flash, and I forced myself to follow her.

When I was down on the ground at last I could hardly stand. I'd read the phrase 'My legs had turned to jelly' in umpteen books, but I'd never really understood it before. My legs wobbled ridiculously inside my jeans, so much so I wasn't sure they would actually hold me up.

'Wow, Rosalind!' said Robbie, looking at me in awe.

'Like Smash said, it was easy-peasy,' I lied.

Smash was rubbing her arms. She had burn marks from sliding down too fast, and her T-shirt was filthy now, but she didn't seem to care.

'Here, Maudie,' she said, wrestling her away from Robbie and giving her a hug. 'I'm fine, see. You'll be able to climb trees just like Smash when you're a bit bigger. I'll show you,' she said. Then she looked at Robbie. 'It's your turn now.'

'Robbie's too small to climb trees,' I said quickly.

'No, he's not! Go on, Robbie. I dare you,' said Smash.

Robbie looked agonized, his eyes huge.

'You don't have to do dares, Robs,' I said.

'Yes, you do,' said Smash. 'You're a coward if you don't.'

'No, it's much braver *not* to do a dare,' I said – though *I* hadn't been this sort of brave.

Robbie looked at Smash anxiously. She was relentless.

'You're just chicken, aren't you?' she said, and she

started clucking offensively. Maudie clucked too, thinking it was a game. 'There, even Maudie thinks you're a coward,' said Smash.

'I don't care,' said Robbie, but tears were brimming in his eyes.

'Oh, look, he's a crybaby now,' said Smash.

'Leave him alone,' I said fiercely.

'He *is* a baby. He doesn't even dare go halfway up,' said Smash.

'Yes, I do,' Robbie said. 'I'll show you.'

He spat on his hands the way he'd seen tough men do in old films and then he sprang up to catch hold of the first branch. He wasn't very good at springing. He missed the branch entirely and banged his poor nose smack against the tree trunk.

Smash laughed so much she nearly fell over.

'Shut *up!*' I said, and rushed to Robbie.

'I'm *fine*,' said Robbie, scarlet in the face. 'I *meant* to do that. I was mucking about, to make Maudie laugh. Leave me *alone*, Rosalind. I'm going to climb this tree.'

He tried again, stretching for the branch instead of springing, and just about managed to grab hold. Then he scrabbled desperately with his feet, trying to make them walk up the trunk to the next branch. His trainers seemed to have turned into roller skates because he kept sliding down. But he got one foot on to the next branch at long last and hauled himself up. He hovered there precariously, barely above our heads.

'Go *on* then,' said Smash. 'Goodness, Maudie could climb that far!'

Robbie tried again, waving his hands towards the next branch. He got some kind of grip, scrabbled with his feet again, almost made it – and then slipped. He came sliding down the tree and landed bump on his bottom.

'Oh, Robs,' I said, desperate to check he was all right and yet not wanting to humiliate him further.

Robbie got up very shakily. He tested one leg, then the other, and shook his arms gingerly.

'Where do you hurt?' I asked.

He thought. 'Everywhere,' he said. 'I think I might have broken something.'

'I'll go and wake Dad.'

'*No!*' said Robbie, and he limped off towards the sand-pit, desperate to get away from us.

Smash laughed again, but she was forcing it. Maudie put her thumb in her mouth, looking worried.

'Robbie?' she said indistinctly, sucking.

'I *think* he's all right,' I said. I glared at Smash. 'No thanks to you. Stop picking on him.'

'Why? It's fun. He's pathetic,' she said. 'Can't even climb a tree!' She picked Maudie up, and whirled her round and round. 'Cheer up, Maudie. You're on the Smash roundabout now. Wheee!'

I wandered over to Robbie, who was sitting in the sand, his head bent.

'Stop following me,' he mumbled.

'I'm not. I'm simply sitting in the sandpit. Hey, maybe we can make some kind of sandcastle for Maudie. She'd like that.'

'We haven't got any buckets and spades.'

'We'll *improvise.*' I went over to the picnic remains beside Dad and Alice. They were still fast asleep, cuddled up together. I shuddered and picked up a couple of paper cups and plates. They proved useless for digging because the sand was dark gold and heavy – but I had more luck with Maudie's plastic feeder cup. I knelt down and started digging.

Robbie took his lion out of his pocket and encouraged it to roam across the sand. It roared softly in appreciation. He went to fetch his other animals and set them all free in this exciting new desert. I watched carefully, but he wasn't limping. It was peaceful, just the two of us – but after a few minutes Smash came running up, pulling Maudie along with her.

'What are you two doing?' she asked.

'Robbie's discovered a new Serengeti and I'm building a Taj Mahal,' I said.

'You what?' said Smash, squatting down beside us.

Maudie reached for her feeder cup.

'Want a drinkie,' she said, and cried when she saw it was covered in sand.

'It's okay, Maudie. I'll wash it out for you in a minute – but now we're digging, see? I'm making you a lovely sandcastle.'

Maudie peered at my little heap of sand as if it might just rearrange itself into a fairytale palace. Nothing happened.

'Want a *drinkie*,' she insisted, reaching for the cup again.

'In a minute, just wait until I've dug a little more,' I said. 'Help me, you two!'

Robbie obediently herded his animals back into his pockets and started scrabbling with his fingers.

'You're useless,' Smash said unkindly. 'Like *this*!' She got down on her hands and knees and started digging determinedly. 'See?'

'It gets up my nails if I dig like that,' said Robbie.

'Oh, poor little diddums,' said Smash, who didn't have any fingernails to speak of, because she bit them so badly. She went on digging, throwing up a storm of sand all round her. Then she suddenly stopped, and gave a little scream.

'What? What is it? Did you stub your fingers on a stone?' I asked.

'There's something *there*!' she said, sitting back on her legs and pointing.

'Oh, ha ha,' I said, because I thought this was one of her games. 'What *is* it? A rotting corpse out of one of your Marvel O'Kaye horror books?'

'It's alive,' said Smash. 'It was warm and it twitched.'

'An animal!' said Robbie excitedly.

'Take no notice, Robs. She's just kidding us,' I said.

'No, I'm not. *Look!*' said Smash, flicking sand again.

We all looked – and saw a *paw*. A brown furry paw with a pink pad and neat little claws. It scrabbled frantically, attempting to cover itself with sand. Smash reached out and tried to grab it.

'*Careful!*' said Robbie in such a fierce voice that Smash stopped, startled. 'You'll frighten it. Now, let me.' He bent down and spoke very softly. 'There now, little creature. It's all right. We're not going to hurt you. We'll let you hide away in a minute if that's what you want. We just want to check you're all right, so I'll ease the sand away here, very very carefully . . .' Robbie exposed a short stout furry leg, and then rather large hindquarters.

'Whatever *is* it?' I said.

'It's a ginormous rat!' said Smash.

'No, it's too furry,' said Robbie.

'I think it's a meerkat. They bury themselves in sand,' I said.

'It's too fat for a meerkat,' said Robbie. 'I'm not sure what it is.'

'Pussy cat, pussy cat!' said Maudie.

'It hasn't got a tail,' said Robbie.

'It's got a very big bottom!' Smash shrieked.

'Sh! So have you,' said Robbie. 'Now shut up, you're frightening it. There now, little creature. Can you come out just a tiny bit?'

The animal did its best to burrow further in, but Robbie very gently scooped the sand away from its sides and then held it firm.

'Come on now. I promise we won't hurt you,' Robbie whispered.

The legs stopped scrabbling and Robbie pulled very carefully. The creature shot right out of the sand. We stared at it, amazed. It was far fatter than we'd expected. It had an extremely wrinkled face with a very disgruntled expression. Its eyes were on thin stalks and wavered about, peering at us disapprovingly from its upside-down position. Every single one of its whiskers was bristling.

'Is it a very tubby *monkey*?' said Smash. 'Its face is all weird wrinkles, just like a monkey's.'

'Monkey!' said Maudie.

'It *is* a bit like a monkey, but they don't have eyes on stalks – and it hasn't got a tail,' Robbie whispered. 'I don't really know what it is.'

'I do!' I squealed. 'It's a Psammead! It really truly has to be a Psammead, like the one in my book. It's exactly like that. Oh please, *are* you a Psammead?'

'Of course I am a Psammead,' it said, very crossly indeed. 'And there's nothing wrong with my face! My wrinkles simply show my extremely distinguished age. I've always been considered an excellent specimen of my species. Now will you kindly turn me right side up, young man. I do not care to conduct a conversation from this ludicrous position. It puts me at a total disadvantage.'

Robbie righted the creature with trembling hands. We all stared at it, speechless, incapable of conducting *any* kind of conversation. Smash shook her head as if she had water in her ears.

'Did it just *speak*?' she said. She stared at Robbie and me as if we'd somehow performed a brilliant trick of ventriloquism. 'I know it's really you guys, pretending,' she said uncertainly.

Maudie put her finger near the creature. Smash snatched her backwards.

'Don't, Maudie. It might bite!' she shrieked.

'I shall indeed bite if you persist with that ill-mannered, high-pitched squealing,' it said. 'Of course I can speak – and much more eloquently than you, Shouty-Squealy-Person. What is your name?'

'Smash,' she whispered.

'*Smash?* Dear goodness, names have become very short and brutal in this new age. Are you a girl person or a boy person?'

'I'm a *girl* – and my real name's Samantha, but I hate it,' Smash muttered.

'I *thought* you were a girl, but your short hair and coarse trousers confused me,' it said. The eyes on stalks wavered in Robbie's direction.

'And I presume you are a girl too?'

Smash sniggered.

'No, I'm a boy,' said Robbie. 'I'm Robert.'

'Well, thank you for handling me so gently, young Robert. Some children would have tugged violently.'

It waddled forward on its hind paws and shook the

rest of the sand out of its fur. Maudie laughed and clapped her hands delightedly.

'You're a merry little person,' it said, its small fierce face softening. Everyone always loved Maudie – even mythical creatures from storybooks.

'She's Maudie, our little half-sister,' I said.

'Half a sister?' said the creature. 'Do you say that because she's half your size?'

'No, because we're only half related. We've got the same dad, but Maudie's got a different mother,' I said.

The Psammead waved its eyes, absorbing this. They flicked on their stalks to Smash.

'So the shouty Smash girl is your half-sister too?'

'No, she's *Maudie's* half-sister, because they have the same mum, Alice – but *we're* just stepsisters,' I said.

'Hmm! Family life seems particularly complicated nowadays,' said the Psammead.

'Don't you . . . breed?' Robbie asked timidly.

'Alas, I fear I am the very last of my line,' said the Psammead. 'Unless –' He turned towards me, clasping his paws. 'You, young lady with the long hair. What is your name?'

'Rosalind.'

'You said you read about a Psammead in a book. Perhaps I still have surviving family after all, if you have read about them.'

'No, I rather think you're the *same* Psammead. You meet five children in my book – Anthea, Jane, Cyril, Robert and the Lamb.'

'Ah! *Those* children,' said the Psammead. 'I remember, I was particularly fond of the eldest girl, Anthea. You remind me of her a little.'

I was so delighted I blushed deep red.

'So was that old book of hers *real*?' said Smash. 'You're the fairy?'

The Psammead nodded complacently.

'So I'm in a book,' it said. 'Does it give my complete life history?'

'Sort of,' I said. 'You go right back to the time of the dinosaurs, don't you?'

'I do indeed. Is that what you're going to wish for? A megatherium or an ichthyosaurus? They'll make you a tasty dinner for a week,' said the Psammead. 'You're looking a little doubtful. I can summon one up that's freshly killed and skinned and cut into chunks if you're squeamish about butchery.'

'It's very kind of you, but we don't actually eat dinosaurs nowadays,' I said awkwardly.

'But we'd like to *see* one, a real live one! Can you summon up a *Tyrannosaurus rex*? They're really cool,' said Smash.

'Smash, do shut up. The Psammead really can do magic spells. You can't possibly wish for a *Tyrannosaurus rex*. It's the most dangerous dinosaur of all. It would rip us apart,' I said.

'It wouldn't rip *me*. I could climb a tree and get away easy-peasy,' Smash said.

33

'Yes, but what about *us*?'

Smash grinned. 'Maybe you'd learn to climb trees too.'

'So, you're requesting a live *Tyrannosaurus rex*?' said the Psammead, starting to puff itself up.

'No, no, definitely not!' I said quickly. 'Stop it, Smash. How can you be so stupid? What about Maudie? It would eat her up in one gollop.'

'You're the stupid one. Of course this tubby monkey thing can't do real magic,' said Smash.

'Yes, it can. It can grant any wish you like,' I said.

'*Really?*' said Robbie. 'Then – then I wish – I wish I could climb trees even better than Smash!'

The Psammead took a very deep breath and then puffed itself up enormously until it was practically spherical, like a furry beach ball, its stalked eyes straining at the top. It stayed immobile for a moment and then deflated with an extraordinary hiss. It lay back weakly on the sand, clearly exhausted.

'Oh dear! Are you all right?' Robbie asked anxiously.

'Has it had some kind of seizure?' Smash demanded.

'Poor Monkey go pop,' said Maudie.

'Very nearly,' said the Psammead weakly. 'Oh dear, oh dear, I'm out of practice. My heart's pounding!'

'Shall I get you some water?' Robbie asked.

'No! Absolutely not! I am deeply allergic to water,' it said in alarm.

'You can't be allergic to *water*,' said Smash. 'I'm allergic to cats – they make me sneeze like anything.'

'Please don't contradict me, Smish or Smidge or whatever your name is. I *am* allergic to water. Just saying the
dreaded word makes my whiskers quiver. I need a good
sand bath. Good day.' It started burrowing into the sand
head first.

'Oh please, don't go – not just yet!' Robbie begged.
He flexed his arms and kicked his legs about experimentally. 'Have you really granted my wish, Mr Psammead?'

'Are you doubting my wish-granting abilities?' said
the Psammead, lifting his head out of the sand again,
looking outraged. 'I might be a tad rusty as I've been
resting for many years. But I can assure you I have never
yet failed in my allotted task, no matter how tedious.'

'Can you really, really, *really* grant wishes?' said Smash.
'Then *I'm* going to wish for loads of money. A whole
huge suitcase full of fifty-pound notes.'

'I can't possibly grant two wishes in one day,' the
Psammead snapped. 'I have already strained myself to
the utmost. Return in a day or two if you absolutely
must, but I can do no more for a full twenty-four hours.'
It stuck its head back in the sand, scrabbled rapidly and
had totally disappeared in two seconds.

'Come back, Monkey!' said Maudie, squatting down
and poking at the sand sadly.

'Yes, come back!' said Smash, digging in the sand
again.

'Stop it! You must let it rest now,' I said, grabbing hold
of her hands.

'But it's so unfair. Why should Robbie get the wish? *I* was the one who found it,' Smash said.

'Yes, you could have wished for *all* of us, Robs,' I said.

'It's a stupid wish anyway,' said Smash.

'I'm sorry,' said Robbie, looking upset. 'I didn't really think. I don't expect it will actually come true, though.' He stood up and walked to the nearest tree, hanging his head a little foolishly.

'Be careful, Robbie!' I said as he spat on his hands again.

'It won't have really *worked*,' said Robbie.

He reached for the first branch awkwardly. As soon as his fingertips touched the bark his whole body changed. He was off up the tree in a second, climbing like a little monkey, arms up, legs up, effortlessly, over and over again, higher and higher, to the very top.

'**W**ow! Look at me!' Robbie shouted, waving down from the very top of the tree.

'Oh, Robbie, be careful!' I called. 'Please, please, come down now!'

'No fear! I'm going to stay *up*! It's fantastic,' Robbie shouted, pulling on the spindly trunk so that it swayed backwards and forwards. '*Look!*'

'Stop it! You could still fall, you idiot! Oh, come *down*!' I shouted at the top of my voice. I was shouting so loudly I must have woken Dad. He came wandering over to the sandpit, yawning and rubbing his eyes.

'Hey, pipe down, kids, you're disturbing the peace,' said Dad. He shook his head at me. 'Was that you

37

shouting, Rosalind? What are you getting in such a state about?'

I pointed upwards. Dad looked up – and then his head jerked, nearly snapping right off his neck.

'Is that *Robbie*? Oh my God, he's so high! Robbie, come down. Are you crazy? Come down this instant!'

Robbie peered down at Dad.

'Hey, Dad, I can climb trees!' he said. 'Really big tall trees! I did it, easy-peasy.'

'Yes, so I can see. But come *down* now. It's very dangerous to go up so high,' said Dad. 'Come down, son. We can all see you're very clever, but come down *now*!'

'It's not *that* clever,' said Smash. 'I can climb just as far. Look, I'll show you.'

'Oh no, you don't,' said Alice, running over and grabbing hold of her. 'You're staying put, young lady.'

'Are you stuck, Robbie? Shall I come up and give you a hand?' said Dad.

'No, I'm not the slightest bit stuck,' said Robbie. 'Watch.' He suddenly let go and *leapt*. We all screamed. But Robbie didn't plummet to the ground. He flew through the air like a trapeze artist to the topmost branch of a neighbouring tree. He hung there, swinging backwards and forwards, and then clamped his legs round the trunk and flung his arms out.

'Ta *da*!' he shouted. 'What shall I do for my next trick?'

'Robbie, *don't*! You might still fall. The Psammead's wishes can go horribly wrong! Oh, please listen!' I hissed.

'Okay, okay, don't fuss, Ros,' said Robbie, and he started climbing down again.

This new tree was a much harder one, with very few branches, but Robbie walked himself down the trunk in a matter of moments. He jumped neatly into the sandpit, landing beautifully on the balls of his feet.

I rushed to him and hugged him tight. Dad came and hugged him too.

'Oh, Robbie, don't ever do that again! I just about died watching you. Don't you realize how dangerous that is? Just one little slip and you'd be a goner,' he said, clasping him to his chest.

'I climbed a tree here too, Mum,' said Smash. 'I climbed right to the top, just like Robbie. I did it first.'

'Then you're very, very naughty. You could have been killed, both of you. I can't believe you can be so stupid and irresponsible,' said Alice, picking Maudie up. 'What sort of an example is this to your sister? You were meant to be looking after her.' Smash certainly wasn't going to get any hugs out of her.

'I still can't quite believe it,' said Dad, holding Robbie at arm's length. 'Have you *always* been able to climb like that?'

'Not really,' said Robbie truthfully. 'But now I seem to have got the hang of it.'

'I'll say!' said Dad. 'You were amazing! I mean, it was very silly of you, because it was immensely danger-ous, and I agree with Alice, a very bad example to your sisters – and yet you've got such skills, such balance, such strength for such a skinny little boy.' Dad picked Robbie right up and gave him a kiss on his forehead. 'I'm so proud of you, son,' Dad said.

Robbie went bright pink, looking as if he was going to burst with pride.

'I can climb trees *much* better than Robbie,' Smash muttered sulkily.

Maudie started wailing for a drink, and then wailed harder because her special cup was covered in sand.

'Come on, let's go home,' said Alice, starting to gather up the picnic things. 'Give me a hand, Rosalind.'

'Just a minute,' I said. I ran over to the sandpit and crouched down in what I hoped was the right spot. 'Thank you, dear Psammead,' I whispered into the sand. 'You've made Robbie so happy. But please, please, please let him *stay* happy. I can't bear it if it's all going to go wrong.'

There was no reply. I looked at the surface of the sand hopefully, but there was no sign of a furry paw. I patted the sand even so, and retrieved Robbie's lion, who was still roaming his Serengeti.

Robbie barely thanked me. He tossed the rest of his animals higgledy-piggledy into his paper sack, busy chatting to Dad.

'You should have seen me climb the first tree, Dad. I did it in *seconds*, truly,' he boasted. 'Look, let me show you!'

'No, Robbie! Simmer down, son. You mustn't,' said Dad, but he sounded as if he were wavering. 'Maybe – maybe just go up a *little* way, no higher than my head, and I'll stand underneath so I can catch you, okay?'

'Okay, okay,' said Robbie. 'Watch then.'

He spat on his palms, leapt for the lowest branch of another tree – and missed. He very nearly bumped his head on the trunk.

'Oh, Robs!' I said.

'Whoops!' Smash shouted.

'Watch out, Robbie,' said Dad.

'You'll hurt yourself,' said Alice.

'Robbie go bang,' said Maudie.

But Robbie was laughing hilariously.

'Fooled you! I *meant* to do that,' he chortled – and this time he was telling the truth.

He leapt effortlessly high in the air, caught hold of another branch and swung himself up swiftly and gracefully – then up and up and up again.

'Not too far!' Dad called.

'You're a Worry-Pop!' Robbie called daringly, edging along a branch. Then he suddenly jumped, making us all scream again – but he clutched the branch with his hands and swung there nonchalantly, then kicked harder and swung himself right up and over the branch.

'My goodness, did you see that?' Dad shouted. 'You're better than any circus boy, son! No, you're like a little Olympic gymnastics champion. We're going to have to start you training straight away. You've got the most astonishing potential. Don't you agree, Alice?'

'Look, watch me! I'm sure *I* could do that, easy-peasy,' said Smash.

'Oh, for heaven's sake,' said Alice. 'No more tree-climbing. Come down now, Robbie, and stop showing off.'

'He's got something to show off about,' said Dad – and when Robbie jumped down Dad picked him up and perched him on his shoulders.

'Here comes the champion!' Dad shouted, panting along, bearing Robbie aloft.

We trailed after them, Alice grumbling because she was carrying too many bags, Maudie whining because she was tired and thirsty, and Smash in a foul mood, kicking her way through the pine needles – and kicking *me*, accidentally on purpose, when I got too near her.

I walked along after them, my head spinning. I couldn't believe the Psammead was *real*. I'd longed for storybooks to come true all my life. When I was Maudie's age I'd kept a keen lookout for Wild Things and Gruffaloes and wanted a Tiger to come to tea. As I got older and read my way through Mum's old Puffins, I played going to stage school with Pauline, Petrova and Posy, and I told stories in the attic with poor starving Sara Crewe, and I spent Christmas Day with Meg, Jo, Beth and Amy – but these were all pretend games, even though I imagined them vividly enough.

If I'd encountered the Psammead on my own, I might have thought I'd imagined it too – but the others had all seen and heard it themselves. It really had granted Robbie his wish. My heart thudded hard as I watched Robbie and Dad together. I was so happy for Robs – though a mean little bit of me wished it was *me* making Dad so pleased and proud. I knew the Psammead could grant wishes. I should have got in first and wished that *I* could do something extraordinary to impress everyone. I knew something else from reading the book. The wishes always stopped working after sunset. I felt I had to warn Robbie – but he was so over the moon and stars with happiness I couldn't spoil things for him just yet.

Dad got tired after lugging Robs on his shoulders for a minute or two, so Robbie jumped down and they marched along together. Every now and then Robbie ran ahead, leapt up at a branch and swung madly round and round, while Dad cheered until he was hoarse.

When we got back to Dad's house at last, Robbie rushed out into the garden to climb the lime tree.

'*No*, Robbie. You've done enough climbing for today. Just simmer down and stop being so boisterous. I don't know what's got into you,' Alice snapped.

'Hey, hey,' said Dad. 'Leave the boy alone. He's not doing any harm. He's just happy.'

They usually took painstaking care not to criticize each other's children.

'Look, we agreed, climbing trees is dangerous. We got

cross with Smash because she did it, so it's not fair that you're positively encouraging Robbie to climb trees now,' said Alice.

'Look, the lad's really gifted – surely you can see that. Just look at him!' They both stared out of the kitchen window as Robbie practically *ran* up the lime tree vertically, while two magpies flew out of the branches in alarm.

'Yes, I'm looking – and I'm trying to be a responsible adult here. He could fall and break his neck,' said Alice.

'Yes, I know. You're right.' Dad opened the kitchen window. 'Come down this minute, son. You're scaring your stepmother.'

'Don't *call* me that!' said Alice. 'All the stepmothers in fairy stories are mean old witches.'

'Well, nobody could mistake you for a mean old witch. You're my fairy princess,' said Dad.

Smash and I looked at each other – and then we both mimed vomiting. Dad and Alice went out in the garden arm in arm to supervise Robbie, while Maudie toddled after them, sucking on her newly washed beaker.

'Oh, *yuck*!' said Smash. 'I can't stand it when they act like that.'

'Me neither,' I said.

'Fairy Princess!' said Smash, in a silly man's voice – and we both fell about laughing.

It felt as if we were almost friends instead of deadly enemies.

'Still, your mum *does* look like one with all her lovely golden hair,' I said, fingering my own meek mousy plaits. 'She doesn't actually look like a mum at all – she looks so young and she's got such a fantastic figure.'

'She has Botox injections every six months to smooth out all her lines – and she's got false boobs,' said Smash.

'She *hasn't*!' I said. I started to feel a lot better. 'Well, my dad still thinks she's wonderful, anyway. And I wish he wouldn't go *on* about it.'

'It's okay for you. You've just got to put up with one parent acting like an idiot. Your mum hasn't met someone else, has she?'

'No. She tried dating someone she hooked up with on the Internet but it didn't work out.'

'Well, my dad's gone off with this really, really young girl. Everyone thought it wouldn't last, but now he's *married* her. I can't stand her.'

'Is she horrible to you?'

'Not really. She acts all nicey-nicey, and says we'll be just like sisters together, but I know she doesn't really want to be lumbered with me.' Smash's voice went croaky, as if she might start crying.

'You were a bridesmaid at their wedding, weren't you?' I asked quickly, to distract her.

'Yes, and it was awful. I had to wear a stupid dress and have my hair all curly. I looked *ludicrous*.'

'What colour dress? I've always longed to be a bridesmaid,' I said.

'Blue silk, and matching shoes with silly little heels,' said Smash.

'Oh wow, are you allowed to wear proper heels? I wish I had heels, but Mum won't let me,' I said.

'Hey, you can wish for them tomorrow then!' said Smash. 'Just ask that Psammead thingy and it'll puff up and those old Tesco trainers will turn into wicked high heels. Isn't it amazing? We can have magic wishes! And I found it, don't forget.'

'Yes, but I *identified* it,' I said.

'Let's have a deck at your book then, and see what those other children wished for,' said Smash, grabbing it.

'They wish to be beautiful,' I said.

'Well, that's a waste of a wish,' said Smash.

'I'd quite like to be beautiful,' I said wistfully. I had once heard two teachers discussing me at school. One wasn't sure who I was, and the other one – my *favourite*, who started up our school library – said, 'Oh, you know Rosalind, she's that pale plain little kid with the pigtails.'

'Well, you be beautiful then – but *I'll* be rich,' said Smash.

'You'll have to be more specific than that. The children in the book wished to be rich and they were showered with old gold coins and they found they couldn't spend them anywhere.'

'I shall be *ultra* specific. I'll wish to be rich and *famous*,' said Smash. 'Then I can have my own show on television. I'll have my very own penthouse suite with staff so I won't need to live with my dad or my mum. I'll get driven around everywhere in this huge great limo and all the paps will chase after me and people will scream and want my autograph all the time. When Maudie's older, she can come and live with me too, and I'll buy her everything she wants and take her to amusement parks during the day and out to a show every evening.' Smash paused. 'Why are you looking at me like that?'

'Smash, the wishes don't *last*. Only until sunset,' I said. 'At least, the wishes don't last in the book for the other children.'

'Well, that's a bit of a let-down,' said Smash. 'It's scarcely worth having them if they're all over and done with in an afternoon.' She looked out of the window again, where Robbie was swinging and whooping. 'Does Tree Boy know?'

'I don't think so,' I said uncomfortably. 'Oh dear, he's going to be so disappointed tomorrow. *And* Dad.'

'Are you going to tell him?' asked Smash.

'Not just yet. He's so happy,' I said. 'Don't you tell him either, Smash, please.'

She hesitated, but then shrugged. 'Okay.' She looked out of the window once more. 'Oh yuck and double yuck! The Fairy Princess and your dad are *kissing*.'

'Yuck, yuck, *yuck*,' I said, and we both giggled together and made disgusting kissing sounds.

Smash went on doing it when they came back into the kitchen with Maudie and Robs. Alice glared at her but Dad was too hyper to even notice. He was clapping Robbie on the back and feeling his muscles and calling him The Champion.

'We're going to start you training for the next Olympics straight away, son,' said Dad.

'I didn't know that tree-climbing was an Olympic sport,' said Alice drily.

'Oh, come on, darling! With Robbie's amazing agility and climbing skills he'll make a fantastic gymnast. How old do you have to be to get into an Olympic team? How old was Tom Daley when he started? You might have to wait till the Olympics after next, Robbie, but I'm sure there are junior teams – and they'll make you captain because you'll be the best.'

'Captain Robbie!' Robbie yelled, strutting around the room.

'Three hearty cheers for Captain Robbie!' said Dad. 'Look, I'm going to phone my mate Tim, this guy I know at my gym. He teaches PE at St Christopher's. I know he runs a special gym class in the holidays. We'll pop you down there tomorrow and see how you do on the old wall bars and the ropes.'

Smash and I looked at each other. My heart started thudding.

'Do you do any of that stuff at your school, son?' Dad went on.

'No, we mostly do football – and I'm not much good at it, Dad.'

'Well, never mind. No one's expecting you to be brilliant at everything. Great little footballers are two a penny – but you're truly gifted at gymnastics,' said Dad.

'Dad? Dad, please don't phone your friend,' I said as Dad dialled a number on his mobile.

'Why not, lovey?'

'Because – because Robbie's skills might not last,' I said desperately.

'What?' said Dad.

'You never know, it could be just a fluke, Robbie being brilliant at tree-climbing. Maybe he'll wake up tomorrow and find he's forgotten how to do it entirely,' I said.

Dad looked at me. Then he nodded as if he understood.

'Hey, Rosy-Posy, don't worry. I'm really proud of you too, you know. I'm sure you're going to be clever at all sorts of things. But Robbie's got such a special gift we really do have to take notice now. You want the best for him, don't you?'

Dad thought I was *jealous*! This was so insulting I wanted to punch him – and Robbie made it even worse.

'Maybe I can teach you how to climb trees like me, Rosalind,' he said magnanimously.

I couldn't stop Dad phoning this friend of his and fixing up to take Robbie round to the school at ten the next morning.

49

'We'll show him, eh, Robbie?' said Dad, giving Robs a high five.

'You bet, Dad,' said Robbie, high-fiving back.

I couldn't get Robbie on his own for ages. I had to trail after him to the bathroom and hang about outside.

'Are you following me?' he said, barging right into me.

'Yes! Oh, Robs, listen. There's one huge great fact you need to know. The Psammead's wishes stop after sunset. I'm so sorry – I should have explained. You won't be able to climb trees any more,' I gabbled.

'Yes, I will,' said Robbie. 'I'm brilliant at it – you saw me.'

'Are you *mad*? That was because you wished it.'

'Yeah, but I know how to climb now. I won't forget. I'll still be able to do it, you'll see,' said Robbie. 'It'll be like learning to swim or how to ride a bike. You never forget *how*, not once you've learnt.'

'Oh, Robbie, I don't think it's like that a bit. You'll go back to being hopeless at it, like you were before,' I said, forgetting to be tactful.

'You just want to spoil it all,' said Robbie. 'You want Dad to make a fuss of *you*.'

'Oh, for goodness' sake! I'm just trying to stop you making an utter fool of yourself in front of Dad's friend,' I said.

'I'm going to be just fine, you'll see. Better than fine. I'm going to be absolutely *brilliant*,' said Robbie.

He sounded truly confident – but that night he woke us all up having one of his nightmares.

'What's that weird shouting?' said Smash sleepily.

'Oh no, it's Robbie,' I said, shooting out of bed.

I ran along the landing to Maudie's bedroom and snapped on the light. Robbie was lying down in bed with his eyes closed, but his arms and legs were flailing around in a tangle of duvet and he was yelling. Maudie was sitting up in her cot sucking her thumb, her cuddle blanket wrapped right round her head.

'Robbie shouty shouty!' she said anxiously.

'Yes, it's all right, Maudie. He's just having a bad dream,' I said. I knelt down beside Robbie. 'Wake up, Robs! It's okay – you're just having a nightmare.'

Robbie opened his eyes. He clutched me and I held him tight. He was burning hot and yet shivering too.

Then Dad and Alice came running in.

'What's the matter? Maudie? Are you all right, poppet?' said Alice.

'Robbie,' Maudie mumbled, and started to cry.

'What's up, son? Hey, hey, Dad's here,' said Dad, easing me out of the way. He wrapped his arms round Robbie and rocked him to and fro. 'It's all right, little champ, Dad's got you safe.'

Alice picked Maudie up from her cot and took her back to bed with her. Dad and I stayed looking after Robbie. He was properly awake now and crying.

'I'm sorry, Dad,' he sobbed.

'It's okay, little pal. You're just overtired with all that tree-climbing. My word, you're so wonderful at it. Just wait till Tim sees you!'

'No, no,' Robbie wailed. 'I don't want him to see me. I can't really climb. It was just the Psammead. He granted me a wish.'

'Shut up, Robbie,' I hissed.

'Now then, Rosy-Posy, let him talk it all out. He's obviously had a dreadful nightmare, poor little chap. I used to have terrible nightmares myself at his age. What was granting you a wish in your dream, Robbie? Was it a monster?'

'No, a little furry animal. He was quite nice but a bit cross, like a schoolteacher. He's *real*, though, Dad, just like the one in the storybook. Ros, *tell* him,' Robbie said, knuckling his eyes.

I couldn't tell Dad. To start with, he'd never believe me. He'd think I was dreaming too, imagining it all. I was almost starting to wonder if we *had* made it all up, because it sounded so bizarre and extraordinary. And if it *was* all true, and Dad *did* start to believe in the Psammead, I knew he wouldn't be able to keep it to himself. He'd tell Alice, he'd tell all his friends, and journalists and television reporters would camp out at the sandpit and harass the poor Psammead. Maybe they'd even capture it and put it in a zoo. It would hate it so if it was permanently on display, being prodded into granting wishes all the time. There'd be nationwide competitions to get a Psammead wish, TV game shows, toy replicas of the Psammead, Royal Command performances – while the poor creature longed to bury its head in the sand and burrow down as far as it could go.

All these images flickered in my head alarmingly. I couldn't help Robbie out, not if it meant exposing the Psammead.

'You've been dreaming, Robs,' I said firmly, patting his shoulder. 'Go back to sleep now.'

I slipped his favourite lion into his hand so he could hang on to it for comfort, and he closed his eyes and settled down.

'There now,' said Dad, putting his arm round me. 'You're good with him, Rosy-Posy. I forget how little he really is. I think this is mostly my fault. I got him so overexcited. I just got carried away. He's so brilliant at climbing and I never twigged, all these years. I don't spend enough time with you two nowadays. It's awful, barely knowing my own kids.' Dad went on mumbling away as we crept out on to the landing.

'Dad?' I interrupted. 'Dad, you won't get cross if Robbie isn't very good at climbing tomorrow? Especially in front of your friend Tim? You won't make him do anything he doesn't want to?'

'What? Don't worry, sweetheart. Tim's a really friendly guy. Robs will love him. And I'm not going to *force* him to do anything at all. I just want him to have fun. Don't be such a little worry-pot.'

I did worry, most of the night. I felt dreadful in the morning. Robbie didn't look much better either. He was very pale, with dark circles under his eyes, and he hardly ate any of his cornflakes at breakfast.

'Now then, champ, you need to stoke up that skinny little body,' said Dad.

It was clear to everyone else that Robbie was going to be sick if he ate another mouthful. Even Alice looked concerned. She put her hand on Robbie's forehead.

'Aren't you feeling well, darling?' she asked. 'I think he might be sickening for something, David. Perhaps you'd better ring Tim and cancel the trip to his school. Robbie doesn't look up to it.'

'But I've fixed it all with Tim as a special favour. I can't really back out now,' said Dad. 'I think Robbie's just a bit nervous, but goodness knows *why*. I keep saying, it's going to be *fun*. You're really going to enjoy yourself, son. Apparently this gym at the school is pretty fantastic. The equipment they've got there is out of this world, not just ropes and wall bars – they've got a trapeze and a full-size trampoline. Wait till you try that out!'

'Can we try too?' said Smash.

'Well, Tim's really just assessing Robbie – that's the deal. He'll have a classful of kids on his holiday course. It will seem a bit of a cheek if I take all of you along,' said Dad.

'Can't we just watch?' I said. '*Please*, Dad.' I needed to be there with Robbie. I had to protect him.

'Okay, okay – but just to *watch*, right?' said Dad.

'I don't want them watching me,' said Robbie.

'Don't be silly, Robbie. When you're an Olympic champion, you'll have the whole world watching you,' said Dad. 'And I'll be in the front seat at all your events, cheering you on.'

Robbie smiled at Dad wanly and got up from the table. He walked purposefully to the back door.

'Where are you off to, son?'

'I'm going to climb that big tree at the end of the garden,' said Robbie.

'What? No, no, we haven't time. We've got to be off in ten minutes,' said Dad.

'But I need to see if I can still do it,' said Robbie.

'Of course you can do it, you silly boy. You climbed right up to the very top only yesterday,' said Dad.

'And you mustn't do it again. It's very dangerous,' said Alice. 'No tree-climbing allowed now, all of you.'

Alice stayed at home with Maudie, while Smash and I tagged along in the car with Dad and Robbie. Poor Robbie looked sicker than ever.

'Don't worry, Robs,' I whispered. 'I think you're right. You'll still be able to climb. You'll remember how. You'll be fantastic, you'll see.'

'I don't *feel* fantastic,' said Robbie. 'I've lost all my springiness.' He held out his arms and legs. 'They're just all wobbly jelly now.'

'Oh, don't be such a wimp,' said Smash. 'You can do

it. Look, you were heaps better at climbing than me yesterday. I don't think it had anything to do with that silly old Psammead. You just believed you could do it – so you could.'

Robbie stared at Smash, blinking uncertainly. Perhaps in her own weird way she was trying to be kind to him.

'Really?' he said.

'Really!' she said, thumping him on the back. 'So buck up. You're Tree Boy, the Little Champ. You show them all.'

We got to the school and wandered about looking for the gym. It was a huge room heaving with children in leotards and tracksuits, all zipping up and down the walls, bouncing on the trampoline and somersaulting along the mats.

'Oh wow!' said Smash, her whole face lighting up.

Robbie said nothing at all. I grabbed his hand and gave it a squeeze. Tim came bustling up. He was a tall beefy man with a big grin of white teeth. He made Dad suddenly look surprisingly small.

'Hi, Tim. This is very good of you. Here's the little lad,' said Dad, his hands on Robbie's shoulders.

'He *is* a little lad,' said Tim. 'Right, kiddo, we'll do a few warm-up exercises first, okay?'

'Can *we* warm up?' said Smash. She gave a very fake shiver. 'We're very cold.'

Tim laughed at her. 'I mean you need to warm your *muscles* up so you don't hurt yourself when you start using the equipment. But, okay, you can all three join in if you want. Take your shoes and socks off and we'll give it a go.'

'Hurray!' said Smash, giving Dad a little nod.

Dad shook his head at her. So did I. I didn't want to join in with all these expert kids in their proper gym outfits. But at least I was keeping Robbie company, so I obediently did all the funny stretching exercises, copying Tim. Thankfully they weren't too difficult.

Then we had to do some work on the mats, bicycling in the air and simple head-over-heels stuff. Robbie's never quite got the hang of head over heels. He had a go, but got stuck halfway, his bottom up in the air, Psammead-style.

'Help!' he gasped.

'Roll *over*, son – don't clown around!' Dad called.

Tim gently tipped Robbie into a more dignified position.

'Do you know something, young man? I'm not too good at head over heels myself,' he said comfortingly. 'Don't worry, we can't be good at everything. Let's get you over to the ropes so you can shine. Your dad tells me you love climbing trees, is that right?'

'Well, it was right yesterday,' said Robbie. 'But I'm not sure I like to do that today.'

'Don't you want to have a go?' said Tim gently, putting his arm round Robbie.

'Not really,' Robbie mumbled.

'*I* want to have a go,' said Smash, bouncing about on the mat like a jumping bean. 'Watch me, Tim!'

'Smash! Calm down now. We're not here on your behalf, dear,' said Dad. 'Come on, Robbie! Stop being so bashful. Go over to those ropes and show Tim what you can do. Go *on*.'

Robbie trailed over to the ropes, his head bent. Smash grabbed a rope straight away and started swinging.

'Hey, hey! Not like that,' said Tim quickly. 'You're not in a playground. You have to use the equipment properly. Now, I'll show you the way I want you to climb.'

'I know how to climb already,' said Smash, demonstrating.

She was halfway up in a trice.

'See!' she said, and slid down triumphantly.

'Mmm,' said Tim. 'You're certainly very good at going up – but not so good at coming down.' He took hold of her hands, opening up her fists. 'Look at those nasty rope burns – and you've got more on your legs, you silly girl. They must be really sore.'

'They don't hurt a bit,' said Smash, though we could all see she was wincing.

'I'll show you how to come down without it hurting,' said Tim.

He climbed up, and then let himself down carefully, hauling himself elegantly, his body arched.

'Cool!' said Smash. 'Okay, watch me this time.'

58

'I'll watch all three of you,' said Tim. 'Off you go.'

Smash was off like a rocket, climbing right up to the very top of the rope.

I made a deliberate mess of things, slipping and sliding and shaking my rope to try to divert attention from Robbie.

He spat on his hands desperately, making Dad and Tim laugh, and then jumped up. And down. He tried again – and again and again. He couldn't climb up at all. He was trying so hard the veins were standing out on his forehead and his eyes were popping, but he simply couldn't do it.

'Come on, Robbie!' Dad shouted. '*Try*, son!'

It was painfully obvious to everyone else that Robbie was trying as hard as he could.

'Down you come,' said Tim, helping him. 'Let's do some fun stuff instead.'

He blew the whistle round his neck and called, 'You've all been working very hard, so I think it's time we played a little game. How about . . . Shipwreck?'

Everyone cheered while Tim scattered hula hoops and extra mats all round the room. I looked at Dad. He was staring down at his knees, shaking his head. I edged up to Robbie and tried to squeeze his hand. He snatched it away. His lips were pressed so tightly together they'd almost disappeared, and he was blinking rapidly, trying not to cry in front of everyone.

Shipwreck was a crazy game, but it was great fun,

even if you were useless at gymnastics. You had to run round and round the room, and then when Tim shouted *Shipwreck* you had to leap on to a piece of equipment or jump inside a hoop or sit on a mat. Then when he blew his whistle you had to leap from one to another. If you couldn't reach, you could maybe climb up the wall bars and sidle along and then jump. If you touched the ground, that meant you were out and you had to sit on the rescue boats – long benches at the side of the room.

Robbie played Shipwreck so slowly and cautiously he wasn't out first, thank goodness. I managed to stay in the game until there were only about ten of us left in, but then I skidded off a mat and my foot touched the floor. It looked as if Smash was going to win. She was brilliant at the game, leaping like a gazelle and landing lightly, often climbing her way round the walls. Soon it was just Smash and a tall, fair boy left in. They went round and round the room, so sure-footed it seemed as if they could carry on forever.

'Go, Smash!' I shouted, surprising myself.

Even Robbie perked up a little and watched her properly.

Smash grinned, loving the way we were all looking at her, and decided to show off. She jumped from a mat and clutched one of the ropes. She swung herself to the next rope, building up momentum, so that she could swing herself nearly, nearly, nearly as far as the gym-horse, and then she leapt for it and landed perfectly. She would have been fine, but she flung her arms out in a flourish. We all clapped and she got so distracted she slipped sideways, off the horse and on to the floor.

'Oh, hard luck!' said Tim, helping her up. Then he turned to the fair boy and clapped him on the back. 'But well done, you!'

Smash's face screwed up.

'It wasn't my fault I slipped! They all made such a noise. Can't I have another chance?'

'No, you can't,' said Tim. 'I would have had to disqualify you anyway, because you're not allowed to swing on the ropes like that. I *told* you. You have to do as I say if you come to my gym.'

'Well, I don't want to come to your stupid old gym then,' said Smash.

'Smash, behave,' said Dad curtly. 'None of you will be coming to the gym. Tim, I'm so sorry for wasting your time.'

'Not at all, Dave,' said Tim. 'It's a pity about your daughter – she's got real talent.'

'She's not my –' Dad took a deep breath. 'Oh well. Smash is a law unto herself.'

'And I hope you all had a good time,' Tim went on pleasantly.

'Good time!' Dad muttered in the car. 'I've never been so embarrassed in my life.'

We said nothing. Smash was glowering, I was agonized and Robbie was slumped in shame.

Dad tried to pull himself together as he parked the car.

'Of course it doesn't really *matter*, Robbie. I mean, I'm still proud of you because – because you're my son, and who cares about any silly old gymnastics? But what exactly were you playing at? You were astonishingly brilliant yesterday and a total little duffer today. How come?'

Robbie said nothing.

'Oh well, maybe it was all some magic trick, like you said. Ha ha,' said Dad mirthlessly.

'Ha ha ha,' we echoed.

Alice and Maudie were waiting for us when we got in the house.

'Oh dear, what's happened?' said Alice.

'Don't ask,' said Dad.

'Robbie didn't do well?' Alice persisted.

'*I* did,' said Smash. 'I nearly won that stupid Shipwreck game. I was better than all the other kids. David's pal Tim practically begged me to come and do gym lessons, but I didn't fancy it. He was a right old bossyboots. It would be just like school.'

'Oh, Smash,' said Alice reproachfully, sighing. 'I don't know how you can even *mention* school.'

Smash had apparently been excluded from her school for bad behaviour.

'She's certainly got an appalling attitude. I was ashamed of the way she talked to Tim,' said Dad.

'That's right, everyone pick on me. It's not *my* fault today's gone all wrong,' said Smash.

Robbie hung his head. I squirmed. Even Maudie looked anxious and sucked her thumb, though she didn't know what we were talking about.

'Oh dear, such long faces!' said Alice, visibly making an effort. 'Cheer up, everyone. What would you like to do today?'

'Go on another picnic in Oxshott woods!' we said.

'**Y**ou want to go to Oxshott woods *again*?' said Dad. 'But we went there yesterday. Why don't we go somewhere different today? We could go to Richmond Park, or Kew Gardens. I'm sure we could all squash up in the car somehow.'

'Maybe you could all go for a car trip while Maudie and I stay at home,' said Alice hopefully.

'No, we really, really, really want to go back to that sandpit in the woods,' said Smash. '*Please*, Mum. *Please*, Dave.'

Smash seldom said please to anyone, so this was highly effective.

We helped get the picnic ready. I was in charge of chopping up carrots and celery, Smash had to watch the chipolata sausages under the grill and Robbie made chocolate cornflake crispies. I was busy worrying about wishes and chopped my finger instead of the carrot and had to have a plaster. Smash was also clearly plotting something in her head and burnt the sausages, though she insisted she'd done it on purpose because she *liked* burnt sausages. Robbie melted chocolate and stirred in cornflakes and poured a neat dollop into little cake papers. Chocolate cornflake crispies are the easiest things in the world to make. Maudie could have done it easily. But Dad and Alice reacted as if Robbie had created an elaborate fancy gateau. Dad made kissing noises and fluttered his fingers, and Alice said Robbie would have to teach her how to make them.

'They're just being kind to me because I made an idiot of myself at the gym,' Robbie said to me.

'Yes, but they mean well,' I said.

'When's anyone going to be kind to me?' said Smash. '*I* didn't make an idiot of myself. I was dead brilliant, and yet I still got told off. No one *ever* says, "Well done, Smash, you're fantastic."'

'Well done, Smash-Smash,' said Maudie, smiling at her – so Smash laughed and gave her a hug.

Maudie still gave me hugs too, but not quite as enthusiastically. I tried very hard not to mind. I gave Robbie a hug instead and he gave me a proper grin at last.

We set out for Oxshott woods very cheerfully this time. It didn't seem anywhere near such a trek. Smash ran ahead, I skipped after her and Robbie ambled along, a lion in one hand, a tiger in the other, making them run a race. He was almost his old self again until we got into the woods.

'How about having another go at tree-climbing, son?' said Dad.

'*No!*' said Alice. 'Honestly, David! You're none of you allowed to do any tree-climbing – and that means you too, Smash.'

Dad muttered that he just didn't get it, and we'd all seen Robbie climbing yesterday, and what was the matter with the boy now? He went on and on and on.

'I wish Dad would just shut *up*,' I muttered.

'Careful!' said Smash. 'The Psammead might be listening. We're not going to waste another wish – though it might be good fun seeing your dad with his volume turned down. He doesn't half go *on*.'

'He's okay,' I said awkwardly, even though I agreed with her. 'What's your dad like then?'

'Oh, he used to be *fine*. We'd have such fun. He hardly ever told me off. He'd always buy me whatever I wanted and take me around with him. One time he even took me out in the evening to this posh French restaurant and he let me have three different puddings. He always had girlfriends, but I didn't care. He always said *I* was his number-one girlfriend. But then he met Tessa.' Smash pulled a hideous face.

'Is she the one he's just married?' I asked.

66

Smash nodded. 'I'm not ever, ever, ever getting married,' she said. 'Come *on*, you lot. Let's get to the sandpit!'

We had to have the picnic first, before we could search for the Psammead. It was another very good picnic. There were tuna and sweetcorn rolls and banana sandwiches and Smash's burnt sausages and my chopped vegetables with two different dips, avocado and hummus. Then there were little individual fruit fools and angel cake and Robbie's chocolate crispies, and a big bunch of black grapes to finish things off. We had home-made lemonade to drink and Dad and Alice had wine again. Quite a lot of it. They lay down, feeding each other grapes – and were fast asleep in minutes.

'Hurray!' said Smash. 'Now, let's find that Psammead again.'

'Yes, let's!' I said.

'Yes, and I'm going to wish I can climb trees all over again to show Dad,' said Robbie.

'Oh no, you're not!' said Smash. 'It's not *your* turn to make a wish!'

'Well, I'll wish we can *all* climb trees,' said Robbie.

'I can climb trees already, so that would be *totally* wasted,' said Smash. 'No, *I'm* going to wish this time, as I found the Psammead.'

'Yes, but I got him out,' said Robbie.

'But *I* was the one who identified him,' I said. 'I'm the one who read the book. I'm the one who knows how the Psammead behaves and how the wishes nearly

67

always go wrong if you're not extra careful. I think we'd all be much better off if *I* made a wish for all of us.'

'Oh, you're much too timid and goody-goody, Rosalind. You'll start wishing for something totally mushy, like we'll all love each other, or we'll all be happy, or something impossible, like World Peace or Saving the Planet,' Smash said scornfully.

'I think those are good wishes,' I said, stung, because she'd read my mind pretty accurately.

'But it's not going to make much difference if it all stops at sunset,' said Smash, getting down on her knees and digging. 'Come on, help me, you lot.'

We all knelt down and helped her, even Maudie.

'It might make a *bit* of difference,' I said. 'If we had World Peace for a day, then all the soldiers in all the different countries might like it so much they'd never want to shoot anyone ever again, and then think how wonderful that would be. Pacifists have tried to achieve this for centuries and yet we could do it just by wishing.'

'Oh, rubbish, of course they'd all start again the moment the spell wore off. Look at the British and the Germans in the First World War,' said Smash. 'They had a truce at Christmas and climbed out of their trenches and played football together – and then they went back to shooting and gassing each other the very next day.'

Smash might have missed a lot of school but annoyingly she seemed to know a lot.

'Let's not waste our breath arguing,' I said. 'Let's just dig.'

So we dug some more. We dug until our nails throbbed and our arms ached. We dug so far down we came to much darker sand mixed up with earth.

'The Psammead wouldn't like burrowing right down here, it's too mucky and damp,' said Robbie. 'I think we're digging in the wrong place. Let's try a bit further away.'

'Oh, for goodness' *sake*,' said Smash, but she shuffled over in the sand and started again.

'We should have marked exactly where the Psammead burrowed down so that we could find it again easily,' I said.

'Yes, but then some other kids might come along and poke their noses in and use up all its wishes,' said Smash. 'Come on, *dig*, Rosalind.'

'It's all right for you. The sand doesn't get up your nails because you've nibbled them right down to the quick. It keeps catching under mine and feels horrid. Perhaps I'd better go and fetch Maudie's beaker again,' I said.

'No, *not* Maudie's beaker,' said Maudie firmly. She banged her little fist in the middle of the sand pile. 'Where Monkey?'

'Where indeed,' I said. 'Look, you don't think –' I paused, feeling peculiar. 'You don't think we really imagined it, do you?'

69

'What?' Smash peered at me, wrinkling her nose.

'Well, sometimes I pretend things, and I can make them seem real. So real sometimes I get mixed up and almost believe it,' I said.

'Are you some kind of nutter?' said Smash. 'I haven't got a clue what you're talking about.'

'*I* know,' said Robbie. 'I do that too. Like with my zoo animals – I know they're little pieces of plastic, of course I do, but sometimes it seems like they're great big wild animals roaring and running around me.'

'Total nutters, both of you. It must run in your family,' Smash said. 'Well, *I* don't pretend anything of the sort. I saw that sammy-thingy yesterday and I absolutely know it's real.'

'I am not a "sammy-thingy", if you please. I am the Psammead,' said a voice behind us.

We whipped round. There was the Psammead sitting on the sand, its arms crossed as it contemplated us, eyes swivelling on their stalks.

'*There* you are! Oh, I'm *ever* so pleased you really are real,' I said. I wanted to stroke it, but I didn't quite dare, in case it thought I was being impertinent.

Maudie was much bolder. She shuffled forward on her knees and reached out eagerly.

'*Nice* Monkey,' she said.

'And nice small infant,' said the Psammead, returning the compliment politely, but it edged backwards. It looked at me. 'Could you please wipe her paws if she must touch me? They look a little damp to me. I have a horror of water.'

'Are you like the Wicked Witch of the West? Will you shrivel up if we pour a bucket of water over you?' said Smash.

'Don't you dare try!' said Robbie, springing in front of the Psammead protectively.

'Do not worry, young gentleman. It would be an extremely unpleasant experience, but I would survive – *unlike* your uncouth companion, who would be instantly turned to stone and gush water forever if she dared to do any such thing.'

'*You* would turn her to stone?' I asked.

'Have you never observed fountains?' said the Psammead. 'All those stone maidens with water pitchers and ugly young louts with open mouths? All my handiwork!'

I wasn't sure if it was joking or not, but I did my best to look impressed. I wiped Maudie's sticky hands thoroughly with the bottom of my T-shirt.

'Nice, nice, *nice* Monkey,' Maudie said, and very gently stroked the Psammead's back with one hand.

It quivered a little, clearly not particularly enjoying the experience, but it sat still for her.

'Were you hiding behind us all the time we were digging?' Smash demanded.

'No, indeed. I was snoozing delightfully deep in my sand, when you started excavating the entire pit with such clumsy vigour that you caused a minor earthquake.

I was abruptly woken from my slumbers and tossed hither and yon until I scrabbled free and listened to your not especially interesting philosophical discussion on the nature of my existence,' said the Psammead.

'Well, you obviously do exist and we'd like you to do another wish for us,' said Smash.

The Psammead looked outraged.

'Please,' Smash added.

'I *don't* please, Miss Shouty Person. Why on earth should I exhaust myself granting you wishes when you destroy my sleeping quarters and then threaten to annihilate me with a jug of water?'

'But – but isn't that what you do? Grant wishes? That's your job!' said Smash.

The Psammead gave a little hissing sound, so that puffs of air blew between its sharp little teeth. It might have been a laugh, though it didn't sound very mirthful. It might have been a threat.

'Shut up, Smash. We must treat the Psammead with great *respect*,' I said.

'Because we want a wish?' said Smash.

'Because it's a very, very elderly and amazing magical individual, a myth and a legend and possibly even an immortal,' I said.

The Psammead's mood changed. It positively preened.

'I couldn't have expressed it better myself,' said the Psammead. 'You have a way with words, Miss Rosalind.'

'That's because she's always reading hundreds of

books,' said Smash. 'And she's a creep. But I didn't mean to upset you, Mr Psammead, sir. I wasn't really being rude. I talk like this to everyone. It's just my way.'

'It's a very unpleasant way,' said the Psammead. 'When I last surfaced, the children then had mostly impeccable manners. That was in the good old days when children were supposed to be seen and not heard.' It sighed wistfully. 'I still feel quite affronted. I am not used to shouty people. I think I will have to retire to my bed forthwith.' It started scrabbling in the sand.

'Oh, don't go! Please! I'm sorry, I'm very, very, very sorry. I didn't mean to upset you for the world!' said Smash, trying hard to make her voice pleasant and placating. She sounded weirdly like her mother.

The Psammead didn't look convinced, but then Maudie nestled up to it and stroked its fur again, very gently and soothingly.

'Very, very sorry,' she echoed, though she'd done nothing wrong.

The Psammead stopped scrabbling and stretched a little.

'Yes, yes, small child. Scratch my back a little, my paws don't reach quite far enough. Ah! That's delightful. Now, where were we?'

'Perhaps – perhaps you were about to grant us another wish?' said Robbie.

'Perhaps I was,' said the Psammead.

'Then I wish –' Robbie began.

73

'You've *had* your turn, Robs,' I said. 'No, please, dear Psammead, *I* was wondering about wishing for –'

'No, no! *Please* let it be me. I wish I – okay, *we* – can all be rich and famous,' Smash gabbled.

The Psammead paused, and then nodded.

'Very well. Rich and famous it is,' it said, and started puffing itself up. It grew until its eyes bulged on the ends of its stalks and it became totally spherical – and then it subsided abruptly, scrabbled weakly in the sand, and retreated.

'Thank you so much, dear Psammead,' I said, nudging Smash to do likewise.

But she was distracted by someone approaching.

'Look out!' she said.

A vast man was striding purposefully through the woods towards us. He was very tall and very big, with a very red bald head and very little neck – a terrifying giant of a man in a pale grey straining suit, stamping towards us in shiny brown shoes.

I clutched Robbie and Smash grabbed Maudie.

'Run for it!' she said. 'He looks like a gangster! Perhaps he's going to kill us!'

But when he got nearer he stopped and touched his fingers to his scarlet forehead in a weird kind of salute.

'Good day, Miss Smash, Miss Rosalind, Master Robbie, little Miss Maudie. I hope you enjoyed your private picnic,' he said humbly. 'So sorry if you've been kept waiting.'

We blinked at him.

'Er . . . who are you?' said Smash.

He hung his huge head a little foolishly.

'You're joking me, right, Miss Smash? I'm Bulldog, your bodyguard. If you'll kindly step this way, Bob has the car ready and waiting.'

'What *kind* of car?' said Smash.

'He thought you'd ordered the pink stretch limo today as there are the four of you travelling together – but if you'd sooner the Rolls or the red Ferrari then you've only to say,' he said, clearly anxious to please.

Smash swallowed. 'Oh, I dare say the pink stretch limo will do for today,' she said, giggling. She stood up and shifted Maudie to her hip. 'Come on then,' she said to us.

'But – but we can't go off with a stranger!' Robbie hissed.

'He's not a stranger. He knows us. He *works* for us,' said Smash. 'We're rich and famous.'

'I'll say,' said Bulldog. 'You're in all the papers again, Miss Smash – and the telly people are going bananas trying to get you on their shows. Graham Norton and Paul O'Grady aren't even on speaking terms now – and Oprah's talking about sending her own private jet across the pond just to get you on her programme.'

'Really!' said Smash. 'Come *on*, you two. Let's get in this car!'

'But shouldn't we tell Dad and Alice?' I said.

'Yes, like they'll let us if we say we're going off with some great big gorilla guy to appear on telly,' Smash hissed. 'It's not *real*, Rosalind. It's magic – and it's only for one day. You can stay behind and spoil it if you like, but I'm going to make the most of it.'

'Are we famous too then?' Robbie asked. 'I wish we *could* tell Dad. What am I famous *for*?' He reached for the nearest tree branch experimentally and tried to pull himself up. It didn't work.

'Clearly *not* tree-climbing this time,' said Smash. 'Okay, we're coming, Bulldog.'

She started striding along beside him, still carrying Maudie.

'We'll go with her just to see if there really *is* a pink limo,' I whispered to Robbie. 'Don't worry. I won't let her get in the car, especially not with Maudie.'

We held hands and hurried after them. We could hear a distant murmuring. It got louder and louder – and then through the trees we saw a large crowd of people standing waiting, chatting, jostling each other, mobile phones held above their heads, ready to take photos.

'Whatever are they waiting for?' I asked as we got nearer.

There was a sudden roar. They surged towards us, mobile phones flashing like fireworks.

'They're waiting for *us*!' Smash said.

Bulldog barged forward, arms spread, shielding us, while two more massive bull-headed minders leant hard against the crowd, quelling anyone too eager to get a glimpse of us.

'It *is* us!' I said.

I looked down at myself hopefully, thinking that I must be transformed into some glossy adult celebrity, all tan and glitter and cleavage and high heels. No, I still seemed to be me, with my mousy plaits and my slightly grubby T-shirt and my jeans with a rip at the knees from yesterday's tree-climbing. Robbie was just the same too, his hair sticking up at the back and his glasses slightly askew. Smash was her ordinary self, with her T-shirt too tight and showing her tummy, and her sparkly shoes covered in sandy dust. Maudie always looked delightful, with her lovely blonde hair and big blue eyes and sweet smile, but she had a runny nose and she was sucking her thumb anxiously.

So why were these crowds of people surging forward to see four ordinary tousled children? Smash was grinning all over her face, strolling along, waving to everyone, while they roared her name and begged her to look this way and that and thrust autograph books at her for her to sign. And it wasn't *just* Smash. They clamoured for me and Robbie! They were even mad enough to try to get Maudie to sign stuff, when she can only print a very wobbly M. There were several stupid women crowding up really close to her, giving her presents, great chocolate bunnies, pink teddy bears, an entire herd of Sophie the Giraffe. Maudie was getting poked and pinched as they ooohed and aaahed over her blonde curls and dimples.

Smash tried to fight them off, her arms tight round Maudie, but someone was grabbing at her T-shirt and someone else was pulling at her hair. Bulldog lifted Maudie and Smash up in his huge arms and ran with them, to where an enormous bright pink limo was waiting, surrounded by more burly bodyguards. I screamed and called after them, hanging on desperately to Robbie, while I tried to duck away from someone who was waving books at me – and then two great minders grabbed me, grabbed Robbie and ran with us too.

We were thrust through the open door into the limo and tumbled down beside Smash and Maudie, as the car revved up and shot off like a rocket.

'Phew!' said Smash, laughing hysterically. 'They went *crazy*, especially over me! Did you just hear them!'

'Yes, but – but what about Dad and Alice? They'll go mad when they wake up and find we've all disappeared. And here we are in a crazy car and we don't even know where we're going!' I gabbled.

'Don't worry, Rosalind. I have your full schedule here,' said a pretty woman with shiny brown bobbed hair. Bulldog and Bob the smiley chauffeur were in the front of the limo, but the brown-haired lady was in the back with us. She whipped a BlackBerry out of her huge handbag and consulted it, smiling. 'We're due to arrive at Harrods at two. They're closing the entire store for us, so there shouldn't be any problems.'

'Trust Naomi – she can fix anything!' said Bulldog.

'What's Harrods?' said Robbie.

'It's a huge posh department store,' said Smash. 'So . . . we're going *shopping*?'

'It will have to be a whistle-stop trip, I'm afraid,' said Naomi. 'But you're always such a decisive shopper, Smash.'

'Is this shopping trip *just* for Smash?' I asked.

Naomi laughed. 'Of course not, Rosalind. I've had them pick out some great outfits for you, just you wait and see,' she assured me.

'And . . . shoes? Could I have some shoes a bit like . . . ?' I pointed to Smash's sparkly emerald trainers.

'Certainly. There will be several pairs of trainers, Converse boots, espadrilles to go with shorts, jeans and beach wear – plus little patent pumps for smart dresses and high heels for parties,' she said.

'That's absolutely marvellous!' I said.

'You're not allowed high heels, Rosalind,' said Robbie.

'You try and stop me,' I said.

'High heels, high heels!' said Maudie, thrusting out her feet as if she wanted some too.

'Is this just going to be boring old clothes shopping?' said Robbie.

'Oh, I know where *you* want to go, Robbie!' said Naomi.

'Where *do* I want to go?' asked Robbie.

'I'm guessing you'll want to check out the kitchenware

79

first, but I've given the pet department a ring and they're very much looking forward to seeing you too,' she said.

We were all a little baffled by the reference to kitchen-ware, but the mention of the pet shop made Robbie bounce excitedly on the seat.

'Oh, Smash, this is an *ace* wish!' he said.

'A tad more interesting than tree-climbing,' she said. She was fiddling with buttons in the upholstery, so that music suddenly blared. Then she pointed to a pink bottle with a gold-foil top and four glasses stacked in a little alcove. 'Can we have some of that?'

'Of course you can,' said Naomi. She got the bottle out and expertly popped the cork.

'Smash, that's pink champagne!'

'So?' said Smash.

'Well, Maudie definitely can't drink it. And Robbie shouldn't either,' I said.

'Yes, I should!' said Robbie. 'I've always wanted to know what champagne tastes like.'

'Well, just a sip. We'll all just have a sip,' I said. 'We don't want to end up drunk.'

'*I* do! It's my wish. I can do what I want,' said Smash, taking a long gulp. She snorted a little as the bubbles went up her nose, but she went on drinking steadily until she'd finished her glassful. Then she hiccuped and laughed at me.

'*Smash!*' I said, taking a sip myself. She wasn't quite

as crazy as I'd thought. It wasn't champagne at all, it was extra-delicious pink fizzy lemonade.

We all had some, and shared a wonderful big box of pink and white chocolates. There were ultra-cute pink and white jelly babies too, which we let Maudie have. She insisted on playing with them in between nibbles, so she got very sticky indeed, but Naomi was clearly prepared for every eventuality and produced a pack of wet wipes from her voluminous handbag.

'Come here, Maudie. Let Naomi wipe your hands,' she said.

She wiped Maudie's face too, but very gently and carefully. Maudie usually squirmed and struggled when Alice attacked her with a damp flannel, but she accepted Naomi's ministrations with dignity. When the limo drew up outside Harrods, Maudie put her hand in Naomi's, treating her like a new mummy.

The friendly chauffeur Bob took us to a back entrance, but even so there were more crowds jostling on the pavement, pressing so close to the car that their noses were bizarrely squashed against the black glass. They couldn't see in at us, but we could see them. Robbie clutched my hand tight and even Smash looked apprehensive.

'How are we supposed to get out? They look like they'll tear us apart!' said Smash.

'The boys will protect you,' said Naomi.

Bulldog was whispering urgently into his mobile while looking at his watch.

'Now!' he said suddenly, flinging the car doors open.

He seemed to have summoned up a whole army of Bulldog clones. Very large men in suits manhandled the crowd out of the way, forcing a tunnel to the entrance – and Bulldog hurried us through it. Smash tried to pause for photos and autographs, but this caused such a flurry of people that they were surging all around her, nearly knocking her over. Bulldog caught her up and carried her over his shoulder into the store.

'Excuse the liberty, Miss Smash, but you were getting a bit swamped there,' he said, setting her down gently.

Smash's hair was sticking up and she needed several of Naomi's wet wipes herself, but she thanked him regally, as if she were the Queen, and then waved to the assembled shop staff. We were escorted to the lifts and Smash pressed the button to the fourth floor, clearly knowing where she was going.

There was an enormous toy department on this top floor. Maudie started jumping up and down, Robbie got his lion and tiger out of his pockets to look for friends and I have to admit I got quite excited too, even though I'm really much too old for toys.

Smash let Maudie grab a gigantic blue rabbit and ordered Naomi to pay for it, but then she hurried us on to the clothes department. Robbie moaned and I hung back as well, wishing I'd had a chance to look at the special American dolls properly. I rather wanted one – just as an ornament, not to play with, of course.

But then I got completely distracted by the clothes department.

Mum and I usually go to Primark for T-shirts and jeans. I had no idea you could have vast departments specially for girls under fourteen, with the most amazing designer outfits: slinky shorts and showy halter tops, tiny miniskirts and long flouncy maxis, elaborate party dresses with a froth of pale petticoats all different pastel colours – and the *shoes*! I ran from one pair to the next ecstatically. I tried on a pair of real high heels and wobbled around in front of the mirror, kicking up my legs at an angle to see the shoes to their best advantage.

'You don't half look daft, Rosalind,' said Robbie, but I just stuck my tongue out at him.

Smash was rushing around the rails, helping herself to armfuls of clothes.

'Come on, Rosalind, let's try them all on,' she said, whirling around.

'Oh, this is so *boring*!' said Robbie.

'You choose some clothes from the boys' section, Robs,' I said.

'I don't like those sorts of clothes – they don't look *comfy*,' said Robbie. 'I'm going off to find this pet department.'

'Oh, that's not fair! *I* want to see the pets too – and it's *my* wish,' said Smash.

'If you like, Robbie, I'll get an assistant to pick out an outfit for you, and then we can go to check out the kitchen equipment while Smash and Rosalind and Maudie try on their clothes. Then we should *all* have time to go to see the pets together,' said Naomi.

It was a suggestion that pleased everyone, though Robbie was still surprised that she thought kitchen equipment his top priority. But he went off willingly enough while we had a wonderful time trying on all the outfits. Robbie returned looking utterly astonished.

'Ros, Ros, you'll never guess what! They had saucepans and baking dishes and knives and all sorts of stuff –'

'So? Robbie, what do you think of these clothes? Do you think I look okay?'

He barely gave my outfit a second glance, and simply shrugged.

'I suppose,' he said.

I thought I looked *wonderful*. I'd chosen a deep-blue silky T-shirt with the moon and stars patterned on it, amazing black designer jeans that cost twenty times more than my old ones and a pair of sapphire-blue sparkly sneakers.

'Ros, *listen*,' said Robbie. 'All that kitchen stuff – it was called the Robbie Range.'

'Yeah? Well, you could pretend it's *your* range then,' I said.

'But it *is* mine! It had my face on the packaging,' said Robbie.

'Are you sure?' I said, not really interested. 'Look at my *shoes*, Robbie!'

'They're a bit too sparkly,' said Robbie. He suddenly looked worried. '*I* don't have to wear sparkly shoes, do I? Dad won't like it.'

Naomi had chosen red boots for him, but they were plain canvas, with blue laces. He had new jeans too, and a red-and-blue checked shirt, perfect Robbie clothes.

We'd had a hard time getting Maudie dressed because she insisted she wanted Big Girls' clothes. She didn't just mean styling, she meant sizing too, so all her chosen dresses trailed on the ground and she staggered along in enormous high heels.

'You can choose one long dress and a pair of high heels for dressing up, Maudie. But I think you need something more your size for your show,' Naomi said firmly. She picked out a beautiful little blue and green flowery dress with a tiny blue and green teddy tucked in a pocket in the front.

'Maudie's in a *show*?' said Smash. 'You look great, Maudie! Give us a twirl then to show off your flouncy new skirt.'

Smash's new skirt was the exact opposite, a tiny tight little strip of material that barely showed under her big black T-shirt. It had a great sparkly silver star and the word *Superstar!* embossed on the front. She had black tights and strappy silver heels, really quite high ones. I looked at her enviously, though I'd never have dared wear such an outfit myself.

'Of course, Maudie's in her special television show,'

said Naomi, as she paid the astronomic clothes bill. 'And Robbie has his special show too.'

'What about *me*?' said Smash.

Naomi laughed and pointed to Smash's T-shirt.

'Come on! You're the superstar, Smash.'

'Am *I* in a show?' I asked, my tummy turning over.

Naomi looked surprised.

'No, Rosalind, though I'm sure that could be arranged. Would you like that?'

'I – I don't think so,' I said.

I knew I'd be absolutely terrified of going on television – and yet I didn't really want to be left out either. Perhaps I was the only one of us who wasn't rich and famous at all. Maybe I just hung out with my brother and sisters and helped them. I was surprised to find I minded quite a lot. But then the clothes assistant came over to me.

'I know this is an awful cheek and terribly unprofessional of me – but could I possibly have your autograph, Rosalind? My daughter absolutely loves your books!'

5

Naomi produced a pen and a postcard from her handbag. It was a postcard of *me*, sitting at a desk with one hand cupped under my chin, gazing dreamily into the distance. Underneath the photo there was a little caption: *Rosalind Hartlepool, children's writer*. I managed to sign my name with a flourish, though my hand was trembling. I was a proper published author – so maybe I was rich and famous too!

In confirmation, Naomi consulted her watch and then patted my shoulder.

'Your book-signing is advertised for half past three, so we're cutting it a bit fine – but there should just about be enough time for us to go and see the pets before we set off.'

I was so dazzled by the word *book-signing* that I could barely concentrate on where I was going. Then we entered the amazing Pet Kingdom – and it was just like an animal fairyland. There were rooms full of dinky designer clothes for cats and dogs and an entire pet toy department full of fluffy mini-mice and chewy chickens and little balls and sticks and bendy bones.

We looked through a glass wall and saw a special spa room for pets. We watched the most glorious little York-shire terrier enjoying a wonderfully pampering massage. A loving assistant styled his creamy white coat until it reached honey-blonde silky perfection. He gave a tiny woof of delight and nibbled daintily at a doggy treat.

'Oh, I want *that* little dog!' said Smash, as the assistant carefully tied a bow tie studded with diamonds round his tiny neck.

'You can't possibly have Duffy!' said the manager of the pet department. 'He's actually Sir Duffield, our most important client, and he has his own mommy and daddy who love him very dearly. But we do have a whole room-ful of very precious VIPs – Very Important Pets – who are all for sale. Allow me to show you.'

We gasped at all the animals: gambolling puppies, delicate kittens, floppy-eared rabbits, squeaking guinea pigs, little white mice with pink twitchy noses, a fluffy chinchilla as soft as thistledown, a pair of lovebirds coyly twittering at each other, and a red and green parrot preening itself, murmuring 'Pretty boy, pretty boy!'

'Where monkeys?' said Maudie, looking for another Psammead – but she seemed happy enough with a chinchilla substitute. She wanted to carry him about in her arms, but we persuaded her he'd be safer travelling in his cage. Maudie hugged her blue stuffed rabbit as a substitute.

Smash stalked about excitedly in her high heels, wanting everything, but she eventually chose the parrot.

'I shall teach it to say all sorts!' she said. 'Pretty Smash, pretty Smash – say "Pretty Smash"!' she repeated.

The parrot looked at her shrewdly with its little beady eye, and opted for a quiet life.

'Pretty Smash, pretty Smash,' he chirped.

Smash squealed with delight. He imitated her squeal at top volume, so we all had to put our hands over our ears.

Robbie wondered if there were any pet lions or tigers, but was happy enough in the dog section. He fell in love with an adorable black Labrador puppy with huge brown eyes. An assistant opened up its cage so that Robbie could coax the puppy out and hold him gently in his arms. The puppy looked up at him and licked his nose lovingly.

'Oh, he's so wonderful!' Robbie whispered, tears in his eyes.

Robbie had been begging for his own dog for years, but Mum said she couldn't cope with a pet in our tiny flat.

I wondered about choosing a dog too, but then I saw a

very little cream Siamese kitten with mushroom-coloured ears and paws, and I knew I simply had to have her.

'She's so gorgeous! I just love her to bits,' I said. 'I think I shall call her Tina, because she's so tiny.'

'I'm calling my puppy Giant because he's going to grow up big and strong and growl at all my enemies,' said Robbie.

'My parrot is called Gobby-Bird,' said Smash.

'I think that's highly appropriate,' said Naomi, as the parrot shrieked its head off. 'What are you going to call your chinchilla, Maudie?'

'Monkey!' said Maudie, who didn't seem very skilled at distinguishing between different animal species.

We needed a whole troupe of assistants to accompany us downstairs and out of the back entrance to the car, carrying large padded travelling cages for Tina and Giant and Monkey and an enormous ornate cage for Gobby-Bird. It was quite a trial getting all of us into the stretch limo. It needed to stretch a little *more* for it to be a comfortable fit, but we managed all the complicated manoeuvring at last, while Bulldog and a team of security men fended off the crowds.

'Now for Rosalind's signing!' said Naomi.

'That's ultra important!' said Bob the chauffeur, smiling at me. He quickly drove us the short distance from Knightsbridge to Piccadilly. There was a huge four-storey bookshop there, but it looked as if it would take us hours and hours to get inside, because there was a large queue of children snaking all the way to Piccadilly Circus, round the statue of Eros, and then back again.

'I wonder why they're all queuing up like that to get into the bookshop?' I asked.

Naomi laughed at me.

'They're queuing for you, Rosalind! They want to buy your latest book and get you to sign it.'

'They're queuing for *Rosalind*?' said Smash, stunned.

'Will we have to queue for her too?' Robbie asked.

'Of course not, Robbie. We'll go inside straight away. I'm sure they'll have laid on some refreshments for us,' said Naomi.

'Can Giant have some refreshments too?' said Robbie.

'And Tina?'

'And Monkey?'

'And Gobby-Bird?'

Naomi sighed, sounding a little tired, but she gave us a cheery smile.

'I'm sure that can be arranged,' she said.

We were ushered into the great big bookshop, Bulldog magically summoning up yet more minders to quell any overenthusiastic fans and ferry our unruly menagerie into the shop.

'It's so great to have you do another signing in our shop, Rosalind!' said a lovely thin dark-haired man called Gary. 'I wonder if you could sign a few special dedications for us first?'

He led us upstairs to a special staffroom. There was a

spread of delicious food on a table: strawberries, rasp-berries, little figs, crisps, nuts, olives, and nibble-size chocolate eclairs and cream doughnuts. However, I only had eyes for the books on the table. They had a lovely red-and-gold cover with the title *Four Children and It* picked out in silver, together with my name, Rosalind Hartlepool.

I fingered the cover, trembling. It really was *my* book. There was the same postcard photo of me on the back cover gazing dreamily back at me. I opened the book and started reading.

'It's quite *good*!' I said, astonished – and then I blushed scarlet because I sounded as if I was showing off.

'It's *very* good,' said Gary. 'Could you sign on the title page? I've got a list of special customers. I've got the names all written down here. Perhaps you could sign one each for Brooklyn, Cruz, Romeo and Harper Seven, another two for Junior and Princess, ditto for Apple and Moses, a joint copy for Maddox, Pax, Zahara, Shiloh, Knox and Vivienne, one for Bluebell, another for Suri, and one for Lourdes because she's still a big fan.'

I signed busily, while Smash and Robbie and Maudie ate some of the refreshments and supervised the feeding and watering of the pets. Maudie insisted on feeding her stuffed blue rabbit too. Tina the kitten curled up on my lap as I signed, nestling into me.

'There, that's brilliant,' said Gary. 'Are you ready to face your fans now?'

He escorted me down to the ground floor. As soon as

people caught sight of me, there was an amazing squeal and stir and flash of cameras. I was led to a chair almost like a throne with a canopy above it, declaring I was *Rosalind Hartlepool, Child Wonder Writer*. I sat down on my grand chair, selected a pen from a handful waiting on the table and smiled at the girl first in the queue. Gary beckoned her over and helped her get her *Four Children and It* open at the title page.

'Hello, what's your name?' I asked.

'I'm Rebecca, probably your biggest fan,' she whispered shyly. She was shy of *me*!

I wrote *To Rebecca, with love from Rosalind Hartlepool* on her book in my best handwriting and she thanked me as if I'd given her a wonderful present. She walked off clutching her book to her chest, saying, 'I've met Rosalind Hartlepool!' over and over to her mother.

It was so astonishing I could barely believe it. Well, I knew it was only happening because of the Psammead, but it seemed real all the same. I smiled and spoke and signed for each child in the queue in such a bubble of happiness I felt I'd rise up like a balloon any moment and hover above everyone. Every now and then Robbie and Smash and Maudie came over and peered at me incredulously.

'How come *you've* written this silly book when it was *my* idea to be rich and famous?' said Smash.

'I like writing stories too. Maybe I could write a book one day,' said Robbie.

'Ros read me story,' said Maudie, trying to climb on to my lap alongside the kitten.

Naomi had to take them all back upstairs. She was looking at her watch rather worriedly.

'Try to speed it up just a little, Rosalind, or we'll be late for the live television show,' she murmured.

My bubble burst. 'I haven't got to be on television, have I?' I said. I was fine talking to all these lovely bookworm children one by one, but the thought of looking into a television camera and talking to millions of viewers at a time made me feel sick with terror.

'No, no – it's *Robbie's* show,' said Naomi.

She helped get Robbie, Smash, Maudie, and all the animals and one loudly squawking bird into the limo while I signed like crazy until I reached the last child, who was crying because she thought she'd never get to see me and have her book signed. I gave her a big hug and put lots of kisses under my signature, thanked Gary fervently for all his help and then let Bulldog pick me up and run with me to the car.

We drove frantically fast through the traffic to White City. Robbie clutched me in the car, looking pale.

'I feel a bit sick, Ros,' he whispered. 'I don't *really* have my own television show, do I?'

'Look, it should be *my* show, seeing as it's my wish,' said Smash. '*I'll* go on television. I'm sure I'm more rich and famous than you are, Robbie. You can't do anything.'

'That's not fair, Smash. Stop being mean to him,' I hissed fiercely.

'I'm not being mean, I'm actually trying to be kind and stop Robbie embarrassing himself. *Again.*'

But Robbie didn't embarrass himself at all. He wasn't famous for singing or dancing or telling silly jokes. He was famous for *cooking*. He was Robbie the Teatime TV Child Chef.

'So *that's* why all those pots and pans had my face on!' he said when he was led on to his own stage set in the television studio. It was a proper little kitchen with a big cooker and a sink and a dresser holding a hundred and one Robbie Hartlepool kitchen utensils. All these little Robbies had shiny smiles – and my Robbie smiled back at himself, thrilled to bits.

The television crew greeted Robbie with great respect, running backwards and forwards with microphones and drinks of water. A make-up lady even dabbed a little powder on Robbie's face because he'd gone pink and shiny with excitement. Then we were all told to be very quiet. Smash held Maudie on her lap and put her finger up to her mouth.

'Sh, Maudie!' she whispered.

'Sh, sh, sh!' Maudie said loudly – but when Robbie's signature tune started up Maudie shut her mouth tight and didn't make a sound.

Robbie smiled straight at the camera, his new red-and-blue checked shirt neatly matching the red and blue curtains hanging at the kitchen window above the sink. He hadn't had time for any rehearsal, he hadn't even been told what to cook – but somehow here in the studio Robbie knew exactly what to do.

'Hi, everyone,' he said. 'Today I'm going to show you how to make some really scrumptious cakes. They're all extra easy-peasy to make. I'll start off with chocolate crispy cakes.'

He reached for a packet of cornflakes and a large bar of chocolate.

'These are great to eat as a snack when you get in from school. You can make a boxful as a present when you go to visit your granny. You can take them on a picnic as a chocolatey treat after you've munched all your sandwiches.'

He set about making the chocolate crispies, and poured the mixture carefully into little cake wrappers.

'Now, while these are cooling, we'll make a five-minute sponge cake,' said Robbie. 'You need some butter and sugar, and some flour and one egg and a little milk. You just mix them all together. You don't need a proper cake mixer. You just stir them round, beating until they're smooth. Just think of your worst enemy at school, or the meanest teacher, and beat and beat and beat. It's great fun, and you won't even have to do much washing-up afterwards because I guarantee you'll want to lick the bowl clean.'

Robbie made his own sponge cake, and when he'd

put it in the oven he showed his viewers how to make buttercream for the filling and lemon-flavoured icing for the topping.

'I *like* lemons,' said Robbie. 'Let's make some lemon tarts too. We'll make a batch of extra fruity jam tarts, some with lemon, and some with blackcurrants – a yummy way to get lots of vitamin C. First we make the pastry and then we roll it out and cut it into tart shapes.'

He had some little scrappy pieces of pastry left over.

'I'm not going to waste them,' he said. 'I'll make a little pastry man for my baby sister and when he's cooked I'll give him a lemon coat and blackcurrant trousers.'

'A little pastry man for *me*!' Maudie whispered.

'Want to see what they'll look like?' said Robbie. 'Here're some I made earlier!'

He couldn't have made them earlier, because he was with us, but he walked confidently to a table spread with a plate of chocolate crispies, an iced sponge cake, another plate of fruity jam tarts – and a cute little pastry man.

'Mine!' said Maudie, and she broke free of our grip and went running on to the set. 'Mine, Robbie, my munchy man!'

'It's little Polly-Wally-Doodle!' the television crew muttered, laughing, as Robbie gave Maudie her pastry man and she bit off his head. The signature tune played and Robbie waved to the camera. Maudie waved too, munching happily.

'Brilliant!' said the director, clapping Robbie on the back. 'And a perfect ending, though you'd better scoot to the studios next door, little Polly-Wally. You're being interviewed on the *Start-at-Six Show*.'

'Why do they keep calling Maudie *Polly*? And why is *she* on the *Start-at-Six Show* and not me?' said Smash. 'It's not fair. All you lot are having a chance to be rich and famous and I'm being totally left out. I'm sure that Psammead fixed it this way on purpose.'

'You really *were* brilliant, Robs,' I said, clapping him on the back. 'The way you carried on, natural as anything, with all the patter! I couldn't have done that in a million years.'

'I'm sure you could, Rosalind,' said Robbie. 'You've made chocolate crispie cakes hundreds of times – *and* sponge cake. Still, you think it went all right? I didn't sound too much of a fool?'

'You were wonderful!' I said.

'Well, you were pretty special with all those girls wanting you to sign their books,' Robbie said generously.

'For heaven's sake, pass the sick bucket,' said Smash.

'You feeling sick, Smash?' said Maudie.

Smash sighed, but gave her a cuddle. She looked at Naomi.

'Is Maudie really on the *Start-at-Six Show*?' she asked. 'She's only a baby.'

'It's just a tiny five-minute interview, with several film clips from the show,' said Naomi. 'Come on then, you lot. We have to swap studios, sharpish. Thank goodness Bulldog's looking after the animals for us.'

We all helped ourselves to one of Robbie's cakes and then dashed off to the *Start-at-Six Show* studio. Naomi let Maudie finish her pastry man in the green room, then wiped her hands and face carefully and brushed her blonde hair.

'Good luck, Maudie!' we all whispered as we crept into the studio.

The new director saw us and fanned his face in a pantomime of relief. Another man tickled Maudie under the chin and fixed a little microphone to the front of her dress.

'Now, no prizes for guessing the show just voted the most popular television sitcom,' said the presenter. 'The ratings have gone through the roof, and no wonder. We all *love* the Doodle Family, don't we? And there's no question who's stolen the show too. It isn't Mum or Dad or crusty old Grandpa. It's isn't Paul or Primrose, the two schoolkids. No, it's pint-size Polly-Wally Doodle, the little girl who's captured all our hearts. Just take a look at this clip.'

They showed an excerpt from a TV show where the family are all on a day's outing to the zoo, and the trip is going horribly wrong. Mum and Dad are arguing, Grandpa is crochety, the teenage girl is sulking and the boy is scowling too – but Polly (*our Maudie!*) is skipping along happily. She waves to each and every animal in the cages and with a bit of trick photography the animals all wave their front paws back at her.

'I just *love* that clip,' said the female presenter. 'And I love Polly-Wally Doodle – expertly played by little Maudie Hartlepool. Come and wave at *us*, Maudie.'

Maudie was gently led along to their sofa. The two adults waved at her – and Maudie politely waved back, though she looked a little bemused.

'It's a delight to have you with us, Maudie,' said the man. 'Did you like making that little film at the zoo?'

Maudie nodded.

'Which animal did you like best, Maudie?' the woman asked.

'Monkey!' said Maudie. 'Funny monkey in the sand.'

'In the sand, Maudie?' said the man presenter doubtfully.

'I know! Maudie means the meerkats!' said the lady. 'I like them too, Maudie, they're very cute.'

'I think our Maudie is the very definition of cute,' said the man presenter. 'Do you like acting in the *Doodle Family Show*, Maudie?'

'It's fun,' said Maudie.

'How ever do you remember all your lines?' asked the man.

Maudie thought hard.

'I just say stuff,' she said.

'Well, we think you say your stuff brilliantly, Maudie. Do you think you'll carry on acting when you're a big girl?'

Maudie nodded.

'Let's hope it stays fun for you, sweetheart. Well, it was lovely to talk to you, Maudie. Shall we wave good-bye too?'

They both waved, grinning away, and Maudie smiled sweetly and waved both her hands to be extra polite.

'Aaah!' said the presenters as Maudie skipped out of view.

We all gave Maudie a proud hug.

'Well done, Maudie!' said Naomi. 'You were a little star.' Then she looked at Smash. 'Time for our big star to start twinkling,' she said.

We went down to the private car park where Bulldog was taking Robbie's puppy, Giant, for a little walk. My kitten, Tina, and Maudie's chinchilla, Monkey, were both curled up asleep in the cages in the car, but Gobby-Bird the parrot was wide awake and squawking away.

'That blessed bird sings even louder than you, Smash,' said Bulldog. 'It's been doing my head in sat in the car with it.'

'I sing loudly, do I?' said Smash.

'I reckon you don't even need your microphone to give the whole O2 arena an earful,' said Bulldog, laughing.

'We'd better set off there straight away. It's a really tight schedule today,' said Naomi.

'We're going to the O2 – that huge great arena where all the stars sing?' said Smash.

Naomi and Bulldog laughed as if she was joking.

'And – and *I'm* singing there?' said Smash.

Naomi took a flyer out of her handbag. It had the word *Smash* in big jagged letters and a photo of a girl in an extraordinary silver costume with silver high heels. She was clutching a microphone and singing her heart out, her head thrown back.

Smash stared at it. We'd never seen her speechless before.

'Your concert starts at half past seven tonight,' said Naomi.

'Have they sold a lot of tickets?' Smash whispered.

'It's a sell-out. Twelve thousand.'

We all blinked.

'Twelve thousand people, all coming to see me!' said Smash. 'Then I *must* be rich and famous! More famous than Rosalind and Robbie and Maudie! Oh wow!'

It was extraordinary driving to the O2 arena, seeing the crowds milling around, all of them there to see our Smash. They started chanting when they spotted our car: 'Smash! Smash! We love Smash!'

Bob the chauffeur had a very hard job driving us up to the stage door, and Bulldog and yet more security men had an even harder time getting us – and all the animals – safely out of the car and into the building. They escorted us along a maze of corridors, O2 staff in special T-shirts smiling and nodding and saying, 'Good luck, Smash!' as we went.

We were led into a large dressing room with a huge mirror and a rack of glorious stage costumes, silver and shocking pink and canary yellow and scarlet, and black lace, all with matching high heels.

'My *costumes*!' said Smash, stroking each one, and trying on the shoes.

There was a table laid with elaborate cupcakes with buttercream to match the costumes: some vanilla cream with silver balls, some pink with raspberries, some pineapple yellow with cherries, some studded with little scarlet strawberries, and some deep blackcurrant with rainbow sprinkles.

'Yummy!' said Smash, and ate one in three quick bites.

There were soft leather sofas and a special large pen for Maudie's chinchilla. My little kitten and Robbie's puppy roamed freely, playing tag with each other. Gobby-Bird the parrot had an enormous gilded cage at one end. It hopped on its perch and started squawking, 'Smash! Smash! We love Smash!'

'He loves me,' Smash giggled. 'They *all* love me.'

'Time's getting on, Smash. Better start getting ready,' said Naomi.

Smash sat down in front of the big mirror and a make-up lady in a blue overall came and worked on her face, outlining her eyes, putting sparkles on her cheeks and giving her a bright red Cupid's-bow mouth. We were fascinated, watching Smash being transformed. Even Robbie had his mouth open, staring.

'Maudie wants some sparkle too!' Maudie said, so the make-up lady dabbed a little on the tip of her tiny nose.

'Which costume will you be wearing first, Smash?' the make-up lady asked.

'Mmm, probably the silver one,' said Smash, barely moving her mouth because she was scared of smudging her lipstick.

The make-up lady combed Smash's short hair back, attached a huge ponytail exactly the same dark colour, and then fixed little silver slides on either side. Then Smash went behind a curtain to try on the silver costume.

'Oh help, it's like wearing an elastic band!' she said. 'I can't get *into* it!'

She tussled behind the curtain for ages – but when she emerged we all clapped. I'd worried rather, because the costume was very skimpy, not much more than a swimming costume, and there was a great deal of Smash, but it was cleverly constructed to squeeze her in the right places so that she looked almost slim. She wore astonishing fishnet tights and the silver high heels. She strutted around the dressing room, swinging her new ponytail, hands on her hips.

'Oh, Smash, you really look a star,' I said.

'I *am* a star!' said Smash.

'Star, star, star!' squawked the parrot, and Smash bowed to him.

Then there was a knock on the door.

'You're due onstage in five minutes, Miss Smash!' a stagehand called.

'Oh help!' said Smash. She suddenly looked like a little girl again.

'You'll be fine,' I said, and I reached out and took hold of her hand. It was icy cold. She gripped me fiercely.

'You've read the book, Rosalind,' she whispered. 'Do wishes *always* go wrong?'

'This one won't go wrong for you,' I said – though my tummy was churning and I felt sick with nerves myself.

Smash started singing little warm-up tunes, staring at herself in the mirror, turning this way and that, as if she still couldn't believe that the silver rock star reflected was really her.

Then Bulldog and more security staff came to take her backstage. Naomi and Robbie and Maudie and I were led down a different corridor, out to our special seats in the auditorium. We caused quite a stir in the audience. We heard them saying our names excitedly, craning their necks to look at us. Then the lights went down and music started up and everyone stared at the stage expectantly. It was so dark you couldn't see a thing – and I suddenly wondered if it was dark *outside*.

I clenched my fists.

'Please don't let it be sunset just yet!' I whispered. 'Please let Smash get to sing. Stay light for ages and ages, *please.*'

We heard a roll of drums. A great spotlight shone on the stage, and there was Smash, standing right in the middle, head tilted, one hand on her hip, smiling at everyone. There was a huge roar of approval and clapping and cheering.

Smash opened her scarlet mouth and started singing. It was a song I'd never heard before, but the audience shrieked their approval and sang along with her. Smash finished with a great flourish, and then a whole troupe of dancers came leaping onstage too, dressed in black with silver stars on their leotards. Smash started dancing along with them, singing a new song, never missing a beat, even when they seized her and whirled around the stage with her.

She danced fantastically, not wobbling once in her silver shoes. When she finished that song-and-dance number, she changed the pace and sang a soft sad ballad and all those thousands of people held their breath, not making a murmur until Smash sang the last melancholy line – and then there was another roar of applause.

Smash grinned and immediately started another song, a really shouty rock song with such an insistent beat you really couldn't help clapping. There was dancing too – the dancers in black and bright pink this time. Smash whirled around with them for a while, but then the girl dancers did a very acrobatic routine without her until suddenly the boys came onstage again in a tight bunch, and in brilliant time to the music stepped aside, one after the other, to reveal Smash in shocking pink, with pink feathers in her hair and amazing pink platform heels. She sang, she danced, she even did a handstand, kicking her heels in the air and waggling her legs.

There was a huge surge forward from the crowd then, all of them yelling her name in unison. I was suddenly very scared, wondering if the wish was starting to go wrong now. Smash looked so small and vulnerable on that vast stage, and there were so many thousands of people. How on earth would Bulldog and his henchmen keep them away if they all ran at the stage at once? The fans didn't want to hurt Smash, they all clearly adored her, but she could be crushed to death in seconds if they all surged at once and fought over every last little piece of her . . .

But Smash herself put up her hands, waving them a little, cool as a cucumber.

'Sit down, guys,' she said, shaking her head at them as if they were naughty toddlers – and they all did as she said and sat back sheepishly in their seats.

Smash started singing again, this time a song that was obviously everyone's favourite, because they all roared again after the first line. It was a great powerful ballad with a soaring chorus. Smash sang it facing square to the audience, her arms in the air, her legs braced, clearly giving it her all. She sang of once being an angry little girl that no one liked, but she'd always known she was born to fame and now here she was, on the stage, singing her heart out. She sang that it meant the world to her because we were all her friends now. Everyone in the audience reached out to her, echoing the chorus fervently – until suddenly the spotlight went out and the whole stage was plunged into darkness.

Robbie clutched me and Maudie started crying.

'What *is* it? What's happened?'

'Don't like the dark!'

'It's okay, it's all right, there must be some kind of power cut. They'll put the lights back on in a minute,' I gabbled, putting my arms round both of them. 'Shall we try and go backstage, Naomi, or shall we sit it out?'

But Naomi didn't answer me. She was strangely silent. Then I realized *everyone* was silent. The raucous people in that enormous audience were all still as statues. I felt the seat in front of me – and it was empty. I stood up, feeling frantically, able to see a little now my eyes were adjusting to the darkness. No one was there. The entire audience had vanished. Naomi was gone. So was Bulldog. We were all on our own in this vast arena.

'Hello? Hello, what's happened? Please, someone put the lights back on!' It was Smash talking, her voice a mouse squeak without her microphone.

It was all over. It must be sunset. The wish had finished. We were no longer rich and famous. And we were stuck in the middle of the O2 arena in the dark by ourselves.

6

'I want it all back! Listen, Psammead, wherever you are, I want to be rich and famous again!' Smash shouted.

'It's no use, Smash,' I said, hoisting Maudie up on my hip and running down the aisle to the stage. 'The wish is over for today. It must be after sunset.'

'But why aren't we back in Oxshott woods?' said Robbie, running after me.

'I don't know. It's just the way the magic works. When the children in the story wished they had wings, they ended up stuck on the top of a tall tower after sunset.'

'Wings would be quite a cool thing to wish for,' said Smash, holding out her arms and swooping about in

109

the gloom, momentarily distracted. 'Maybe I'll wish for that next.'

'It's not your turn. You've already had your wish. And look where it's got us,' I said, starting to panic as the full realization hit me. 'How are we going to get *home*? And what are Dad and Alice going to say? They'll go *spare*. We've been missing for hours and hours.'

'Let me look at my mobile,' said Smash. 'Oh, it's horrible to be back in my boring old jeans – I *loved* that costume. Didn't I look great in it?' She tapped on the screen of her mobile and then sucked in her breath. 'Whoops! Fifty-seven missed calls! And goodness knows how many texts. *Where are you? We're getting very worried, come back now! If you're playing a silly game it's very very naughty of you. Smash, PLEASE, answer me! Is Maudie all right? Is Maudie with you? Smash, Maudie's only a baby. You need to bring her back right now. We're phoning the police!* Oh God, it goes on and on and *on*.'

'Maybe I'm glad my mum won't let me have my own mobile yet,' I said. 'You'd better phone Alice then, Smash. She sounds like she's going frantic.'

'She's not frantic about me, she's just worried about Maudie – and she *is* all right, isn't she? Maudie?' Smash called into the darkness, her voice suddenly sharp.

'Smash-Smash,' said Maudie sleepily, her head lolling on my shoulder.

'It's okay, I'm holding her. Can you get down off the stage, Smash? It's so dark I'm worried you'll fall,' I said.

'I didn't fall in those amazing platform heels, did I? Oh, they were so glorious! Didn't I look grown-up in them? And did you hear me singing?'

'I think all of London heard you singing!' I said.

'I can remember some of the songs. Listen! *I was an angry little kid.*' Her voice sounded small and scratchy, *like* an angry little kid's.

'It doesn't work without the magic,' said Robbie. 'I couldn't climb trees after, remember?'

'Yeah, but you're just hopeless. It does *so* work. It just sounds a bit weird because I haven't got a mic on now,' said Smash fiercely – but she sounded like she might be crying.

'Never mind. You *did* sing fantastically, and everyone absolutely adored you. You were a superstar,' I said.

I waited for her to say *I* was a superstar too, a brilliant best-selling author – but I waited in vain.

'Anyway, let's phone Dad and Alice and – and I suppose Dad will drive all the way over and fetch us home,' I said. My stomach lurched at the thought, but I knew we should do it immediately.

'He'll go nuts. He hates driving in London,' said Robbie. 'I can't stand it when he shouts at us. Can't we call Mum instead?'

'She's at her Summer School. We can't drag her out of it – and she hasn't got her car with her anyway,' I said.

'We don't need a car,' said Smash. 'We'll go home by

ourselves. Then maybe we can sneak in somehow and nip up to our bedrooms and pretend we were there all the time.'

'What planet are you on, Smash? As if that could happen in a million years!' I said.

'As if I could have a sell-out concert at the O2 arena!' said Smash. 'Now shut up and let's try and find our way *out* of here.'

She jumped down off the stage. We all held hands in the dark and stumbled to an exit door.

Please don't let it be locked, I said inside my head, my heart beating fast – but the door opened easily enough.

We stood blinking in the brightly lit corridor.

'But aren't we in the wrong bit? We need to get back to that dressing room. We left Giant there,' said Robbie.

'Giant?' said Smash.

'My *dog* Giant,' said Robbie. 'Do you think Bulldog might have taken him for a walk?'

'Don't be daft, Robs. Giant doesn't exist any more – or Bulldog for that matter.'

Robbie bent his head.

'I *loved* Giant,' he mumbled.

'Look, I loved my little kitten –'

'I'm quite glad that parrot's not real. Gobby-Bird was a bit *too* gobby,' said Smash. 'But I do miss my clothes and those glorious shoes. Have I still got any of my make-up on?' She rubbed her face experimentally. 'No, worst luck!'

'Monkey!' said Maudie mournfully. 'Want *Monkey*!'

We didn't know if she meant the chinchilla or the Psammead itself. Perhaps Maudie didn't either. She just knew she was tired and hungry and stuck in a strange corridor, feeling lost and miserable. She started crying.

'Don't cry, darling,' I said, shifting her to the other hip.

Maudie cried harder.

'She wants *me*,' said Smash, grabbing her. 'You want your Smash-Smash, don't you, Maudie? Come on, we'll go home and tomorrow you'll see Monkey again. We can wish for heaps of monkeys if you like and you can play with all of them.'

'I thought it was *my* turn to make a wish – though I suppose Maudie can go first as she's little,' I said.

'I think we should all wish Dad doesn't get cross,' Robbie sniffed. 'Because he will be, especially with me. He just always is.'

'No, he'll be crossest with me, because I'm the eldest,' I said, sighing. 'Look, can't we just text him, Smash, to let him know we're safe and on our way home? Though how are we going to *get* home? We can't walk, it's miles and miles and miles, and we don't even know the way.'

Robbie and Maudie were already crying and I felt very near tears myself.

'You are pathetic, you lot,' said Smash. 'Follow me.'

I don't think she really knew where she was going, but she strode along the corridor determinedly, shifting

Maudie so that she was riding piggyback. Robbie and I shuffled along after them.

'Hey! What are you kids doing here?'

A security man stood right at the end of the corridor, staring at us in astonishment.

'How did you lot get in?'

It was going to be a waste of time trying to explain.

'Run!' said Smash.

So we ran for it.

Robbie and I can't run very fast, and Smash was carrying Maudie, but he was still a long way away. We thundered back down the corridor, saw a door and hurtled through it – into a busy complex of shops and restaurants.

'Keep on running!' Smash yelled, though he didn't seem to be following us now. We saw a sign overhead: *To the Underground*.

'Aha!' said Smash. 'Come on, you lot! We'll get the tube.'

'By ourselves?' Robbie said.

Smash snorted contemptuously.

'I suppose you two always go everywhere with Mumsie-Wumsie,' she said.

'Shut up! Of course not,' I said – though she was right.

Smash marched forward confidently and we bobbed along in her wake.

'What are we going to do about tickets?' I asked

anxiously, wondering if Smash was planning to try jumping over the gate.

Smash rolled her eyes.

'I suppose I'll have to donate some of my pocket money,' she said.

She took a plastic Mickey Mouse purse out of her jeans pocket.

'But it'll cost heaps,' I said.

'I've *got* heaps,' said Smash, fingering a little wad of paper money.

She asked for two children's travel cards at the kiosk, and handed one to me.

'What about Maudie and Rob's?'

'They're too little to need tickets. Don't you know *anything*?' said Smash.

I *didn't* seem to know anything, even though I was a year older. Though I'd travelled on a tube in London before I had no idea which platform to go to or where to get off, but Smash just glanced at a strange underground map and worked it all out in a flash.

The underground was quite crowded and several couples stared at us.

'Are you children all by yourselves?' one middle-aged lady asked, looking concerned.

'Yes, we are,' said Smash. 'But it's all right. I'm looking after them.'

I blushed furiously, aware I was taller than Smash and clearly the eldest.

'Does your mother *let* you travel around after dark by yourselves?'

'She doesn't have any choice,' said Smash. 'She's got this illness and she's in a wheelchair and our dad cleared off ages ago.'

'Oh dear!' said the lady, taking her seriously. 'But surely – surely there must be someone who could help?'

'We don't need help, thank you,' said Smash.

The tube train rumbled into the station, making Maudie suddenly start whimpering in alarm.

'There now, Maudie, it's okay, darling. It's just a funny train,' said Smash, jogging her up and down. 'On we get.'

Robbie didn't like the tube either. He wouldn't get on. He froze like a statue, his foot hovering over the gap. He peered at the dark track below anxiously.

'We could fall down,' he said.

Smash would normally have groaned at him, but now she coaxed him gently.

'Come on, Robs, it's quite safe, honestly. You can't fall – and if you do I'll catch you!'

Robbie didn't look convinced, but the woman seemed very impressed.

'What an amazing plucky little girl,' she murmured.

Smash smirked at me, enjoying herself enormously. I wasn't so sure she'd become a rich and famous singer in the future. It seemed more likely she'd become a rich and famous actress. Or even a London Tour Guide – she seemed to be able to find her way around instinctively. She signalled for us all to get off the tube at Waterloo and led us along mystifying tunnels.

Maudie had nodded off to sleep, but Robbie was ultra wide awake and fearful still, hating the tube noise and the tunnels and the muffled announcements to mind the gap and stand clear of the doors. He didn't like the escalators up to the mainline station either. I had to practically drag him up with us.

Smash consulted the indicator board. I did too, of course, though I wasn't even sure which station would be nearest to Dad's house. While my eyes were still swivelling up and down the lists of places, Smash shouted triumphantly, 'There! Platform eight. Come on!'

The train was quite crowded and again people stared at us. Someone else asked if we were on our own and Smash started her poor-plucky-little-me story all over again. She overdid it a little, killing our mother off altogether and inventing a cruel stepfather who shouted at us all the time and hit us if we dared argue with him.

'He's especially mean and cruel to my little brother here, making him join a gym club and then getting at him because he's so hopeless,' said Smash. 'He's terrified of him, aren't you, Robbie?'

Robbie went bright red.

'Dad isn't really like that!' he hissed when the woman got out at the next station.

'I know. I was just telling her a *story*,' said Smash.

'Well, don't tell stories about our dad,' I said. 'He *isn't* mean and cruel.'

'Then why are you both so scared of him getting cross with you?' said Smash. 'You're practically wetting yourselves over what he'll say when we get back.'

'No, we're not. We'll explain it wasn't really our fault,' I said.

'So you're going to explain we've been all round London in a limo and you've done a book-signing and Robbie's done a cookery programme and Maudie's been on the *Start-at-Six Show* and I've been a megastar at the O2 arena?' said Smash. 'Oh yes, of *course* he'll understand.'

'So what *can* we tell him?' I said.

'We've got to make them feel scared and sorry, and not blame us,' said Smash. 'I know! We could tell them this creepy guy attacked us in the woods and dragged us to his van and drove away with us and locked us up in this awful shed, but I managed to climb out of the window and let all you lot out and we just ran for it. Yeah, let's say that!'

'No, we can't, because he'll call the police and we'll all be questioned and Robbie's useless at lying – he just goes red and cries.'

'I do *not*,' said Robbie, going red and nearly crying.

'And they'll want statements and descriptions and we'll end up perjuring ourselves in court and we'll be put into some awful children's prison,' I said.

'That might be quite good fun,' said Smash. 'I bet it wouldn't be nearly so bad as this boarding school my mum sent me to – though I sorted out all the other kids and got to be boss of the dormitory. Even the big girls used to do what I said.'

'I can well believe it,' I said wearily.

'Look, it's okay. I'd look after you lot,' said Smash. She cradled Maudie, who was still fast asleep. 'I'd especially look after Maudie.'

'We don't need you to look after us,' I said haughtily.

When we got off at the right station and stood uncertainly on the forecourt, not really sure which way to go, an older man came up to us.

'You kids look a bit lost,' he said, and he put one arm round Smash and one arm round me. 'Look, I've got my car parked over there. I'll give you a lift home, shall I?'

'*Stranger danger!*' Robbie and I mouthed to each other.

'No thanks, there's our dad over there!' said Smash, pointing into the darkness.

We ducked away from the stranger and ran.

'Is Dad *really* here? I can't see him,' Robbie panted.

'We just needed to get away from that weirdo,' said Smash.

'Look, Smash, you *must* phone Dad and Alice now!'

'No fear! I'll have to pretend I've lost my mobile. Who's got pockets? Come here, Robbie.' Smash thrust her mobile into Robbie's pocket, squashing it up with his lion. 'There now. They won't search you. Come on, I think we go down that road over there. It's not too far.'

'But what are we going to say when we get home?'

'Leave it to me,' said Smash.

'Yes, that's what I'm worried about,' I said. 'You can't go making up one of your mad stories. How about us keeping it really simple? We were in the woods and we wandered off and we got lost. And then we got tired and went to sleep and when we woke up it was dark, and we've been trying to find our way home ever since. And you lost your phone somewhere in the woods – it just fell out of your pocket.'

Smash and Robbie blinked at me, not looking particularly impressed at my sudden brilliant inspiration. Even Maudie snuffled disapprovingly in her sleep, her head lolling against Smash's shoulder.

'It's a bit *lame*, that story,' said Smash. 'It makes us all sound like little kids Maudie's age.'

'Yes, but then they won't be so cross with us,' I said.

They were cross anyway. Very, very cross, though first there was a lot of hugging and crying. Dad held Robbie in one arm, me in the other, and hung on to us hard, as if he would never let us go. Alice cried all over Maudie, and then Dad pulled them close too. We were all in an embracing huddle – except Smash.

Then Dad had to phone the police, because they'd

been out searching for us. They'd even sent a *helicopter* up to hover over the woods.

'Oh wow! I wish we'd had a ride in it!' said Smash.

She didn't seem to mind a bit when Alice shouted at her and said she was incredibly naughty and irresponsible and a bad influence on all of us. She just stood there, smiling, going, 'Yeah, yeah, yeah,' until Alice shook her.

'How *dare* you behave like this!' said Alice. 'I was going out of my mind with worry.'

'Only because you were scared something had happened to Maudie,' said Smash. 'You don't care tuppence about *me*.'

We were sent to bed in disgrace. Smash pulled the covers over her head and seemed to go to sleep straight away – but when I woke up hours later I heard little sad snuffling sounds coming from her bed.

'Smash?' I whispered.

The sounds were muffled, but I could still hear them.

'Smash, are you crying?'

'Of course not, you idiot. Shut up, you've woken me now,' Smash whispered fiercely.

I struggled with myself. Why did she always have to be so rude and horrible? I really couldn't bear her. Then I heard another little sob.

I got out of bed and bent over her. I felt her cheek. It was very wet.

'Oh, Smash,' I said gently.

'I'm just furious because I didn't get to carry on sing-ing at the O2,' said Smash.

'Yeah, yeah, yeah,' I said, deliberately echoing her. I searched for my shoulder bag in the dark. I found a wad of tissues and my purse. I gave Smash the tissues and started clinking in my purse for some money.

'I haven't got enough to repay you for the train fare,' I said. 'But look, take this.'

I found her hand in the dark and pressed two coins in it.

'What's this?'

'Two pence. *I* care. About you.'

'No, you don't. You hate me.'

'I do sometimes. But then I hate Robbie sometimes too, and he's my brother. Well, I suppose you're my sister now. And you were great singing during the wish. And *really* great getting us home safely.'

Smash snuffled again, but she squeezed my hand in the dark.

'I'm going to wish we're rich and famous all over again tomorrow,' she said.

But we didn't get a chance to wish anything at all. We were still deeply in disgrace and weren't allowed out.

'Couldn't we just have a *little* picnic in the woods for Maudie's sake?' Smash said. 'She *so* loves going there – and she hasn't done anything naughty at all. Well, *we* haven't either. We couldn't *help* getting lost – and we promise, promise, promise we won't get lost again.'

'You can promise till you're blue in the face. You're not going on another picnic,' said Alice.

'Couldn't we go to that lovely sandpit place *without* a picnic?' I said. 'Or you and Dad could take some food and wine while *we* have to go without. That would be a fantastic punishment for us.'

'Be quiet, Rosalind. You're not going in the woods again. You're not going anywhere. You can't be trusted,' said Dad.

They remained adamant. We were stuck at home. To be truthful, it would normally be my idea of bliss to stay indoors all day, so long as I had enough books to read. Robbie likes reading too, or he's happy to play a long complicated zoo game with his animals. But this was a nightmare for Smash. Alice wanted to punish her particualrly, convinced it was all her fault yesterday. She confiscated her laptop so she couldn't play any games, and wouldn't let her watch any DVDs. We had to stay in our rooms while Dad and Alice played with Maudie downstairs.

'Well, they can't keep *me* cooped up here,' said Smash, going to the window. 'I'm going to climb out and walk to the woods. I'll find the Psammead. I'll wish . . . I'll wish my mum gets warts all over her face and your dad goes bald and they'll both get really, really fat and disgusting and hate the sight of each other and then they'll have a breakdown and get locked away in separate loony bins. *We'll* stay here with Maudie and get wishes every day. How about that?'

I went to the window too. We were only on the first floor, but it was still a very long way from the ground.

'Don't be mad, Smash. *You'll* be smashed if you try to jump for it.'

'If only there was some way I could get down,' Smash fretted. 'I just need a rope or something.'

In boarding-school stories they always escaped from the dormitories by knotting sheets together, but this still seemed a highly dangerous idea, so I didn't share it with Smash.

'I don't think escaping would work. *Or* magic spells against Dad and Alice. They'd get even crosser with us after sunset and keep us locked up forever. No, we've got to make them think we're really sorry. When Robbie and I have a fight with Mum, we always write her a letter afterwards saying sorry and it makes her cry and forgive us straight away.'

'I'm not writing a stupid letter!' said Smash.

'Don't then. But I'm going to. And I'll get Robbie to write one too. Robs, come in our room. I need you to do something,' I called.

I carefully tore a couple of pages out of my drawing pad and opened my big tin of coloured pencils.

'Let's do the friezes first,' I said to Robbie, drawing his margin for him because he always wobbled the ruler.

I drew little flowers and trees and bluebirds and squirrels and rabbits in my frieze. Robbie drew lions and tigers and elephants and giraffes. His animals were so big their necks and paws and trunks and tails burst right out of the frieze, but he was good at drawing so it still looked reasonably artistic.

Smash stood over us and commented caustically.

'Who do you two fancy yourselves as, Walt Disney?' she said. 'Honestly, Rosalind, exactly how old are you? Still drawing cute little bunnie-wunnies!'

'Shut up. I'm not drawing them for *me*. It's to charm my dad. And he always thinks of me as much younger than I actually am. He gave me a *doll* last Christmas.'

'He didn't!'

'Well, it might have been the Christmas before. But still,' I said, drawing steadily. I didn't feel the need to tell Smash that I'd been secretly *thrilled* with this beautiful American doll and I'd dressed and undressed her and combed her long hair and played tentative little games with her in secret.

'*My* dad gives me really cool presents, like designer clothes and my iPod and my phone. Can I have it back, Robbie? I need to see if there are any texts from him. He's been sending me *heaps* from the Seychelles.'

Smash consulted her phone and looked disappointed – but read out several texts even so. It was obvious even to Robbie that she was making them up.

'Heaps and heaps of texts,' Smash mumbled.

'Your *mum* sent you heaps and heaps of texts last night,' I said meanly.

'Stupid old bag,' said Smash, busy deleting them.

'Why don't you *try* writing her a letter?' I said. 'You don't have to mean what you put.'

'I'm not a creep like you two,' said Smash.

'Okay, we're creeps – and if it works they'll take Robbie and me to the sandpit and *we'll* get the next Psammead wish all to ourselves while you stay stuck at home,' I said.

Smash considered this.

'Give us one of your pages then,' she said, sitting down on the floor beside us.

She drew a very big frieze and spent a very long time filling it in with little pictures of herself. She drew a small Smash climbing a tree all the way up the page, another jumping on the trampoline at the gym, another dancing in high heels, and yet another wearing a black and silver costume, singing into a microphone.

'She'll think I'm simply fantasizing,' said Smash, sighing. 'But tomorrow when I wish I'm rich and famous all over again I'm going to have Mum right at the front of the auditorium. And Dad. And your boring old dad and my dad's silly new wife. And all my old schoolteachers and that stupid therapist and everyone else who's ever nagged and moaned at me. They'll all goggle at my performance and say, "Oh, *now* I understand. It's just Smash's artistic temperament – isn't she wonderful!"'

'You do talk drivel at times,' said Robbie, adding delicate stripes to his tiger.

'I'm ready to do my letter now,' I said. I drafted it out

carefully on a rough piece of paper so I wouldn't make a mess of it.

Dear Dad and Alice

I am so so sorry we worried you so much yesterday and wasted everyone's time, including the police. We truly didn't get lost on purpose but I suppose it was our fault for wandering off.

We just love going to the woods so much but if we're ever lucky enough to go there again we solemnly promise we'll stay by the sandpit. It's so good of you to take time off work to look after us and it's been such fun to stay in your house.

Please can we keep on coming to stay because you are such a special dad and stepmother.

Love from Rosalind

'Oh *yuck*!' said Smash, reading over my shoulder. She did a pretend vomit all over my head.

'I agree,' I said. 'I don't *mean* it.'

Robbie's letter was much briefer, but covered the same ground.

Dear Dad and Alice

I'm ever so sorry. I won't get lost again. I really am ever so ever so sorry.

Love from Robbie

Smash decided her letter would be briefer still. It consisted of one word: *Sorry*. But she wrote it over and over again in all different handwritings, using a new coloured pencil each time, so that it irritatingly looked most effective.

'There! See, I'm making my point without doing any loathsome grovelling,' she said. 'That's what you are, Rosalind. The Loathsome Groveller.'

'No, I'm not,' I said.

'The *Loathsome Groveller*,' Smash repeated in a silly affected voice, and she started doing a very unkind imitation of me, with her lips stuck right out revoltingly.

'Stop it! Why are you pulling that stupid face? I don't look anything like that,' I said. 'Especially not my lips.'

'Yes, you do. These are your sucky lips because you keep sucking up to my mum and your dad even though you don't like them any more than I do. You're just a gutless creep.'

'I am *not*,' I said, though my heart was banging in my chest.

'It's a waste of time anyway, because it doesn't work,' said Smash. 'They just think you're pathetic. You're so stuck up and nerdy and boring. No wonder your dad walked out on you. He got sick of you and your stupid brother. My dad *wanted* me.'

'You shut *up* about my dad,' I said.

I couldn't believe she was being so horrible, especially after I'd done my best to comfort her last night. I knew it wasn't really true – or was it? Smash was just being horrid because she was bored and fed up that her precious dad still hadn't contacted her – but somehow her words seemed to have crawled right into my head. They wriggled around there, making me feel scared and panicky.

I picked up *Five Children and It* again to distract myself. I needed to reread it to remind myself how Cyril, Anthea, their Robert and Jane had coped with the Psammead. It was hard concentrating, because Smash made up a Loathsome Groveller song, circling round me, sucking and smacking her lips and doing a special bent-over creep walk.

When we were called downstairs for lunch, we gave Dad and Alice our letters.

'You mustn't think you're getting round us just like that,' Dad said gruffly – but then he gave us a big hug.

He was careful not to leave Smash out this time. In fact he made a huge fuss of her, saying *her* letter was incredibly artistic. Smash grinned smugly and I wanted to slap her.

We were allowed to stay downstairs in the afternoon, although Smash's computer was still confiscated.

'See if I care,' she said to Alice, and she took my coloured pencils again – without asking – and started crayoning all sorts of pictures for Maudie.

'Draw Monkey!' Maudie begged.

So Smash drew a reasonably accurate picture of the Psammead, much to Maudie's delight.

'That's not a very good monkey. It's much too fat and it's got weird things sticking out of its head,' said Alice.

'Nobody asked *your* opinion,' said Smash crossly, and she scribbled all over her picture with the brown pencil until it broke.

'Smash! That's *my* pencil,' I said.

She pulled a face at me, and when Alice wasn't looking she deliberately broke a green and a blue pencil too.

'You pig! Give them back. I never said you could borrow them,' I said, snatching them back.

'Hey, hey,' said Dad, coming into the room. 'Rosalind, what are you doing? Can't Smash share your pencils?'

'No, she can't – they're *mine*,' I said, knowing I sounded like a spoilt baby. 'She's ruining them all, look.' I was a telltale now, which was even worse.

'Keep your silly crayons then,' said Smash. 'Come on, Maudie, shall we play with all your teddies? Let's give them a plasticine picnic. We're sick of silly crayoning anyway, aren't we?'

Smash played an inventive game of Teddy Bears' Picnic with Maudie. Robbie helped make all the plasticine food, which I thought was intensely disloyal of him. I sharpened all my coloured pencils until they had perfect points and then coloured in some of the pictures in *Five Children and It*.

I did it very slowly and carefully, even doing proper shading. I chose exactly the right shade of brown for the Psammead and coloured his little eye stalks rose pink. I added a tweedy design to Cyril's and Robert's clothes and gave Anthea and Jane patterned pinafores. I was particularly fond of Anthea, because she was the eldest, and she had the best ideas. I'd have liked to have her as a special friend. I wished she was real.

Smash's game of teddy bears got wilder and wilder after tea. She made all the teddies growl at Maudie, and then she made them be naughty, throwing their plasticine jam tarts everywhere.

'*Stop* that, Smash! You're getting little bits of plasticine stuck all over the carpet!' said Alice, outraged. 'And you're getting Maudie much too overexcited.'

Maudie was shrieking with laughter, but in such a high-pitched way it was almost like crying.

'Hey, hey, calm down, little Maudie,' said Dad, squatting beside her. 'Perhaps we're all getting a bit het up because we've been cooped up indoors all day. How about a little walk before bedtime? Shall we go to the pond in the park and feed the duckies?'

'No! No, go Ocky woods and feed *Monkey*,' said Maudie.

'We're not going anywhere near those wretched woods ever again,' said Alice firmly. 'You've been far too naughty and irresponsible ever to be trusted there again.'

Maudie stared at her – and burst into floods of tears.

'No, no, Maudie. I didn't mean *you*, darling,' said Alice, picking her up.

Maudie wept harder, flinging herself around hysterically.

'Hey, Maudie, don't cry, sweetheart. Let Daddy-Pops take you. There!'

Maudie arched her back and screamed louder, kicking her legs.

'She's gone past being sensible. She's overtired from all those silly noisy teddy games. Come here, I'll put her to bed,' said Alice.

'No bed, no bed – want walk in *woods*!' Maudie screamed.

'Did you hear that? Perhaps you ought to give in to her. She'll never get to sleep in that state,' Smash said quickly. 'You want a little walk in Oxshott woods, don't you, Maudie?'

'Yep!' said Maudie, stopping crying instantly.

'See that!' said Smash.

'Yes, but we're not giving in to her. We don't want to encourage her to start screaming whenever she wants her own way. We've got one spoilt brat in the family already,' said Alice crisply.

'Please, Dad-Dad,' said Maudie, snuggling up to him. 'Please go walky in woods.'

'Well, perhaps we *could* go for a quick stroll – *if* we all stayed together and you older guys absolutely promised not to wander off,' said Dad, unable to resist her.

'Brilliant, Maudie!' said Smash as we all set off. 'We'll just about get time for one more magic wish before sunset. I bags it this time.'

'But you had yesterday's wish. It's *my* turn,' I said.

'Who says we have to take it in turns? And, anyway, yesterday's wish was for all of us. We all got to be rich and famous, didn't we? I want my own wish now. I'm going to wish my dad sends me a mega-long text and I shall save it so it'll last even after sunset.'

'It won't last, it'll just disappear,' I said.

'No, it *won't*. You don't know everything. I wish *you'd* disappear,' said Smash.

'You shut up. *You* disappear, you mean beast,' I said.

'Mean beast! Is that the worst you can call me? You sound like those prattish children in your silly story-book,' said Smash, sneering at me.

We quarrelled all the way into the woods, while Robbie ran ahead talking to his lion, and Dad and Alice held Maudie's hands and swung her in the air every few steps.

'Maudie flying!' she squealed happily.

'Yes, and Mummy's arms are aching like mad!' said Alice. 'I think we'd better go back home now before it gets dark.'

'Oh no, *please*, Mum. Let's go to the sandpit. Maudie wants to have just a teeny-weeny play in the sandpit, don't you, Maudie?' said Smash.

'Yes, yes, yes!' said Maudie.

'Who's your favourite sister then?' said Smash, dancing round and round her and pulling funny faces. 'Is it Smash-Smash?'

'Smash-Smash! Smash-Smash!' Maudie cried, laughing at her.

'See!' said Smash, poking her head at me. She picked Maudie up and gave her a piggyback, jumping her up and down.

'Careful, Smash! You might trip,' said Alice. 'Put her *down*!'

'She likes it, don't you, Maudie?' said Smash. 'She likes me. She *loves* me!' She jumped even higher, forgetting that Maudie was higher still.

Maudie bumped her head on a low tree branch and started crying.

'I *told* you, you stupid careless girl!' said Alice, rushing to pull Maudie away and cradle her in her arms.

'You *idiot*, Smash, you could have taken her eye out!' Dad shouted, forgetting all his resolutions.

'I didn't *mean* to. I didn't see the stupid tree. You're all right, aren't you, Maudie?' said Smash.

Maudie was actually fine. She just had a tiny scratch from a twig on her forehead. It wasn't even bleeding. But she'd had a shock, and like any toddler she decided to make the most of all the attention. She cried noisily all the way through the woods. When Alice suggested returning home at once, she cried even harder.

Smash stumped along beside Robbie and me, glowering.

'I don't think Maudie loves you *now*,' Robbie remarked.

'You shut up, Tree Boy. Absolutely nobody *at all* loves you, you're so pathetic,' said Smash.

'Don't you dare say such horrid things to him! Take no notice, Robbie, it's not true at all. Mum loves us like anything, you know that – and Dad loves us too,' I said.

'No, he doesn't. He loved me when he thought I was good at tree-climbing, but he doesn't really like me much at all now,' said Robbie dolefully.

'Yes, he *does*,' I insisted.

'No, he doesn't,' said Smash, smirking.

We squabbled about it all the way to the sandpit. Dad and Alice sat down beside it. Maudie clamoured 'Smash-Smash!' but Alice hung on to her tightly.

'No, no, darling, you stay with Mummy and Daddy, sweetheart. You don't want to play with the big ones; you'll only get hurt. Mummy will play in the sandpit with you.' She started digging in a desultory fashion, very careful of her manicured fingernails.

'She wants to play with *me*, Mum,' said Smash sulkily. 'Won't you *listen*?'

'Don't talk to your mother in that tone of voice, Smash!' said Dad.

'You can't tell me what to do. You're not my father,' said Smash.

Maudie was scrabbling in the sand too – and seemed to have found something. It looked like a little clenched paw.

'Smash!' I said pointedly.

'You can shut up too,' said Smash, misunderstanding. 'I'm sick of you. I'm sick of being stuck in this stupid new family. I wish my mum had never ever met your dad.'

The entire Psammead surfaced, swelling rapidly. Smash saw it and gasped.

'No, that wasn't a proper wish!' she said, but it was too late.

The Psammead grew into a sphere, gave a little wheeze and then deflated rapidly. It burrowed back down into the sand immediately, not pausing to say a word. We were all speechless too. We stared at each other, Smash and Robbie and I.

'It didn't *do* anything, did it?' Smash asked.

We looked round. Alice was still sitting by the sand-pit – but where was *Dad*? And Maudie! As we watched she faded rapidly, a little ghost girl on Alice's lap. Her mouth was round in a silent scream. She lifted her wispy little arms helplessly – and then vanished completely.

'Maudie!' Smash screamed, and scrabbled at Alice, trying to grab Maudie back.

'Where is she? Where's David? What's *happening*?' said Alice.

She stood up and started shouting their names frantically.

'I didn't wish that they'd disappear!' said Smash, white with shock.

'You wished Dad had never met your mum, so he's disappeared – and Maudie doesn't even *exist* now,' I said, starting to cry.

136

'But I didn't mean it! Oh please, Psammead, *stop* it! I want Maudie back!'

'And I want my *dad*!' said Robbie. 'I love him even if he doesn't love me much.'

'Maudie! David! Where *are* you? Come back! Don't play silly games – it's getting dark!' Alice shouted, running frantically this way and that.

'It's getting *dark*!' I echoed, looking up at the sky.

I saw the pink rays of the setting sun above the tree-tops. Then Dad suddenly came running back into the clearing, looking utterly bewildered – and Maudie appeared again, bouncing on Alice's lap.

Robbie and I hugged Dad, and Smash hugged Maudie. Then we hugged little Maudie. Smash didn't go as far as hugging Dad, but she did ask him worriedly if he was all right.

'Well, I think so. I just had the weirdest kind of waking dream,' Dad said, shaking his head and looking dazed.

'Were you playing a silly trick, hiding from us?' said Alice. 'I was terrified. How did you make Maudie disappear like that?'

'*I* didn't make her disappear,' said Dad.

'But she suddenly wasn't there! One minute she was on my lap – and then she vanished,' said Alice, clasping Maudie close.

'Maudie went pop!' said Maudie, blinking.

Smash suddenly burst into tears. We all stared at her, astounded.

'Don't cry, Smash-Smash. Maudie back now,' said Maudie, smiling heroically.

Smash ducked her head and covered her eyes. She wouldn't say a word to any of us on the way home. I tried talking to her when we went to bed, but she pulled the covers over her head and wouldn't answer.

7

Smash kept picking Maudie up and giving her huge smothering hugs the next morning.

'Will you stop squeezing her like that, Smash, she's only little,' Alice snapped. 'Why do you always have to be so rough with her? If you want to play with her, why don't you sit and read her a story from one of her picture books?'

'Stories are boring,' said Smash. 'We want to play bears, don't we, Maudie?' She hunched over and growled.

Maudie jumped, startled. She'd usually have clapped her hands and giggled, but perhaps she was tired from her unexpected disappearing act last night. She backed away instead, her bottom lip trembling.

'There! Look, you're making her cry!' said Alice. 'I *told* you, read her a story.'

'And *I* told you, no,' said Smash, turning her back on her.

Alice looked at me.

'*You* read to her, Rosalind, while I sort out the washing, there's a dear,' she said.

This was clearly a tricky one – but Maudie looked at me pleadingly, going, 'Story, story, story!'

'Okay then,' I said, glancing nervously at Smash.

Maudie nestled up beside me and I started reading her *The Tiger Who Came to Tea*. Maudie chuckled and chanted along with the words, knowing most of it by heart.

'There, Smash! You see! Maudie loves being read to. *Thank* you, Rosalind,' said Alice.

Smash chanted the words too, in a niminy-piminy voice, clearly imitating me.

'Smash!' said Alice warningly.

'I'm *reading* it, aren't I? Why is it wrong if I do it, but okay for her? Oh, silly me, I forgot the sainted Rosalind can do no wrong, can she?' Smash said, sitting down beside Maudie and me.

I carried on reading self-consciously. Smash went on mumbling, one beat behind me.

'If you don't stop, Smash, I'll send you to your room,' said Alice grimly, stuffing clothes in the washing machine. She looked as if she'd like to stuff Smash in there with them.

'Alice had better watch out. Smash will be wishing her to disappear too,' Robbie whispered to me.

Smash had sharp ears.

'You shut up, Tree Boy. I *didn't* wish Maudie to disappear,' she hissed. 'But don't tempt me with possibilities. I might just wish *you* disappear, and your suck-up swotty sister.'

'Look, will you shut up, Smash? Just because you're feeling guilty about wishing Maudie away you don't need to take it out on us,' I said.

'I *didn't* wish her away! Stop saying that! It was all a mistake, you stupid little nerd.'

'*I'm* not the one who's stupid! *I'm* not the fool who wishes stuff right in front of the Psammead,' I said, losing my temper at last.

'Stop it!' said Smash, giving me a shove.

'*You* stop it!' I said.

'Don't you shove my sister!' said Robbie.

Maudie started wailing anxiously.

'Hey, hey, what's all the racket?' said Dad, breezing into the kitchen. 'What are all these grumpy faces? What are we going to do today? Shall we have a day out in London? We could take the train and go and see the sights, and maybe do some shopping?'

He expected us to whoop enthusiastically. We couldn't very well explain that we'd been driven all round London in a stretch limo the day before yesterday and *we'd* been one of the sights.

'It's very kind of you, Dad,' I said cautiously. 'But wouldn't it cost too much money?'

'That doesn't matter, not if that's what you'd like to do,' said Dad.

'Well, actually, what we'd really like would be to go on another picnic.' I paused. 'Locally. In Oxshott woods.'

'No,' said Dad. 'Not again.'

'Definitely not,' said Alice. 'That place really spooks me. First you three get totally lost – and then poor little Maudie disappears too.'

'Not for very long,' said Smash.

'And we absolutely promise we wouldn't get lost this time,' I said.

'Yes, we totally promise,' said Smash.

'You bet,' said Robbie.

'*No!*' said Dad. 'And that's an end to it.'

But it wasn't an end, because Smash picked up Maudie and whispered to her. We already knew Maudie had the potential to be an actress and say her lines on cue.

'Want to go to Ocky woods,' she said earnestly. '*Please*, Daddy-Pops. Please, Mum-Mum. Want to go to Ocky woods and sandpit and play Monkey. Want *Monkey*!'

'Monkey?' said Alice. 'Why do you always go on about this monkey, darling? There aren't any monkeys in Oxshott woods. Don't you mean you want to go to the zoo?'

'Monkey in woods!' said Maudie.

'It's a game we play with her. We pretend a monkey lives in the sandpit,' I said. 'She loves that monkey game, don't you, Maudie?'

'We've had enough games in that wretched wood,' said Dad. 'We'll take you to the zoo and show you real monkeys, Maudie. You'd like that, wouldn't you? See the funny monkeys?' Dad did a terribly embarrassing monkey imitation, capering about, scratching himself. He was clearly trying to make Maudie laugh, but she started crying instead.

'Want *my* monkey in Ocky woods,' she sobbed.

'Oh, for heaven's sake,' said Alice. 'Stop it, David. You look ridiculous and you're frightening her. All right, Maudie, we'll take you to the woods.'

'But if you three come you must not wander off and get lost,' said Dad. 'You must solemnly swear not to worry us like that again.'

'We swear,' I said.

'I *love* swearing,' said Smash.

'I swear, Dad,' said Robbie – but he got me on one side later, while we were helping Alice prepare yet another splendid picnic.

'Is it really bad if you break a swear, Ros?' he asked.

'Yes, it is, but it's all right. We won't get lost and we won't worry them, so we'll be keeping our promise, okay?'

'Aren't we going to ask the Psammead for a wish then?'

'Yes, of course we are – but I've thought of a good way to do it,' I whispered.

This time the picnic consisted of pieces of chicken breast with crunchy carrot, almond and tomato salad and big chunks of granary bread, a cherry tart with cream, soft white cheese with black grapes and savoury biscuits, a peach each and little bars of white chocolate. Alice packed a bottle of pink lemonade for us – just like the lemonade in the limo! – and a bottle of rose-pink wine for her and Dad.

Then we set off for Oxshott woods. Robbie took his zoo monkeys with him. He held a gorilla in one hand and a chimpanzee in the other, and when we got to the woods he helped them climb up ferns and bushes as if they were tall trees in the jungle.

Robbie looked up at the real trees wistfully several times. Dad looked wistful too, but managed not to say anything. Smash held Maudie's hand carefully, singing her own song to her, to the 'Ring a Ring o' Roses' tune.

> 'Going to see the monkey
> Going to see the monkey
> Sandpit! Sandpit!
> We all make a wish!'

We were so keyed up we ate the picnic as quickly as we could.

'Don't bolt your food like that! You'll get chronic

indigestion,' said Dad. He was savouring his own food, but only sipping his wine, and Alice didn't have any at all. When they'd cleared the picnic things away, they didn't lie down and doze off in the sunshine. They sat bolt upright, staring at us. Alice kept a firm hold of Maudie, even though she tried to wriggle away.

'What are they *doing*?' Smash muttered. 'Why don't they cuddle up and go to sleep?'

'They're keeping an eye on us. But maybe they'll get tired in a little while,' I whispered.

They didn't seem at *all* tired, even after another half-hour. Maudie fidgeted and moaned and refused to listen to a story and wouldn't play Round and Round the Garden with Dad. She kept looking at us and looking at the sandpit, murmuring 'Monkey!' in a melancholy fashion. Yet we were in full view of Dad and Alice. If we dug up the Psammead right in front of them, then doubtless Alice would scream her head off and Dad would catch the Psammead and stuff it in the picnic bag and carry it off to London Zoo or wherever . . .

I knew what to do when the Psammead surfaced. I just had to stop Dad and Alice seeing him first.

'They won't go to sleep this time because they're so scared we're going to wander off again. So we'll have to dig the Psammead up without them seeing,' I whispered to Smash and Robbie. 'If we all line up with our backs to Dad and Alice they won't be able to see what we're doing, not properly.'

We stood up and sauntered ever so casually into the sandpit.

'Where are you going?' Dad said immediately.

'We're just going to play in the sand, Dad,' I said.

'We're – we're pretending it's a wild terrain for my animals,' said Robbie.

Dad pulled a face. He obviously thought we were too old for pretend games now.

'Me too, me too!' said Maudie, struggling free of Alice. 'Monkey, Monkey!'

'Yes, here's the funny monkey,' said Robbie, holding out his gorilla to Maudie.

Alice let her go reluctantly. Maudie came charging over and squatted in the sand. She looked at the plastic gorilla, her face screwed up.

'No! *Monkey!*' she said.

'Yes, I know, Maudie. We're trying to find him,' I muttered. 'Let's all dig.'

We scrabbled in the sand, our backs to Dad and Alice.

'So is this the famous monkey game?' Alice called.

'Shall I come and help you dig?' Dad offered.

'No, we're fine, Dad. I know it looks a bit daft, but Maudie loves this game, don't you, darling?' I said.

'Where *Monkey*?' said Maudie.

'There!' Robbie hissed, suddenly uncovering a familiar little paw.

Maudie shrieked delightedly.

'What's that? Why is Maudie so excited?' said Alice.

'Tell Daddy-Pops,' said Dad, getting to his feet, clearly about to come over.

'Oh, dear Psammead, can you hear me? This is an emergency! Could just *part* of our wish be that Dad and Alice don't notice any magical thing, ever, no matter what happens? Oh please, *quick*, before Dad sees you,' I gabbled.

The paw twitched. There was a great heaving and scuffling of sand as the Psammead surfaced, puffed up like a ball.

'What on *earth*?' Dad said, but then his voice faded away.

The Psammead hopped right out of the sand but Dad didn't even blink. He rubbed his eyes.

'Just for a moment I thought I saw this ugly little furry animal,' Dad muttered. 'But it must have been a trick of the light.'

'*Ugly little furry animal!*' the Psammead repeated, insulted. He spoke up indignantly – but Dad didn't hear him.

'Oh well, have a good game, kids,' Dad said, and went back to join Alice.

'*Monkey!*' said Maudie, holding out her hands joyfully.

'Is she clean and dry?' said the Psammead anxiously.

'Sort of,' I said, giving Maudie another quick wipe with my T-shirt.

'So Mum and Dave can't see or hear you now? Wicked!' said Smash.

'I am *not* wicked. I am the most benign of magical beings – though I can be severe if I'm not properly respected, and when attacked I retaliate with a very powerful bite,' said the Psammead, showing its sharp teeth.

'Smash didn't mean to be disrespectful, dear Psammead,' I said, glaring at her. 'She didn't mean you were really wicked, it's just a slang way of saying you were wonderful. And you *were* wonderful, getting that wish in just in time.'

'Yes, it's quite a feat, initiating a wish upside down, head first in one's sandy bed – but I achieved it,' said the Psammead. 'Will that be all then?'

'Oh no! We wanted another wish!' said Smash.

'I did say, could *part* of our wish be that Dad and Alice don't notice anything. I know it's a bit of a cheek but we did hope we could have another part of a wish – if you'd be so nice and kind,' I said.

'Monkey *very* nice,' said Maudie, and she put her arms round the Psammead and gave him an enthusiastic hug.

It wriggled uncomfortably, its eyes right out to the end of the stalks, but it patted her gingerly with one paw.

'Yes, nice, nice, nice Monkey – I mean Psammead – so please can we be rich and famous all over again today? Please,' said Smash.

'No,' said the Psammead.

'But I said please – twice – and I was ever so respectful,' Smash wailed.

'That is a matter of opinion,' said the Psammead. 'But it is not in my power to grant you that wish, even if I wanted to.'

'But why? You granted it before!'

'Exactly. You can never have the same wish twice. It would become tedious for both of us,' said the Psammead.

'So can't I *ever* be good at tree-climbing again?' Robbie said dolefully.

'Perhaps you might wish to be good at something else?' said the Psammead. 'But I don't believe it is your turn to choose today.' He shuffled sideways to face me. 'Do you want to complete your wish, Rosalind?'

'Oh yes, please!' I took a deep breath. 'I wish we could meet up with those other children, Anthea and Jane and Robert and Cyril, the ones in my storybook.'

'Very well,' said the Psammead, and started puffing itself up.

'How can you wish us into a storybook?' said Smash. 'Those children aren't real. It won't work.'

'The Psammead's in the book, and it's real, so why can't it work?' I said, as the Psammead expanded.

'You could have chosen a *better* storybook then,' said Smash. 'One with vampires and monsters and aliens.'

'This one's got a boy called Robert, like me!' said Robbie. 'Is he a nice boy, Ros?'

'He gets to be a giant in the story – and in another story about the same children he carries a magic phoenix around in his jacket. I think you'll like him a lot,' I said, as the Psammead grew bigger and bigger. 'Oh goodness, be careful! Don't burst!' I said anxiously.

But then the Psammead breathed out with such a gust that he blew himself head over heels – and then alarmingly *we* were tumbled about too, somersaulting in thin air in a world gone suddenly dark. I cried out, trying to catch hold of Robbie and Maudie. I was sure Smash could look after herself. Then I was suddenly in bright sunlight again, staring at the sandpit – but it was a *different* sandpit. This was much bigger and made of brown gravel, great mounds of it, with purple and yellow flowers at the top, and little holes for sand martins to hide in.

'Oh goodness! This is the gravel pit in the story!' I said.

I whipped round – and saw four strangely familiar children staring at me. There was a tall boy in a tweedy jacket, a smaller boy in a sailor suit, and two girls in floppy hats and pinafores.

'It's Anthea and Jane and Robert and Cyril, it really is!' I said. 'But I meant them to come to *us* in our time, so I could keep my promise to Dad and not leave our sandpit.'

'They look so *weird*!' said Smash, giggling.

I was relieved to see she had firm hold of Maudie – and I was clutching Robbie by his T-shirt sleeve, so at least we were all safe.

'If you don't mind my saying, *you're* the weird ones,'

said Cyril. He looked Smash up and down. 'You're a rum sort of boy.' He looked at me. 'And you're even odder, with your long hair.'

'We're not boys at all!' I said.

'*I* am!' said Robbie.

'How do you know our names?' said Anthea.

'I know them because – because I've read about you in a book,' I said.

'A book!' Jane squeaked. 'Oh goodness, are we famous?'

'Nowhere near as famous as me. Or rich. *I've* starred at the O2 arena,' Smash said, her chin jutting.

The children looked blank.

'It's – it's a bit like a very big music hall,' I said.

'Oh, I've *always* wanted to go to a music hall, but Father says we're not allowed,' said Robert.

'Are you Robert? I am too,' said Robbie. He peered hopefully at Robbie's sailor top. 'Have you got your golden phoenix tucked away in there?'

'What golden phoenix? I *haven't* – but I jolly well wish I had,' said Robert.

'The phoenix happens in the *next* book,' I said to Robbie. 'I wonder where we are in *Five Children and It*?'

'There are only four children,' said Smash.

'Our little brother is having his nap just at the moment,' said Anthea. She bent down beside Maudie and smiled at her. 'Hello! My little brother's about your age. What's your name then?'

'Maudie,' said Maudie.

'Perhaps you'd like to play with the Lamb?' Anthea looked at me. 'We call him that because –'

'The first word he said was "Baa"!' I said.

'This is so strange!' said Anthea. She glanced at the sandpit. 'It's some kind of magic – so this is surely something to do with the Psammead, isn't it?'

'Shut *up*, Panther!' said Cyril. 'Don't tell them!'

'We *know* about the Psammead. It's *ours*, because I found it,' said Smash.

'Look here, you might know about it, but it's definitely *our* Psammead. We've been coming to the gravel pit every day these hols and we've never seen you here *once*,' said Robert.

'We're not usually *here*. We come from way in the future, more than a hundred years,' I said. 'And the Psammead lives in a sandpit in Oxshott woods now and I wished we could meet all of you, because I've read about you.'

'So does it tell all about us in this book?' said Robert. 'Does it tell about the day I became a giant and frightened the baker's boy?'

'Oh, I should so love to be a giant and frighten people!' said Robs. 'Perhaps I could have that as my next wish!'

'Did you read about us being as beautiful as the day? I had blue eyes then and long red hair.' Jane ran her hand through her limp brown curls wistfully.

'That was a completely wasted wish,' said Cyril. '*I*

liked it best when our house became a besieged castle and we poured water down on the enemy.'

'That sounds cool,' said Smash. 'Maybe I'll wish that. Isn't it meant to be boiling oil, though? Water sounds a bit tame.'

'You're a rum sort of *girl* too,' said Cyril.

'Cyril! You might try to be polite,' said Anthea. She looked at me. 'So you really wished to meet *us*?'

'Yes, I always thought we might – we might be friends,' I said, blushing and feeling a fool.

'Oh, how lovely of you! Of *course* we'll be friends,' said Anthea. 'Look, you must come back home and have tea with us. So your name is . . . ?'

'I'm Rosalind. This is my brother, Robbie – and you've met Maudie – and this is my stepsister, Samantha, though we all call her Smash,' I said.

'Your *step*sister, like in *Cinderella*?' said Jane.

'Yeah, I'm like really mean and spiteful and ugly,' said Smash, pulling a hideous face.

Jane took a step back, thinking she was serious.

'She's just fooling around,' I said quickly. 'Her mum married my dad.'

'Worst luck,' said Smash.

'Did your mother die then, Rosalind?' Anthea asked sympathetically.

'Oh no, she's fine. Well, she is now, though she was ever so upset at first, when they got divorced,' I said.

The four children blinked as if I'd said a rude word.

'You poor *thing*!' Anthea said, patting my arm.

'But she's fine now. She's away at an Open University Summer School and –'

'Your *mother* is at university?' said Anthea. 'Oh my goodness, she must be immensely clever.'

'Not really. She just wanted a bit of a change. She's hoping to get a different sort of job when she's got her degree. She's a bit fed up working in the bank,' I said.

'Your mother works in a bank?' said Jane, sounding incredulous. 'Oh, how lovely! Does she bring you home lots and lots of money? *We* had money once, great big heaps of gold coins, but we couldn't spend them anywhere, so it was a total swizzle. We so wanted to be rich. You must be extremely rich, though, because banks have lots and lots of money.'

'Stow it, Jane!' Cyril hissed. 'Their people must be very *poor* if their mother has to work.'

'Life's different in our time,' I said awkwardly. 'In lots and lots of ways. Women go out to work because they want to.'

'But who looks after the house? Do you have lots of servants?' Anthea asked.

'We don't usually have servants. Well, my mum has Bridget, our cleaning lady, but she only comes once a week,' said Smash.

'We all do our share,' I said. 'Our dad does the vacuuming, doesn't he?'

'What's that?' said Jane.

'He – he sweeps the carpet with a special machine.'

'Your *father* does that?' said Robert, sounding astonished. He looked at my Robbie. 'So in the future do boys do housework too?'

'Yes – I do stuff like loading the dishwasher.'

They looked blank.

'That's another machine that washes up the crockery,' I said.

'Oh, what fun!' said Jane. 'I like the sound of all these machines – and I especially like it that boys have to help in the house like girls. Oh, can *we* ask the Psammead to wish us into *your* time?'

'So long as we don't have to do all this housework!' said Robert.

'But first you're our guests here, so please come up to the house,' said Anthea, taking hold of my hand.

Anthea, Jane, Maudie and I walked up the little path from the gravel pit. Cyril and Robert climbed up the edge. Robbie tried to copy them, but kept slipping back and had to follow us along the path. Smash climbed up too, and beat Cyril and Robert to the top. She showed off considerably when she got there. Anthea didn't say anything, but she looked at me. We both rolled our eyes and then grinned. I *knew* we would be friends!

It was quite a long walk up the hill to the house, through a little brambly wood. I ended up carrying Maudie.

'Are you allowed out by yourselves like this, or will

your dad be cross with you when we get back?' said Robbie, trying to brush the gravel off his T-shirt.

'Oh, Father's nearly always away on business, worst luck,' said Robert. 'But he lets us go anywhere, doesn't he, Cyril?'

'So long as I keep an eye on everyone,' said Cyril, with a lordly air. But then he held out his hand to Robbie in a friendly way. 'Come on, little chap. Come with us boys.'

Robbie went pink, so pleased to be included, even though he hadn't managed gravel-climbing. We went through an orchard and picked an apple each, munching as we walked, and then into a proper garden smelling wonderfully of white jasmine. Anthea and Jane picked some jasmine and wound it round their hats like ribbon.

'Would you like some jasmine in your hair, Rosalind?' asked Anthea, and made me a little crown of it. She politely offered some to Smash too, but she pulled a face at the idea.

The French windows were open at the back of the house so we could wander in. It was very dark inside, out of the sunlight, probably because there were thick net curtains and heavy velvet drapes at every window. The rooms were crowded with big dark furniture so that it looked very grand but a little gloomy.

'Mother's out visiting an old friend, so let's have tea up in the nursery,' said Anthea. 'Jane, run and tell Cook that we have four guests and ask for two kinds of cake if possible.'

'You've got your own cook?' said Smash, looking impressed. 'Can you tell her to cook anything you want? What fun! Could we have *three* kinds of cake – or even four?'

'Cook's not always very obliging,' said Jane. 'Do I have to be the one to ask her? She'll be feeling extra grumpy today.'

'Yes, but you know you're her favourite. If anyone can get round her, you can,' said Anthea.

'Go on, Jane, be a sport,' said Cyril.

Jane sighed, but ran off obligingly.

'Why is your cook feeling really grumpy today?' Robbie asked.

'She's in a bit of a stew with us because we used up all her pots and pans for helmets when we were playing battles, and we were hitting each other on the head with ladles and they got a bit dented – the saucepans, not our heads. Though I did have a big bump on my head too, actually,' said Robert. 'Do you like playing battles, Robbie?'

Robbie looked uncertain.

'I suppose you *can't*, not properly, if you've only got sisters,' said Robert. 'Never mind, I dare say you could play with Squirrel and me.'

'Thank you!' said Robbie.

'No battles today, or we won't get any tea at all,' said Anthea. 'Come upstairs, everyone.'

There was a wide staircase with a shiny polished banister.

'We're not supposed to play on the banisters because I fell off and bumped my head – again,' said Robert.

'But we do,' said Cyril. 'So feel free to have a little ride on the banister if you want to.'

Smash wanted to very much, of course. She ran to the top of the stairs and then simply whizzed down, shrieking with laughter.

'Sh now, what's that dreadful noise! You've only gone and woken up his little lordship, when I've just got him off to sleep!' A rather fierce-looking woman came out on to the landing, glaring at all of us.

'I'm so sorry,' I said, because I wasn't sure that Smash would apologize.

'Is that your mother? I thought you said she'd gone out to tea? Does she get *very* cross?' Robbie asked nervously.

'That's Martha, our nurse,' said Robert. 'Don't worry, she's often cross, but she doesn't really mean it.'

'Why do you have a *nurse*? Are you ill?' Robbie asked.

'Well, she looks after our little brother now,' said Robert. 'We chaps can look after ourselves, mostly.'

We could hear wails and a small voice saying determinedly 'Wanty Panter!'

Maudie looked up, smiling. 'Who that?'

'You might as well let the Lamb get up to meet our guests, Martha, seeing as he's awake,' said Anthea cheerily.

She led us all into a beautiful nursery bedroom with

a dog on wheels and a scrap screen and little compli-cated white clothes airing on a fender. A small boy stood up in his cot, shaking the bars, eager to be lifted out. He had fair curls and big blue eyes and very pink cheeks and looked extraordinarily like a little boy version of Maudie. Both toddlers pointed at each other, laughing.

'There now! Let's get you out, my little duckie,' said Anthea, lifting him up.

'He'll likely be grizzling and grumbling all afternoon now because he hasn't had his nap,' said Martha, but the Lamb seemed in an exceptionally sunny mood. He nodded at all of us and gave Maudie a delighted hug.

'We're going to have nursery tea today, Martha,' said Anthea. 'Why don't you go downstairs and have a nice cup of tea with Cook? We'll look after the Lamb for you.'

'Well, see he doesn't get into mischief. And that goes for the rest of you too.' She frowned at Anthea and Cyril and Robert, and positively glared at all of us.

'I don't know where you met up with those strange children, but they don't look like proper gentlefolk at all. Look at the rags they're wearing! They're scarcely decent. I don't know what your mother would say, Miss Anthea,' said Martha.

'She'd say, "How lovely to meet you and I hope you have a splendid tea,"' said Anthea.

'Off you go now, Martha,' said Cyril – and she did.

I wondered what it would be like to order adults around

like that. Smash looked as if she'd like it tremendously.

Anthea picked up the Lamb and led us into the day nursery next door. There were chairs and a table and a rag rug and brightly coloured religious pictures on the walls – but we only had eyes for the toys. We saw an enormous rocking horse with a long mane and tail and a red leather saddle, a Noah's ark with painted wooden animals parading along the lino, a fort with a troop of little lead soldiers, and a group of dolls sitting in a cluster with miniature cups and saucers and plates, having a meal of daisies and grass and broken matches.

'They're eating fried eggs and green beans and chipped potatoes,' said Anthea. 'Jane and I gave them a feast yesterday and they're still eating it.'

'You play with *dolls*?' said Smash.

'We love our dolls,' said Anthea, without a hint of embarrassment. 'Why, what do you play?'

'I don't play with any kind of *toys*,' said Smash – though I knew for a fact she had a little toy mouse that she slept with. She hid it under her pillow or up the sleeve of her pyjamas, but when she was asleep she snuggled it against her nose like a comfort blanket.

'I love your Noah's ark. Look, my animals can join in the parade,' said Robbie, taking out his lion and tiger.

'But they're different species,' said Cyril. 'They can't be a pair.'

'Yes, they can – and if they breed they can start a whole new species of tions and ligers,' said Robbie.

160

Robert laughed.

'That's a great wheeze, Robbie! Let's mix all the animals up!' He seized a giraffe and a zebra. 'Look, here's Mr Giraffe and Mrs Zebra and they're going to have a splendid family of little gee-ebras.'

They carried on mixing up the animals, roaring with laughter. Cyril looked a little scornful and lay on his stomach, idly assembling the lead soldiers into a platoon. Smash sat a little way away, watching. Then she deftly rolled a marble – and half Cyril's soldiers keeled over.

'Do you have to be such a pest?' said Cyril.

'It was a cannonball. I've declared war,' said Smash.

'You want to play battles?' said Cyril. 'All right, you can have half my soldiers.'

'Not the dead ones!' said Smash, squatting down beside him. 'What can we have for weapons?'

They started a battle game that became increasingly traumatic. Smash kept up a running commentary as if she was a war correspondent, describing every wound and injury.

'Your sister's very bloodthirsty,' said Anthea. 'You don't want to play battles, do you, Rosalind?'

'I'd much sooner play dolls with you,' I said.

I thought Maudie would like to play dolls too, but she had invented a new game with the Lamb called Walky Doggy. They took turns pushing the dog on wheels, running fast and frequently ramming it into the furniture – or us.

Jane came skipping up from the kitchen.

'I got round Cook! I threw my arms round her and said she was a dear, kind, lovely Cook and could we possibly have an extra jolly tea as we have special guests, and she's busy icing a sponge cake and whipping up a batch of scones too!'

'I could make chocolate crispy cakes if you like – they're very yummy,' said Robbie.

'You can make cakes?' said Robert, amazed.

'I'm actually quite good at it,' said Robbie. 'I got to be a rich and famous chef on television. Well, it was a Psammead wish, but it was still me making all the dishes.'

'What's television?' asked Robert.

'Well, it's – it's this big moving picture thing and you watch stuff,' said Robbie.

'Ah yes, Father's told me all about moving pictures,' said Robert. 'Well, fancy *you* being in one! Lucky you, Robbie!'

'Let's dress the dolls and put them to bed now, seeing as they've been eating this meal all day long,' said Anthea. 'Have *you* been in a moving picture, Rosalind?'

'No, but when we were rich and famous I found I wrote books,' I said shyly, carefully undressing the biggest doll. These dolls wore far more intricate clothing than my old Barbies. It was quite a struggle getting her little button boots off, and her pinafore and dress and petticoats.

'Here's her nightgown,' said Jane. 'Cover her up

quickly. She's blushing because she's only wearing her unders!'

'You write *books*?' said Anthea.

'It was just part of the Psammead wish. I expect I ended up writing books because I love reading so much,' I said.

'Oh, so do I!' said Anthea. 'What's your favourite book? I like *Little Women*.'

'Oh, I *love* that book too. I especially like Jo, don't you? And isn't it sad when Beth gets ill?'

'I cried and cried,' said Anthea.

'So did I,' said Jane. '*And* I cried in *What Katy Did* when she fell off her swing. I never thought she'd get better.'

'I didn't like the Cousin Helen part much, though. She was so saintly I wanted to slap her,' I said.

'Oh, me too, me too!' said Anthea.

'It's so *lovely* to meet girls who like my sort of books!' I said. 'I think my all-time favourite is *A Little Princess*, though.'

Anthea and Jane looked blank.

'Ah, I don't expect it's been published yet. Well, look out for it. I think you'll *love* it. Sara has a very special doll in that book. She's called Emily and she has hundreds of different little outfits. I read that part over and over again, I liked it so much. And then there are lots of really sad scenes where Sara has to be a servant, and she's starving in an attic and the only friend she has left in the world is this little rat Melchisedec.'

'Oh, I should so love to have a pet rat,' said Jane. 'Or any kind of pet at all, come to that.'

'I had a pet Siamese kitten called Tina. I loved her so much, even though I only had her for one day,' I said.

'Of course, we have the Psammead,' said Anthea. 'But it doesn't really belong to us and it certainly doesn't *behave* like a pet. Though it did cuddle up on my lap once.'

'It's not really a *bit* cuddly with Robbie and me,' I said. 'And certainly not with Smash. But it did let Maudie pat him a little.'

'Shall we go back and see him after tea? There's still heaps of time before sunset to make a wish,' said Anthea.

'But we've already *had* our wish,' I said. 'It only wants us to have one wish each day.'

'Yes, but *we* haven't had our wish yet!' said Anthea. 'Jane and I had to go shopping with Mother this morning and then we played battles with Cook's pots and pans after lunch, so we're very late with our wish today. We were just getting round to it when you all popped up and stopped us – and of course it was a lovely surprise,' she added politely.

There was a knocking on the nursery door.

'Come and give us a hand then, Miss Anthea and Miss Jane. My arms are being pulled right out of their sockets, this tray's so loaded.'

The tray was filled with a pot of tea with milk and sugar, a plate of little triangles of bread and butter, another of golden scones with a pot of strawberry jam, and *three* kinds of cake: iced sponge, lemon squares and little fancy cakes filled with chocolate cream and a crystallized violet topping each one.

'I hope this passes muster,' said the cook, sniffing. 'It would be nice to have a little warning next time you take it into your heads to invite home all and sundry.'

'Oh, dear Cook, you've totally turned up trumps,' said Jane, giving her another hug.

'Now, now, Miss Jane, calm down,' said Cook, but she gave Jane a little hug all the same. It was clear Jane was her favourite.

Anthea laid cups and saucers and plates on the nursery table and spread out our feast. We all sat round and started tucking in. Maudie and the Lamb could only sit still for two minutes. They grabbed a handful of cake each and tottered round the room 'feeding' the dog alternately.

'This is a really lovely tea,' I said. I crunched on the crystallized violet and licked at the milky chocolate cream. 'I especially like these cakes! I wish we had them in our time.'

'What sort of cakes do you have at teatime then?' asked Cyril, biting into a huge slice of sponge.

'We don't really have any cakes,' said Smash, cutting herself an even larger slice and stuffing all of it in at once.

'We *do*,' said Robbie. 'I make chocolate crispy cakes

– and maybe when we get home I could make sponge. I *like* sponge.'

'So what do you mostly eat at teatime?' asked Robert.

'We don't have a teatime as such. If we're hungry – which I always am – we might have crisps or cookies, or sometimes I hang out round McDonald's after school and have a burger and French fries,' said Smash.

All four Edwardian children looked puzzled.

'You've never heard of *McDonald's*?' Smash said incredulously. 'Don't you have fast-food places?'

'What's *fast* food?' said Cyril.

'Meat in buns, and doughnuts, and pizzas, and fried chicken and chips. They're all yummy,' said Smash. 'Look, come back with us and try some.'

'Oh, yes please!' said Jane. 'Let's go and ask the Psammead right this minute.'

'But – but as we're in the past, I wonder, shouldn't we take a look around? Maybe go into the nearest town and see all the differences? Imagine what great marks we'd get for a history project,' I said.

They all looked at me as if I was mad – except Anthea.

'You are *such* a sad swotty little nerd,' said Smash.

I blushed, feeling foolish.

'No, you're not, whatever that means,' said Anthea. '*I* like to get good marks too. I *love* history – and English, but I'm pretty useless at algebra, and hopeless at Latin too.'

'Goodness! Well, you must be much brainier than me, because we don't even study algebra and Latin at my school,' I said.

'I don't even *have* a school at the moment,' said Smash. 'They keep expelling me. It's totally cool.'

'Aren't your mother and father in a terrible bate about it?' said Cyril.

'You bet,' said Smash cheerfully.

'Don't you *mind* upsetting them?' said Robert.

'Look, they don't mind upsetting *me*. They just want to get rid of me. I hardly ever see my own *mother* and my dad's away heaps,' said Smash. 'You have no idea what it's like being a modern child. You don't know how lucky you are.'

'Well, our father is away a lot on business and Mother is often ill and has to go abroad, but *we've* managed not to get expelled,' said Cyril. 'Perhaps you should do lessons at home like a little kid.'

'I'm not little,' said Smash, giving him a shove on his shoulder.

He happened to be washing his cake down with a cup of tea at that precise moment.

'Ouch! I've practically scalded myself! Stop that!'

'Well, you stop insulting me,' said Smash, and gave him another push.

'Look here, if you were a boy I'd fight you for that,' said Cyril.

'Go on then! I'd like to see you try,' said Smash.

'I can't fight *girls*,' said Cyril.

'Why not?' Smash demanded.

'Well, it wouldn't be gentlemanly,' said Cyril.

Smash laughed unpleasantly. 'You are *so* pathetic. Girls can fight. See!' she said, and she thumped him hard in the chest.

'Right, that's it! You need teaching a lesson, girl or not!' said Cyril.

'Oh, please don't, Cyril, she's just being aggravating on purpose,' said Anthea. 'And watch the tea things, for goodness' sake!'

Cyril stood up and raised his fists.

'Stand up and fight like a man then,' he said to Smash.

'No! Don't, Smash. Oh please don't be so *silly*,' I said, but of course she didn't listen.

She punched Cyril and he punched her, not really *fiercely*, but it was enough to make her stagger. She punched him back and then suddenly they were rolling around on the floor, wrestling with each other.

'Oh, I say, stop it, Cyril. She's our guest!' said Anthea.

'Stow it, Squirrel,' said Robert.

'Oh dear, she's getting hurt. I can't bear it,' said Jane, and she threw herself at her brother to try to stop him. She got thumped herself and screamed.

'Oh, Jane, I'm so sorry!' said Cyril, sitting up and giving her a hug.

'Come on, you can't stop fighting. Nobody's won yet,' said Smash.

'Poor Jane!' said Anthea, rushing to her. 'Don't cry, darling.'

'Look, never mind Jane, I got hit heaps of times and *I'm* not crying,' said Smash.

'No – well, good for you,' said Cyril. He helped Jane to her feet. 'So sorry, Jane, though it really was your own fault, you know.'

'So, have I won the fight?' said Smash.

It had been clear to all of us watching that Cyril was winning. I'm sure it was clear to Cyril too, but after hesitating a second he held out his hand. 'Yes, well done, Smash, you've won the fight.'

'Hooray!' said Smash, shaking his hand and then strutting round the room. 'I *told* you girls can fight. I'm an absolutely champion fighter.'

The rest of us sighed.

'What?' said Smash. 'Come on then, you lot. Let's go to see the Psammead and whizz back to our time. I want to show you all sorts of stuff. Wait till you see my Xbox, Cyril, and my computer *and* the television. We can watch Sky Sport. Which football team do you support?' She chatted away to Cyril nineteen to the dozen all the way to the sandpit, clearly trying desperately to impress him, even though she'd been about to punch his face in five minutes ago.

'If you don't mind my saying, your sister's very *strange*,' Robert said to Robbie.

Robbie screwed his finger against his forehead. 'She

is seriously loopy, I agree. But she's not my *real* sister, thank goodness. That's Rosalind. She's a totally ace sister.'

I was so touched I nearly hugged him, but didn't want to embarrass him in front of the others. I always worried that I was a very irritating boring older sister, always fussing about things and trying to keep us out of trouble.

'Psammead? Are you there, Psammead dear?' said Jane, down on her knees in the sand.

'Will it be *our* Psammead or theirs?' said Robert.

'I think it will be the *same* Psammead. I think there's only one of it, and it can pop up any time it likes, a bit like Doctor Who,' I said.

'Oh yes, wait till you see our television – you'll absolutely love *Doctor Who*, Cyril, especially the stone angels. They are seriously creepy,' said Smash.

'I don't like them one bit,' said Robbie. 'We don't watch when they're on, do we, Rosalind?'

'Oh, I might have known!' said Smash. 'You two are such sad little wimpy *babies*. Hey, Psammead, where are you? You haven't got stuck in a time warp, have you?'

'Don't!' I said. But then I thought about it. Perhaps it wouldn't be so bad being stuck in the past. I seemed to fit in here. Nobody minded if I liked reading or playing pretend games. I could even play dolls without anyone laughing.

'*There* you are, dear Psammead!' said Anthea, uncovering his cross little creased face. It seemed to have just as many lines, even though he was more than a hundred years younger here. 'We are so sorry to disturb you, but could we possibly see what it's like in the future, with our new friends? We'd like it most awfully.'

'Though it's lovely being here too,' I said dreamily. 'In fact I wish I could live here forever.'

'Oh, Rosalind, be careful!' Anthea cried.

I saw the Psammead wriggle right out of the sandpit, its bat ears flapping. It looked directly at me with its eyes on stalks and then started puffing up. I couldn't believe I'd been so foolish – especially after Smash had made the same stupid mistake.

'No! No, I didn't really mean it! It wasn't a proper wish!' I said, but the Psammead took no notice.

It puffed up even further. Then suddenly I saw a dark tunnel and the others were all sucked into it, whirling round, spinning head over heels. I screamed, flailing around, trying to catch hold of Robbie and Maudie, but I could no longer see them in the terrifying darkness. Then the light came back and I found myself on my knees in the sandpit – but I was totally alone.

8

'Robbie? Maudie? Smash?' I shouted.

No one answered.

'Anthea? Jane, Cyril, Robert? Oh please, *some-one* hear me!' I shouted again.

The sandpit stretched out in every direction at the bottom of the gravel pit. I had no idea where the Psammead was. I scrabbled in the sand, hurting my fingernails.

'Psammead? Oh please, I didn't mean that wish, not really and truly. I don't want to be here in Edwardian times, not *forever.*'

I tried to tell myself that I only had to wait until sunset and then I'd be whizzed back to my own time, but I couldn't be sure of that. I'd read *The Phoenix and the Carpet,* the sequel to *Five Children and It.* In that book the

children's cook wished to stay on a tropical island forever
– *and she did*. She didn't mind at all, because the natives
on the island mistook her white cap for a crown and
made her their queen, and later on in the story a kindly
burglar came along and he got to be their king, and *he*
stayed forever too, sunset after tropical sunset.

'Please, Psammead, you know I didn't really mean it,'
I said, digging frantically for him in the sand. 'I'm so
sorry. I know I should have been more careful. I simply
wasn't thinking. Look, leave me here till sunset if you
must, just to teach me a lesson, but please, please, please
let me go back to my own time then.'

There was still no sign of the Psammead, not a paw,
not an ear, not even a whisker. I knelt there in the sandpit for a good half-hour, begging the Psammead to take
pity on me. Then I started wondering if it had hurtled
into my time with the others and was now in its sandy
pit in Oxshott woods. I started to panic, but I was sure
Robbie would wish me back as soon as he could, though
the Psammead had made it extremely plain it was only
prepared to give us one wish per day. Maybe I'd have
to wait till tomorrow.

I took a deep breath and wiped my eyes with the hem
of my T-shirt. I feel a bit of a fool admitting it, but I'd
been crying quite a lot.

'Pull yourself together, you idiot,' I told myself fiercely,
standing up and brushing the sand off as best I could.
'Of *course* you'll get back to your time soon enough, so

make the most of things now. Go and have a look around the village. See what sort of shops they've got. Look out for all those ponies and traps. Make a long list of all the differences you can spot. Come *on*, this is your big opportunity, Rosalind Hartlepool. Don't be a total wimp.'

I started walking briskly up the hill, out of the gravel pit. There was no point trying to find my way back to the house because I knew for a fact Anthea, Jane, Cyril, Robert and the Lamb weren't at home – and everyone might be in a fuss wondering where they were.

I set off down a lane instead. My neck prickled when I heard the clop of horses' hooves behind me. I turned, and there was a man in a cart wearing a funny cap, flicking the reins at an old nid-nodding horse. I scuttled to the side of the lane and watched it go past. It was like stepping into the pages of a history book.

'What are you staring at, you young varmint?' the man shouted.

I was stuck for any kind of answer.

'You're up to no good, I'll be bound,' he said. 'Little ragamuffin!'

I thought he was incredibly rude. It wasn't *my* fault I was stuck in the wrong kind of clothes, with a rip in my jeans and sandy smudges all over me. I chose to ignore him and walked on haughtily.

I was at the edge of the village now. The houses looked pretty normal, little huddled-together terraces of red brick. They seemed especially bright, because the houses were all newly built. The street got wider and busier, edged with strange curly street lamps. I stared around at the people passing by: an old lady with a shawl and a skirt down to her ankles; a younger lady in a blouse with great puffy sleeves and a hat sitting sideways on her hair; two children running along in pinafores, bowling a hoop. They looked just like people in a period television film, but their clothes were faded and more crumpled. I stared, fascinated, until one of the children put her tongue out at me.

I stuck my tongue out at her, and she giggled.

'Hello! That looks fun,' I said, pointing to her hoop. 'Can I have a go?'

She shrugged, so I took that as a yes. I tried bowling the hoop. It wobbled around a lot at first, but I soon got the hang of it, though it seemed a bit of a pointless occupation.

'Hey! What are you doing with my Jessie's hoop? How dare you!' A very cross-looking woman came bursting out of a house, actually shaking her fist at me.

'I'm just *playing*. I'm sorry. Don't be cross!' I said, but she took hold of me and started slapping me about the head. I couldn't believe she would be so hateful. She was really hitting me. I'd never been smacked in my life before and it felt awful.

More women came out of their houses to see what was going on, but no one tried to rescue me.

'He tried to steal our Jessie's hoop, the dirty little stranger!'

'Looks like a gypsy to me. You have to watch them, they'll steal anything.'

'Look at the length of his *hair*! Who's he trying to look like, Little Lord Fauntleroy?'

They all burst out laughing. I tried to seize my chance and run for it while they were distracted, but the slapping woman clung on to me. I struggled, and one of my flailing arms hit her hard in the chest.

She screamed, doubling over. Someone else seized hold of me and pinned my arms behind my back.

'He's got the temper of the devil! Better call for the police. Did you see the way he flew at her?'

'No, please, I'm sorry! I didn't mean to hurt anyone. Please let me go,' I begged, but the little gang of women marched me along the road.

'Now then, what's all this?'

A policeman rounded the corner, wearing a very large helmet and a tunic buttoned right up to the neck. All the women started talking at once, pushing me towards him.

'Oh, please, officer, it's all a terrible misunderstanding. Of course I didn't try to steal that little girl's hoop. I was just trying to play with her. She didn't mind in the slightest,' I gabbled, but he wouldn't listen to me.

'You come along with me, you young off-scouring! I'll teach you to frighten all these respectable ladies and their children! Don't you worry, ladies, I'll take care of the dirty little tyke.'

He took hold of me by the *ear* and pulled me along the road in a manner that was both painful and horribly humiliating. I started crying again, and he gave me an extra tug on my poor throbbing ear.

'Stop that caterwauling! Bear up like a little man,' he commanded.

'But I'm not a little man, I'm a girl!' I wept.

'Then what are you doing in those rum clothes?' he said. 'You're up to no good, boy *or* girl. You come with me.'

I got dragged all the way to the police station and pulled inside. Everything seemed such a crazy nightmare. I fully expected to be thrust in a cell, maybe even shackled to the wall – but instead he sat me down in an ordinary room with a table and chairs.

'Now then, stop your snivelling. Make a clean breast of things and tell me the truth,' he said.

'But I *am*. I truly didn't try to take that little girl's hoop. It's all been a misunderstanding. I've never stolen anything in my life!'

'A likely story! Now tell me your name, laddie, and where you've come from. The truth now, or I'll get really severe with you.'

'My name is Rosalind Hartlepool and – and I live most of the time with my mum in Stoke Newington in London, but I'm visiting my dad in Oxshott in Surrey,'

I started, trying terribly hard to tell the exact truth, without thinking of the consequences.

'So what are you doing in Kent then, hm? You've been travelling around a lot. Are your folks gypsies?'

'No, my dad works in an accounts office and my mum works in a bank,' I said.

'So shall we send for one or t'other of these fine folks of yours?' said the policeman.

'I wish you *could*, but – but it's not possible,' I sobbed.

'No, it's not possible, because they don't exist, do they? You're clearly a beggar or a thief, up to no good in our village, stealing from little children and lying your head off now you're caught. Well, there's only one place for you, little lad or lass. That's the work-house, where they'll work you hard, clothe you decent and learn you a lesson.'

'Oh no, please! Look, I'm not really a stranger here. I know the family in the White House, they're special friends of mine. There's Anthea and Jane and Cyril and Robert and the Lamb!'

'I'm not interested in your stories of strange kiddies and their livestock. Now you'd better come along with me.'

'I *do* know them. You just have to ask at the house,' I said.

'What's the surname of this family then?'

'I – I don't know – but I swear I know *them*. Just ask Anthea. Oh, wait a minute! I don't think she'll be at home just now, or the others – but you could try Martha, their nurse, I'm sure she'd remember me.'

'Oh, stop your babbling. It's getting on my nerves. Come along with me.'

'Don't take me to the workhouse, oh please, don't! It's a terrible place,' I cried.

'Ah, so you've been in one before, have you?'

'No, but – but I've seen the show *Oliver*, where that poor little boy begs for more gruel.'

'Stop carrying on! You don't get gruel nowadays. You get a nice bowl of porridge for breakfast with a mug of cocoa, and good bread and mutton and tatties for your dinner. The casual ward opens at six, so we'll hurry you along and you'll be in time for a good supper.'

I had no choice. I had to go with him.

'But, please, don't pull me by the ear. It hurts so,' I begged.

'You've got two ears. I'll pull you by the other one,' he said, but he was only grimly joking. He took me by the arm and elbow and steered me along the way, through the village. Here was my chance to observe typical Edwardian shops, but I was in such despair I could hardly take anything in until we reached the portals of a big stone building.

The policeman tapped on the large knocker, keeping a tight grip on me with the other hand. A thin matron in a long apron opened the door and peered at me, her eyes narrowed.

'Another young lad up to no good?' she said.

'Well, he *says* he's a girl. I'll leave you to ascertain whether he's lying or not,' said the policeman.

The woman sniffed as if she didn't much care if I were one or the other; it was all the same to her.

'Come with me,' she said, pulling me in.

'Please, ma'am, I *am* a girl – and I haven't done anything wrong. It's all been a terrible mistake,' I said. 'I just want to go *home.*'

'So where *is* your home?' she asked.

I could hardly expect her to believe my two homes were more than a hundred years in the future. Mum's flat and Dad's house hadn't been built yet. They hadn't even been born. Their parents and their parents' parents hadn't been born either. I wondered wildly whether I had great-grandparents who might somehow recognize me as some kind of kin and take me in, but it seemed extremely unlikely.

'*Well?*' said the matron.

'I – I don't suppose I *have* a home now,' I said.

'Then come with me to the receiving ward,' she said.

It was a small grim room with two large stone baths at the end.

'Get those dirty rags off, quick sharp,' she said.

'But – but I – I don't want to!' I said feebly.

'You need a bath. You're filthy dirty and no doubt infested too. I can't have you infecting all my other residents,' she said, running the tap in one of the baths.

Shrinking with embarrassment, I took off my jeans and T-shirt and underwear. She stared at my clothes in astonishment, shaking her head, then gathered them up with the tips of her fingers and deposited them into a wicker basket.

'So you *are* a girl – though why you choose to wear strange boy's garb I'll never know,' she said. 'Come on, stir yourself. Get in that bath and start scrubbing hard.'

I put one foot gingerly in the bath and shrieked.

'It's freezing cold!' I gasped.

'Oh, for goodness' sake, get *in* and stop making such a fuss,' she said. 'Do you think we've got time to heat a bath for each new inmate? Now get a move on – there'll be ten more coming before midnight, I'll be bound.'

I bathed myself as quickly as I could in the terribly cold water, crouching instead of sitting, because the bottom of the bath was gritty and disgusting. The soap smelt terrible and stung my eyes.

'Give that long matted hair a good scrubbing too,' said the matron.

There wasn't any shampoo so I had to wash it as best I could with the soap and then duck my head in the bathwater to rinse it out. I was given such a small frayed piece of cloth to use as a towel that I was still dripping wet when I put on the clean clothes the matron provided: a strange harsh petticoat and long scratchy drawers, a coarse grey dress and apron much too big for me and a pair of boots that didn't fit.

'Excuse me, I don't think these are my size,' I murmured, but the matron didn't care.

'Come with me,' she said, pulling me along.

She led me through a nursery full of infants and small children, but she must have thought me too old for this category because she hurried me through the room. One little girl about Maudie's age tried to clutch at my skirts, clearly wanting to be picked up and cuddled, but the matron unhooked her, tutting.

We ended up in a long bleak room full of women sitting in neat rows. Most of them were very old with white hair and toothless mouths. They were all dressed identically in institution grey.

'There now, you can sit here until supper time,' said the matron. 'You will be number one hundred and twenty-one. You will sleep in that designated bed in the dormitory. Then tomorrow we will put you in the French-polishing unit. Don't look like that! It's really quite easy pleasant work. You will soon get used to it.'

'But what about lessons? Won't I go to school?' I asked.

'Can you read and write and figure?'

'Yes, ma'am.'

'Then you don't need any lessons, do you?' She shook her head at me and walked off briskly, out of the room.

I didn't like her at all, but I wished she would stay even so. I was left with all these strange immobile old women and I didn't know what to say or what to do. I crept up and down the rows, trying to find a spare chair. Did I have to find chair number one hundred and twenty-one? None of them seemed marked in any way.

One old lady nodded at me in a vaguely kindly way, so I bent down beside her.

'Please, can you tell me where to sit?' I whispered.

'Sit right there, my child,' she said, gesturing as if there were several comfortable armchairs to choose from.

'Thank you, but *where* exactly?' I said, dithering.

'Pray join me in my humble repast,' said the old lady, regally offering me an invisible plate.

'I'm sorry?'

'Don't take any notice of old Sarey, she's totally dottled,' said the woman beside her. She was much younger, maybe only in her thirties, but her face was hard and pinched and there were sharp lines creasing her forehead. 'Half the old girls here are dottled,' she said matter-of-factly. 'Maybe it helps.'

'Is it truly awful here?' I asked.

The woman shrugged. 'Well, it ain't *my* idea of home – but I have no other,' she said.

'Do we *have* to stay here? Are we locked in?' I asked.

'Where are you going to go then? The gutter's even harder than a workhouse bed, and a sight colder too,' said the woman.

'But – but can't we work hard and earn enough to get our own places?' I asked.

The woman stared at me. 'You don't get no earnings, missy. You work for your bed and your board.'

'But it's just like prison, and I haven't done anything wrong, truly,' I said.

'You're poor and you're homeless. You don't need to do anything wrong to qualify,' said the woman. 'You've got a lot to learn.'

'Can't we *ever* start again outside?' I said.

'Well, if you're one of Matron's favourites she *might* just recommend you if a job in service comes along, but you have to suck up to her something chronic, and that ain't my way.'

'You mean, be a maid?'

'Well, what else could you do?'

I thought of all the different alternatives I had in my own life in the future and felt sick with despair. I looked up at the windows. I kept looking at them all that long, lonely evening as the light gradually faded.

We were led into another large bleak room with long tables and benches, where we sat in rows again, eating stale bread and drinking watery cocoa with lumps that made me shudder as I swallowed. No one talked at the table. Perhaps it wasn't allowed. There was just the sad sound of old mouths munching their bread to pap.

Then a bell rang and all the women got up obediently and shuffled off again. There was a visit to an unspeakably disgusting privy block, queuing for ages, and then we were led off to bed, though it still wasn't completely dark. I thought we would sleep in a great dormitory, but we each had a separate cubicle, very like a cell. Cubicle one hundred and twenty-one was so small I could touch both walls as I lay on my hard cot. There were no sheets, not even a pillow, just a dirty grey blanket.

There was no proper window, but a small air vent in the brick above my head showed a tiny patch of sky. I watched it desperately until I could see nothing but black. It was obviously well after sunset now – but I was still here, in the workhouse, in the past. I was trapped here forever.

I started crying again and someone banged on the wall. 'Stop that snivelling! You're keeping me awake!'

I tried to cry more quietly. I could hear several other women weeping too, and further away a baby wailed forlornly. I curled up tight, my hands over my ears, wondering how I would ever bear this dreadfully bleak life. Then it suddenly got much darker. I was tumbled out of my bed, tossed and turned in the air, and then I fell and landed with a great thump . . . in my own bed at home! There was Smash, sitting on the end of my bed, grinning at me.

'Oh, Smash! Am I truly back? Oh, you'll never *believe* what happened! I was stuck in the past because of my own stupid wish and it was so *awful*. I ended up in the workhouse! I thought I was going to have to stay there forever. How on earth did I get back?'

'*I* got you back,' said Smash, bouncing up and down.

'We all thought you'd come back automatically after sunset so we didn't fuss too much. I thought it might teach you a lesson, actually, as you had the cheek to call *me* a fool for making an accidental wish in front of the Psammead. We had great fun with those storybook kids. Cyril *loved* my computer, and when he saw Dad's car in the garage he was just over the moon – Robert too. And Anthea and Jane liked all your books and stuff and tried on some of your clothes.'

'Oh, I *wish* I'd been there!'

'Don't you start wishing again, you idiot! Anyway, they all suddenly disappeared completely at sunset and we peered all round everywhere, looking for you to come back – but you didn't. Robbie got a bit tearful. He was sure he'd heard you wish you could stay in the past forever, see, but I told him not to worry, we'd wish you back tomorrow when we went for another picnic, but he went *on* worrying. You know what he's like.'

'What about Dad? Did he go spare? Did he phone my mum?'

'No, he didn't seem to notice you were missing, just like we wished, but he kept looking round and scratching his head as if he was looking for something but he couldn't remember what. Alice didn't seem too fussed, though, but she wouldn't care even if *I* went missing. She certainly didn't miss me tonight.'

'What do you mean?'

'Well, Robbie was going on and on about you,

wondering if you were all right. I started wondering too. You're not very good at looking after yourself, are you? And then I heard my mum telling your dad that she wants to take Maudie to this children's Fun Day in some park tomorrow, so probably we won't be able to go to the woods and see the Psammead. Robbie was going nuts, scared you might not *like* being stuck way back in the past on your tod. I was getting a bit fed up too without you, actually. Your Robbie isn't exactly a bundle of fun, is he, and Maudie's lovely but you can't really hold a conversation with her, can you? So I decided to get you back.'

'But how did you *do* it, Smash?'

'Simple. I waited till bedtime. Your dad was even weirder then, he kept putting his head round the door and staring at the empty bed, though the wish was so strong he still couldn't remember he had a daughter. It was like he knew *someone* was missing, but he didn't know who it was. So, I waited till he settled down in his room at last, and I reckoned Robbie had cried himself to sleep and Maudie was out like a light. I didn't want to get them involved, so I just got dressed again and crept downstairs and found the big camping torch and pocketed the spare front-door keys from the kitchen dresser and let myself out.'

'You went *out*? In the *dark*? By *yourself*?'

'Yep!' said Smash. 'I went all the way to the sandpit to see if the Psammead could get you back.'

'Oh, Smash! Weren't you scared?'

'Not in the slightest,' said Smash.

'But it's so dangerous to go out at night by yourself. You could have been attacked.'

'If anyone tried anything with me, I decided I'd whack them on the head with the big torch,' said Smash. 'It *was* a bit weird in the woods. I did think I might get a bit lost in the dark – but I was fine.'

'Oh, Smash! I just can't believe this. You risked everything to rescue me. You're a true *heroine*,' I said, and I gave her a hug.

'Get *off* me, you big softie,' said Smash, squirming, but she looked pleased.

'And did you find the Psammead straight away?'

'No, I had to dig in the sand for ages – but I figured it could hear me. I went on and on about you being stuck in the past and probably very scared. I said I knew the Psammead didn't think much of me, but couldn't he take pity on *you*, because you're always so nicey-nicey – and it worked. It suddenly stuck its head out and started talking to me. It was terribly *grumpy*, mind, because I'd woken it up. It gave me a right telling off and said it had already given us a wish for today and did I want to exhaust it utterly. I begged it to give us tomorrow's wish right now. I pointed out that if it would only grant me my teeny little wish it could burrow down in the sand and go back to sleep in a jiffy, whereas I'd carry on and on pestering it if it didn't. I put in a lot of pleases and thank yous because it's so fussy about manners, and *eventually* it said, "Very well." I wished that you and I were safe back in our bedroom and it puffed itself up and then I was wibbling and wobbling all over the place in the dark until I landed right back here in the bedroom, as requested – and you did too!'

'You are the best sister in all the world!' I said. 'Oh, Smash, I think I'd have *died* if I'd had to stay in that terrible workhouse. It was so awful. Let me tell you all about it.'

But Smash was fast asleep and snoring in less than a minute. I lay in my soft pyjamas in my clean comfortable bed, still scarcely able to believe I was back.

9

When Robbie came running into our room in
the morning he gave a great whoop of joy
as he saw me. He hugged and kissed me so
enthusiastically he nearly crushed me to death. When
I told him how Smash had rescued me he tried to rugby-
tackle her into a hug too.

'What do you two think you are – *bears*?' said Smash.
'Too much hugging! And if you try and *kiss* me, Robbie,
you are *dead*, I'm warning you.'

Maudie was satisfyingly pleased to see me too. 'Rosy
come *back*!' she kept saying.

Luckily, Dad and Alice didn't seem to hear her. Dad
still didn't know I'd ever gone missing, but he made a
big fuss of me at breakfast-time even so.

'My Rosy-Posy,' he said, ruffling my fringe and pulling my plaits. 'You're such a funny little thing. Sometimes I hardly know you're there. You always wander off and nobody knows where you are. I can barely remember seeing you yesterday! Where did you get to?'

'Oh, I – I expect I was stuck in some storybook,' I said.

'I wish *you'd* read more, Smash,' said Alice. 'Still, you *do* like those awful Devil Child adventure books, and I think the author, Marvel O'Kaye, is giving a talk at this special Children's Fun Day. You'd like to go to that, wouldn't you?'

'No,' said Smash. 'I'd sooner have my own adventures.'

We got the train up to London, and then the tube to the park, which was a bit of an adventure in itself for Robbie. He was still very nervous in tubes and had to hold my hand tight all the way. But somehow it all seemed a bit tame after our London travels in the pink stretch limo when we were rich and famous.

The Fun Day wasn't really tremendous Fun either, because we weren't part of it – we just had to watch. Alice took Maudie to see a nursery-rhyme puppet show for the under-fives, while Dad took Smash, Robbie and me into this big marquee to listen to Marvel O'Kaye.

'It sounds as if he writes really scary books,' Robbie whispered to me. 'I'd much sooner go and watch the puppets with Maudie. Shall I ask Dad?'

'Better not,' I said. 'Don't worry, Robs, I'm sure Marvel O'Kaye won't be too scary. He'll just tell us where he gets his ideas from and how long it takes to write a book, stuff like that.' I was quite interested, just in case I ever did write a book myself.

However, when Marvel O'Kaye came onstage he grinned at all of us in a wicked sort of way. When we'd stopped clapping, he said, 'Hi, I'm Marvel. I write the Devil Child series, but don't worry, I'm not going to bore you by telling you how I get my ideas or how long it takes to write one of my books. I'm going to tell you *stories* – and they're going to be s-c-a-r-y!'

Almost every child in the tent squealed in delight. Robbie groaned and hunched down in his seat.

'Now, what are you really scared of?' Marvel asked. 'Come on – you, little kid in the blue T-shirt. What are you frightened of?'

'Rats!' she squeaked.

Robbie breathed a sigh of relief.

'I'm not frightened of rats, I *like* them,' he said. 'Fancy being frightened of lovely interesting creatures like rats! They're just like big friendly mice.'

Marvel O'Kaye pointed at some other children.

'I don't like dentists,' said one.

Marvel rolled his eyes.

'I'm scared of SATs tests!' said another.

'Per-lease!' said Marvel.

He pointed at our row now, looking straight at Smash.

'What are *you* scared of?' he asked.

'Nothing!' she said, sticking her chin up.

Then he pointed at me.

'I'm scared of being smacked about the head and having my ears pulled,' I said, remembering being stuck in the past.

Dad looked anguished.

'Rosalind! You've never *ever* been smacked,' he hissed. 'Oh lordy, what will people think!'

Marvel O'Kaye was pointing at Robbie now.

'What are *you* frightened of?' he demanded.

'Oh dear, we'll be here all night now,' said Smash.

'I don't like the underground very much,' Robbie mumbled.

'Ah! Nice one,' said Marvel. 'Okay, okay, I think we've got enough ideas for our s-c-a-r-y story.'

He started making up this story about a girl who said she wasn't scared of anything. Smash laughed delightedly. Marvel said this girl sat some exams at school and had three big fillings at the dentist, and yet she didn't even flinch.

'I like this story!' said Smash.

'But *then*,' said Marvel O'Kaye. 'Then she had to go home on the *underground*.'

He described the girl going into the tube station, and down a whole series of steep escalators. He said there wasn't anyone else there at all, which made her just a little worried, though she still wasn't really scared. Then a tube rumbled through a nearby tunnel and as the noise faded away she heard this strange squeaking. It got louder and louder.

'It's going to be rats – but I don't mind rats,' Robbie muttered.

'The squeaking got louder still, and the girl looked down on the track and saw a huge black rat with great yellow teeth and a very long slimy pink tail. Then she saw another and another, hideous misshapen creatures slithering and slathering below her. She told herself they couldn't really hurt her there – until one leapt right up on the platform and bit the girl viciously on the leg.'

All the children were squealing now. Smash was laughing uproariously. Robbie was clutching me.

'I think I might be scared of this kind of rat,' he said.

'Don't be scared, Robs. It's meant to be *funny*. Just laugh like the others. It's just his silly story,' I whispered.

'Then the girl heard this strange moaning from down in the tunnel,' said Marvel O'Kaye. 'She peered through the gloom, rats circling her ankles, scrabbling at her legs, and saw a grotesque creature lumbering along the tracks, almost a man, but covered all over in rat hair, and with a long glistening pink tail trailing behind him. He opened his mouth when he saw the girl, exposing his sharp savage teeth, and then he groaned, "Mind the gap! Stand clear of the d-o-o-r-s!"'

Everyone collapsed into laughter – except Robbie.

He had his hands over his ears and was la-la-la-ing fever-ishly, trying to blot out all other sounds.

'It's okay, Robbie. It's a *joke*. It wasn't a really scary monster. He was just saying what those men working in the underground say when you get on a tube,' I said, prising his hands away and doing my best to reassure him.

It was no use. The deserted Underground station and the rats and the monster man were in Robbie's head now, and he couldn't blot them out, no matter how hard he tried.

He'd have been so much happier seeing the puppets with Alice. Maudie was very hyper when we met up with them, singing a bizarre montage of nursery rhymes over and over again.

'Hey diddle diddle, Jack and Jill went up the hill, Atishoo atishoo, We'll all have tea!'

'I think you've got your wires crossed there, Maudie,' said Smash. 'You're singing it all wrong. That's not a proper nursery rhyme.'

'Yes, it is,' Maudie insisted, and sang her own version again, louder.

'That's it, sing up, darling,' said Alice. 'Don't take any notice of Smash. Your sister couldn't sing *any* nursery rhymes when she was your age.'

'She sings wonderfully now,' I said.

Alice and Dad looked at me as if I was crazy.

'Smash doesn't *sing*,' said Alice.

'You should hear her. She's brilliant,' I said. 'She can make up her own songs. They're really moving.'

'Shut *up*, Ros,' said Smash, but she squeezed my hand even so.

Later, when we were all having a pizza, she asked me if I really thought she could sing well.

'Come on! Like you had the entire O2 arena absolutely ecstatic,' I said.

'Yes, but that was just the Psammead wish.'

'I know – but you really got *into* it. And it was *you*, after all.'

'Well . . . maybe you'll end up writing books too. You *read* enough, so you'll probably get the hang of it and have your own published.'

I felt myself blushing scarlet. I knew she was probably just trying to be encouraging back to me, but it meant a lot, even so.

'I know one thing, though,' said Smash. 'It's not ever going to work for Tree Boy.'

'Oh, don't. Poor old Robbie,' I said.

I looked over at him. He was nibbling at the edge of his pizza. It was his favourite, pepperoni, but he was acting as if he'd been given rat-tail topping.

'He *might* end up a chef. He likes cooking,' I said.

'Well, it doesn't look as if he likes *eating*,' said Smash. 'Don't you want that pizza, Robbie? I'll have it if you like.'

'You've had too much already, Smash,' said Alice.

'You eat your own pizza, Robbie. Come on, eat it properly. Stop that prissy nibbling,' said Dad.

Robbie took a big bite and chewed. It was a mistake. I saw his face. I knew he was imagining rat-tails in his mouth. I grabbed him as he turned pale green.

'Run, Robbie!' I said, trying to rush him to the toilets.

We didn't quite make it in time. I mopped him up as best I could, but he really needed a clean set of clothes.

'We'd better go home,' said Dad – but that was a problem too.

Robbie went even greener when he saw the underground sign and threw up again. We ended up having to get a taxi to the station, with Dad paying the cabbie double because he didn't want Robbie being sick in his car.

It wasn't really a *fun* day at all. I heard Alice and Dad whining that it had been a waste of time and effort trying to take us for a lovely day out. They were in the kitchen, but we could still hear them clearly.

I saw Robbie's face and my heart turned over. I went into the kitchen.

'Please stop going on about it!' I said. 'It's not fair. Robbie couldn't *help* being sick.'

'Do you mind, Rosalind? We're having a private conversation,' Dad said coldly.

'But we *do* mind, Dad. You're making us feel bad and it's not our fault,' I said.

'I'd appreciate it if you didn't argue with me,' Dad said. 'You're getting a bit above yourself, young lady. I think we've heard quite enough of your opinion.'

'I can't win, can I? One minute you say I'm quiet as a mouse – and the next I've got too much to say. You're allowed to criticize *us*, but we're not ever supposed to find fault with you,' I said, my voice rising.

'Stop shouting at me! Do you behave like this with Mum?'

'Rosalind's imitating Smash. She's clearly a bad influence,' said Alice, and sighed. 'I don't know what I'm going to do with that girl.'

'I can *hear* you,' Smash called. 'Yatter, yatter, yatter – naughty, rude, disobedient, bad-mouthed Smash – more yatter, yatter, yatter. See if *I* care!'

I wanted Robbie to join in too, but he was still very pale and quiet and shaky. He went up to bed at the same time as Maudie.

Smash and I stayed awake for ages, having a wonderful moaning session about Dad and Alice.

'I always miss Dad so much when I'm not with him – and yet when I *am* he's sometimes so bossy and mean that I can't stick him. I especially can't stand him being bossy and mean to Robbie,' I said.

'I can't stick my mum being bossy and mean to *me* – and she nearly always is,' said Smash. 'I love my dad much more. Well, I used to. He seems to have forgotten all about me since he got married.'

'I think I love my mum more than my dad,' I whispered, though I felt wicked saying it.

'Let's ring them up,' said Smash, fishing for her mobile phone. 'We'll talk to your mum and my dad. I'll go first.'

'Are you sure your dad won't mind, seeing as he's on his honeymoon?'

'Yuck! It's disgusting, a guy his age *going* on a honeymoon,' said Smash, pulling a face.

She selected his number. It rang for a long time, while Smash tutted and tapped her foot impatiently. Then the phone switched to voicemail.

'Hey, Dad, it's me! *Answer* me! I have to talk to you,' said Smash.

She rang off.

'Oh dear. Never mind.' I hesitated. 'Can I ring my mum now?'

'No, wait. He'll ring back,' said Smash. She nodded triumphantly as her phone started ringing.

'Hey, Dad! . . . What? . . . No, I'm fine, I just . . . Look, I know it's past my bedtime, but I don't care what time it is, I need to talk . . . Huh? To tell you stuff, obviously . . . Like what I've been doing. Which is actually pretty weird. You'd never believe the half of it . . . Well – no, I can't really say, you'll think I've gone crazy . . . No, nothing like that. It's just there's this kind of magic stuff . . . Okay, *like* a game, but it's actually real . . . What? *I* don't know how much it costs to phone the Seychelles . . . Don't you *want* to talk to me? Listen, I haven't said all the stuff about Mum – she's being so mean to me . . . Like forever whining about my *attitude*, and making these veiled comments about my *weight*, like she thinks I'm *gross* . . . Yeah, yeah . . . What? *What?* Oh, you obviously don't care! Bye, Dad.' She ended the phone call abruptly. 'I could *make* him care,' she said bitterly. 'They don't realize, my stupid parents. I could mosey down to the sandpit and make one little wish . . . I could wish Dad suddenly hated this awful Tessa and make Mum suddenly hate your dad. I could muck it all up for them. That would be great, eh?'

'No, I think it would make them all worse, especially to us,' I said.

'But if your dad got fed up with my mum he'd maybe go back to *your* mum. Wouldn't you like that?'

'Well, I used to hope and hope it would happen. Robbie and I wished it every single night.'

'There you are then! You can wish it for real.'

I sat still, trying out the idea in my head. It was so weird knowing I could really do it. I thought of Mum, and how after Dad left she'd cried night after night in bed when she thought we couldn't hear her. It would make her so happy to have Dad back, wouldn't it?

'Can I phone my mum now, Smash?'

'Oh yeah, sorry.'

Mum took ages to answer too. I pictured her, shut up in some gloomy college bedroom, so deep in her studies it was a while before it dawned on her that the phone was ringing.

'Hello?'

'Hi, Mum!'

'Ros! Hello, darling. What is it? What's the matter? How are you getting on at Dad's?'

'I'm fine, Mum,' I said.

'And Robbie?'

'He's . . . fine too,' I said, because I didn't want to worry her. I wasn't sure where she was, but there seemed an awful lot of noise her end, music and talking and laughter, almost as if she were at a party.

'Then why are you phoning so late, love?'

'I – I was just worried you might be lonely.'

'Oh, darling, you're so sweet. No, I'm not a *bit* lonely. The Summer School's absolutely great and I'm with a whole lot of friends now and we're letting our hair down a bit. I haven't had so much fun in years.'

'Oh. Right. Well, that's good.'

'What *is* it, Rosalind? There's something on your mind, isn't there?'

'Well, I was just wondering – do you ever wish Dad would come back?' I blurted out.

Mum was quiet for a moment. I heard someone asking her if she was okay, and someone else offering her another drink.

'That's a funny thing to ask,' Mum said eventually. 'Why, has Dad said anything?'

'No, not really.'

'Is he having rows with Alice?' Mum asked, sounding hopeful.

'Not exactly. Well, you know Dad, he ends up having rows with *everyone.*'

'I hope he's not been cross with you and Robs,' Mum said indignantly. 'Shall I talk to him?'

'No, better not. I'm actually supposed to be asleep now.'

'Well, so I should hope. It *is* very late.' Mum paused. 'I don't think it would work now if Dad came back, Ros,' she said very gently. 'He's changed. And I've changed too. I know it's maybe what you and Robs would like, but I'm afraid I don't think it will ever happen.'

'It *could* do, Mum,' I said. 'Look, I know this sounds absolutely crazy, but I know how I could work a magic spell. Well, someone could wish it for me – this magical creature. Do you remember the Psammead in *Five Children and It*?'

'I loved that book. It was one of my favourites when I was your age,' said Mum. 'In fact I'm thinking of writing about it for my children's literature module.'

'Yes, well, the Psammead's real! We've found it in a sandpit in Oxshott woods, but you mustn't tell anyone,' I hissed into the phone.

'What's that? I'm sorry, darling, it's so noisy here I can hardly hear you.'

'We see the Psammead nearly every day and it grants us wishes and I – I was wondering what you'd really like if you could have a wish.'

'Oh, this sounds a lovely game,' said Mum, clearly not believing a word I was saying. 'Okay, I wish that you and Robs have a lovely holiday and that I get the most out of my Summer School.'

'That's not a very imaginative wish, Mum!'

'Well, you're the one with the vivid imagination, darling, not me. I *must* go now – and you must settle down and go to sleep. Night night, Ros. Love you lots.' She made kissing noises.

'Love you, Mum,' I said. I made kissing noises too, and then switched off.

Smash was staring at me. She pulled a face. 'Yuck, what's with all this lovey kissy rubbish?' she said. 'You're talking to your *mum*, not your boyfriend.'

'She didn't believe me about the Psammead,' I said.

'Well, *there's* a surprise,' said Smash.

'She says she doesn't want Dad to come back,' I said. 'She doesn't think it would work. And maybe it wouldn't. He loves your mum more – I can see that. And it's too difficult wishing really big family stuff because we might get it all wrong. It's not actually my turn for a wish anyway. It's Robbie's.'

'Maybe he should wish he could frighten the pants off Marvel O'Kaye. That would be funny!' said Smash.

Poor Robbie had bad dreams in the night and shouted

203

out again. I tried to get to him before Dad, but didn't manage it.

Dad did his best to be kind and tried to give Robbie a cuddle, but Robs curled into a tight little ball, his eyes closed, and wouldn't speak to him.

'Come on, son. You need to talk it out, tell me what's going on in that silly head of yours. That's the only way I can help,' said Dad. He was starting to get irritated. 'Oh, for goodness' *sake*, Robbie. Don't just lie there quivering. What's the *matter* with you?'

Robbie kept quiet, while the rats ran round and round in his head and that voice of doom echoed in his ears. Maudie sat up in her cot and was immediately wide awake and chirpy.

'Playtime!' she said, standing up and bouncing.

'*Sleepytime!*' said Alice firmly, picking her up and taking her off to her own bedroom. We could hear Maudie chuckling and singing to them, long after Dad went back too. She sang her special nursery rhyme over and over again. 'Hey diddle diddle, Jack and Jill went up the hill, Atishoo atishoo, We'll all have tea!' Alice and Dad kept wearily begging her to be quiet and go to sleep.

I stayed with Robbie, sliding into his bed and curling round him to help him feel safe. It wasn't very comfortable, especially as he had most of his zoo animals in the bed with him.

'You go to sleep, Robs. I won't let the bad dreams come back. And tomorrow we'll try to get Dad and Alice to take us back to the woods and we'll see the Psammead, and it's *your* turn for a wish. Have you thought what you're going to wish for? It could be anything at all. Remember, we've wished that Dad doesn't notice anything, so he can't get cross.'

'I wish we didn't *have* a dad,' Robbie mumbled.

'Hey, shut up, don't you start!' I said.

'But I don't like him any more,' Robbie said.

'That's silly. Of course you do.'

'No, I don't. And he doesn't like me.'

'Yes, he does. He loves you. You're his son.'

'But he hates it that I get scared and get sick . . . Ros?'

'What?'

'Do you think Dad left us because of me?' Robbie whispered. 'Because he got fed up with me?'

'No! It wasn't anything to do with you – or me either. Dad just got fed up with poor old Mum, and liked Alice more.' I gave Robbie a big hug. 'Now, stop worrying about silly stuff. You just think up a really, really good wish for tomorrow.'

10

We nearly didn't get to the woods the next day. It rained most of the morning.

'We can't have a picnic in the pouring rain,' said Dad.

'I'm a bit sick of picnics anyway,' said Alice. 'They're too much hard work.'

Smash and Robbie and I begged and pleaded, especially when the rain stopped around noon, but Dad and Alice didn't take any notice of us. However, we had one small ultra-winning ally.

'Picnic?' said Maudie. 'Picnic in woods! Yes, yes, yes!'

'*Again?*' said Alice.

'Again! Again! Again!' said Maudie, jumping up and down.

'Well, I suppose we can always sit on a tarpaulin,' said Dad. 'And *I'll* make the picnic this time, Alice.'

He cut a big French loaf into chunks, wrapped up three different cheeses, took some pears and bananas from the fruit bowl, a packet of chocolate biscuits from the cupboard, and stuck a big box of fruit lollies in the ice pack in the cold bag.

'There!' he said triumphantly.

It wasn't as elaborate a picnic as Alice's, but it was very enjoyable all the same. Alice wasn't at all happy about Maudie having an ice lolly, fussing about food colouring and E numbers, but it was hot now the sun was out and Maudie's eyes were big and pleading. She got her lolly too and licked and slurped happily, getting orange all round her mouth, even in her *ears*, because she kept turning her head to stare longingly at the sandpit.

'Monkey in a minute!' she said.

'Yes, we'll just go and play Monkey with Maudie in the sandpit,' said Smash.

'You and your funny games,' said Alice. 'All right then – but no wandering off, do you absolutely promise?'

'Don't *worry*, Mum. We're never going to do that to you again,' said Smash. 'Come on, Maudie, let's dig in the sand, yeah?'

We all went over to the sandpit, Maudie jumping about gleefully.

'It's your turn, Robbie, remember?' I said.

'*My* turn, *my* turn, *my* turn!' said Maudie.

We all stared at her.

'Well . . . I suppose Maudie *hasn't* had a turn, but isn't she too little?' I said doubtfully. 'What if she wishes something weird and it all goes wrong?'

'Like that hasn't happened to us!' said Smash. She scrabbled in the sand and discovered a Psammead paw. 'Aha! Found you! Come out, little Mr Psammead!' She started pulling at him.

'Gently!' said Robbie.

'Yes, extremely gently,' said the Psammead crossly, pushing through the sand and giving itself a shake. It yawned hugely, showing a very pink mouth and a lot of sharp little teeth. 'I was having such a delightful snooze too. Why did you have to come and disturb me?'

'We want another wish, that's why,' said Smash. 'Go, Maudie!'

Maudie shuffled forward on her knees in the sand, grinning happily.

'Hello, Monkey!' she said.

'I might *look* a little simian in a bad light, but I am a different species entirely,' said the Psammead. 'Oh dear. I am now the only one left of my species – and I fear *I* won't last much longer if you children continue to harass me.'

'Funny Monkey,' Maudie said lovingly, clearly not understanding a word. She reached out to stroke him.

'Careful!' said the Psammead sharply.

Alice hadn't been able to wipe all the ice-lolly stains off her, and she was still a little sticky.

'Nice Monkey. Funny Monkey. Maudie's Monkey,' she said, squatting down right next to him, but taking care not to actually touch him. 'Hey diddle diddle, Jack and Jill went up the hill, Atishoo atishoo, We'll all have tea,' Maudie sang to him.

The Psammead's eyes swivelled on their stalks.

'Maudie's singing you her special song,' I said.

'So I hear,' said the Psammead.

'*Wish*, Maudie!' said Smash.

'I wish for the people,' said Maudie.

'*What* people?' said Smash.

'Jack and Jill and Polly and Sukey and funny cat and doggy and cow and dish and spoon and all the ring o' rosies,' said Maudie.

'But they're not *real* – they're those silly nursery rhymes,' said Smash. 'You can't wish that!'

'Yes, she can,' said the Psammead. It started puffing itself up until it was a great furry globe and then it suddenly collapsed into its own shape again. It peered around with its eyes on stalks, then twitched when it heard a dog barking in the distance. It scurried under the sand immediately, all four paws scrabbling hard.

We were left staring at the strangest assembly of creatures we had ever seen. A brown-and-white terrier dog careered madly around, obviously picking up the scent of the Psammead. The dog tried to dig, but Robbie caught him and hung on to him.

'No! Bad dog! You leave the Psammead alone,' said Robbie.

The dog went on barking, now trying to get at a cat in a scarlet dinner jacket and blue trousers who was sitting on a tussock, a tiny violin under his chin. He fiddled away while a strange metal plate and spoon capered about hand in hand. A large brown cow came trotting through the trees, mooing in time to the music. She kept lifting her head, looking up, her neck straining.

'She's looking for the moon so she can jump over it!' said Smash, snorting with laughter.

'Hey diddle diddle, hey diddle diddle!' said Maudie, and she started jogging up and down to the cat's music.

Then a boy and girl came trudging along, carrying a big pail between them. The boy had a red jersey and blue trousers, the girl a white dress with blue spots.

'Jack and Jill!' I said. They all looked wonderfully familiar. I remembered *Lavender's Blue*, my long-ago nursery-rhyme book, and Mum reading it to me over and over again as she showed me all the pictures. 'Look, Robbie, it's Jack and Jill going up the hill to fetch a pail of water.'

'Better tell them to watch out!' said Smash.

'I should be careful going up that hill if I were you,' I said.

Jack and Jill looked at me.

'Yes, we're going up a hill,' said Jack in a sing-song voice.

'To fetch a pail of water,' said Jill, staring vaguely into the distance.

'Jack and Jill went up the hill!' Maudie gabbled, clapping her hands. 'Me go too!'

'No, you'll tumble down with them, sweetheart, and maybe hurt yourself,' I said. 'Look over there! Shall we join the ring-o'-roses people?'

There was a bunch of little girls and one boy circling the sandpit. Three girls had white dresses, two with red spots, and a third wore buttercup yellow, while the little boy had grey shorts and a blue jersey. They were only a little bit bigger than Maudie and they all had smiles on their faces, so I thought she was safe with them.

'Atishoo atishoo?' she said hopefully.

'Atishoo atishoo!' they all said, bobbing their heads.

Then they all sat down suddenly in the sand, giggling. Maudie sat down too, liking her new friends and their game so much she laughed uproariously.

'Again! Atishoo *again*!' she said.

They scrambled up and started the game from the beginning.

'Ring a ring o' roses –'

'You'd better join in too, Rosy-Posy,' said Smash.

'Try to get them to play over there on the grass, Maudie,' said Robbie. 'The Psammead won't like it at all if they keep on thumping down right over his head.'

He went over to them and bent down to their level, adopting the pose of a kindly uncle.

'I think it would be better if you played over *there*,' he said, pointing.

'Ring a Ring o' Roses,' said the little boy, trying to take his hand.

'Yes, I know you want to play Ring a Ring o' Roses, but let's play it over *there*,' said Robbie, gently leading them.

'A pocket full of posies!' sang the little girls, swinging arms with Maudie.

'ATISHOO! ATISHOO!' she shouted, bobbing her head with them.

'We all fall *down*,' they sang, and collapsed on the grass, drumming their little legs.

Jack and Jill came tumbling down too, back out of the woods. Jack came first, landing on his front, spilling his pail of water, and Jill followed, her arms in the air, legs kicking, looking shocked.

'Oh dear, oh dear,' said Maudie, rushing to pick them up. 'Plaster?' she said to me. 'Plaster to make it better?'

'No, no,' said Jill, getting up gingerly and patting her brother.

'Jack must go to bed and mend his head with vinegar and brown paper,' she said solemnly.

'Yeah, I never did get that bit,' said Smash. 'Vinegar and brown paper? It's like he's a portion of fish and chips.'

'I suppose they didn't have disinfectant and plasters in those days,' I said.

Maudie was still squatting beside Jack, looking anxious.

'It's all right, Maudie. He'll be better soon,' I said.

'Ready to start all over again,' said Smash. 'This is quite a sweet wish, but I feel like I'm stuck in playschool. Who else is going to make an appearance?'

Two shadowy girls in grey and white came out of the woods, one of them holding a kettle.

'What's up with them?' said Smash.

Their faces were white and they had hair in varying shades of grey. They walked over to a little fire in the clearing with its own cosy brick fireplace. The flames were grey and the bricks were off-white.

'I know!' I said, laughing. 'It's Polly and Sukey and they're a black-and-white illustration in the nursery-rhyme book, not full colour like the others.'

They looked pretty eerie in real life and Maudie approached them warily, but Polly smiled at her.

'We'll all have tea?' said Maudie, pointing to the kettle.

'Look, there *is* the tea!' said Robbie.

A grey table had materialized, with a grey-and-white checked cloth, a grey spotted teapot and a grey-and-white cottage loaf.

'Polly put the kettle on,' said Polly, balancing the kettle on the hob over the fire.

'Me too, me too,' said Maudie.

'Careful! No, keep away from the fire, Maudie,' I said.

The flames might be black and white, but I could feel the heat from them and I was sure they could still burn.

'Polly put the kettle on,' Polly repeated, Maudie singing along with her.

'Polly put the kettle on,' Polly said a third time.

'Oh, for pity's *sake*, you're worse than Gobby-Bird,' said Smash.

'We'll all have tea!' Polly and Maudie sang together, going to sit at the table.

'Wait for it,' said Smash, as Polly's pal Sukey went striding up to the table.

'Sukey take it off again,' Sukey sang, predictably enough. She repeated herself. Twice over. Then Polly took Maudie's hand and they ran away from the table.

'They've all gone away!' Sukey sang.

Polly and Sukey and Maudie all burst out laughing.

'Again! Again!' Maudie begged.

'No, no! How many times have we got to put up with this?' said Smash.

'Oh shut up, it's quite sweet, really, and Maudie's loving it,' I said.

Robbie seemed to be enjoying himself too, trying to soothe the poor jumping cow and then stroking the little dog, who barked continuously. I hadn't realized nursery rhymes would be so *noisy*. It wasn't just the mooing cow and the barking dog. The cat played very loudly on its fiddle, the spoon clattered against the dish, Jack and Jill clanked their bucket and tumbled over with repeated thuds, the ring-o'-roses children sneezed explosively, and Polly and Sukey sang with great emphasis, right in our ears.

'Again! Again!' said Maudie.

'I'm getting fed up with this lot,' said Smash. 'Where are all the other nursery rhymes? What about Humpty Dumpty? I want to see him getting smashed up! Then there's that other one where the maid gets her nose pecked off –'

'You and Marvel O'Kaye are clearly soulmates,' I said. 'I don't think Maudie *knows* any other rhymes, just those four.'

'So we're stuck with them singing this stupid stuff again and again?' said Smash.

'Again! Again!' Maudie agreed happily.

'I think I'm going to burrow into the sand along with the Psammead,' said Smash, putting her hands over her ears as all the characters started singing their rhymes simultaneously.

I tried to talk to Jack and Jill as they paraded up the hill with their pail. They listened politely, their little mouths smiling.

'Jack and Jill, why not take your pail to the village pump and get your water that way? Then you won't tumble down the hill and hurt yourselves,' I suggested brightly.

'Jack and Jill,' said Jill, nodding.

'Went up the hill,' said Jack.

'To fetch a pail of water,' they said in unison, and went off to do just that.

I tried Polly and Sukey.

'Polly put the kettle on,' said Polly hospitably. 'Polly put the kettle on. Polly put the kettle on.'

'Yes, thank you, that would be lovely, but could we perhaps come to lunch instead?' I asked.

'We'll all have *tea*,' said Polly.

'Sukey take it off again,' said Sukey, doing just that. 'Sukey take it off again. Sukey take it off again.'

'But what if I don't go away? What if I stay sitting at the table, saying "Please can I have a cup of tea. I'm really thirsty"?' I said.

Sukey frowned at me.

'They've all gone *away*,' she said, stamping her foot.

'You can't have a proper conversation with them,' said Smash. 'It's like trying to talk to Mickey Mouse and Pluto at Disneyland. Robbie, can't you get that stupid dog to shut up?'

'Sh, boy! Quiet! Be a good dog now,' said Robbie, but the dog barked on and on as the little cat played his fiddle, the dish and spoon capered, and the cow kept trying to leap in the air, though the blue summer sky was entirely moonless.

Dad and Alice seemed entirely oblivious to this sudden nursery-land invasion of Oxshott woods. Our wish that they didn't ever notice any Psammead magic was extraordinarily effective. The cat wandered over with his fiddle and serenaded them as they sat on the picnic blanket, the cow tried to leap right over them, the dog barked, Jack and Jill trudged past and tumbled back, the little children danced round them in a circle, sneezing, and black-and-white Polly and Sukey dashed backwards and forwards with their kettle.

Dad and Alice didn't even blink. They smiled fondly at Maudie when she sang along with the nursery-rhyme people, but didn't react in any other way.

We weren't smiling fondly at Maudie by this time. We were getting heartily sick of all four rhymes.

'It's going to be ages and ages and *ages* till sunset,' said Robbie, still trying hard to calm the barking dog.

'Perhaps we can just go home?' said Smash. 'Maybe they won't follow. They'll just stay fiddling and barking and dancing and sneezing and falling over and shoving that silly kettle on and off to their hearts' content deep in the woods, while I play on my computer and you read and Robbie mucks about with his plastic animals.'

'I don't *muck*,' said Robbie. 'I'm trying to develop a kindly zoo environment for wild animals.'

'Which involves taking a lion for a walk up and down, going "Here, Lion, lovely Lion, be a good boy, Lion, and I'll give you a lick of honey"?' said Smash.

'Maudie's having such fun playing with the nursery-rhyme people here,' I said as she shouted, 'Again, again!'

'Well, maybe she can persuade them to follow along behind us and they can all cavort about in the garden

217

at home, while we shut ourselves in the house?' Smash suggested.

It was a very tempting idea, especially as I hadn't brought a book with me. Smash and I tried walking away from all of them. Immediately the dish and spoon clattered after us on their spindly little legs.

A woman walking her dog passed us, and stared in alarm at the capering crockery.

'Whatever's that?' she gasped.

'Oh, it's just a clockwork toy,' said Smash, seizing hold of the dish and spoon.

They didn't like this at all and waved their legs in protest. The nursery-rhyme dog barked and the woman's dog barked back, and she was momentarily distracted, trying hard to keep the two animals apart. Then the cow wandered along, looking up expectantly at the sky.

'Good heavens! I didn't know there were cattle in Oxshott woods,' she said. 'Have they started farming part of it?'

Then she spotted the cat striding along on his back paws, playing his fiddle. Her jaw gaped.

'That's a cat and it's playing a violin!' she whispered. She crept nearer to it and then reached out and touched the cat's tail, which was swishing rhythmically sideways in time to his tune. 'That's not a toy. It's real!'

'It's – it's not a *real* real cat. It's a very little person in a catsuit,' said Smash, which again didn't seem very likely.

Then Jack and Jill went by, seeking a new hill, swaying their pail and singing away. The ring-o'-roses children all sneezed together, circling nearer. Then black-and-white Polly and Sukey appeared.

The woman's dog barked hysterically.

'Run! Run away!' she shrieked at us, and blundered back through the woods, her dog leaping around her.

'Oh no, she'll go and tell someone!' I said.

'Yes, like they'll really believe her when she starts describing what she's seen,' said Smash. 'Look, you dim nursery people, stay near the sandpit, please!'

They wouldn't stay. They wandered wherever we went. It was clear they would follow us if we tried to go home. I thought what it would be like parading down Acacia Avenue with a troupe of nursery-rhyme characters, two of them in black and white.

'Perhaps we'd better just stay here,' I said. 'I think it's less complicated.'

So we stayed, while the cat fiddled, the cow ambled up and down, the dog barked, the dish danced with the spoon, Jack and Jill went up and down their hill, the children revolved round and round in their ring of roses, and Polly and Sukey put their kettle on and off a thousand times. We stayed until the sun slid down the sky and the cow spotted a pale crescent of moon at long long last. It leapt up in the air with a great joyful moo, soared right over it – and then disappeared.

11

Dad called Robbie and me into the living room after breakfast the next day. Robbie pulled a face at me.

'What have we done now?' he mouthed, looking scared.

'We haven't done anything, Robs,' I said, squeezing his hand. 'Don't worry.'

But I was worried inside, wondering what was up. I never knew how to please Dad. I'd never felt quite relaxed with him even when he lived at home with us. Sometimes he seemed to want me to cuddle up and be his little girl, like Maudie. Sometimes he wanted me to grow up and act more sensibly. I sensed he'd like me to have more spirit like Smash – but if I dared cheek him and argue back he got furious. And, if I was floundering, poor Robbie was hopelessly out of his depth. He'd started to flinch nervously whenever Dad raised his voice – which made Dad even madder.

But now Dad was smiling at us in a slightly fierce way, teeth showing, rather like Robbie's toy lion.

'What's up, Dad?' I said, trying to sound bright and bouncy.

'Nothing's up, silly,' he said.

'Have *I* done something, Dad?' Robbie whispered.

'No, no. For goodness' *sake*, kids, don't look so scared. I want to have a little chat, that's all, just us three.'

Alice was letting Maudie wash up her plastic dolly's tea set along with the breakfast dishes, while Smash was emailing her dad.

Our dad sat down on the sofa and held both his arms out.

'Come on, sit down, both of you,' he said, gesturing.

We absolutely hated sitting down on that sofa, because it was where Dad and Alice cuddled up and it made us feel ill. We perched gingerly on the edge while Dad put his arms round us.

'Now then, I just wanted you to know that I'm happy, happy, happy that you're here,' said Dad.

We smiled back at him.

'I do miss you so when you're at your mum's,' said Dad.

He waited for us to say something.

'We miss you too, Dad,' I said.

'I just want to make sure you're enjoying yourselves, kids,' said Dad. 'We don't really seem to be *doing* very much. We seem to spend most days pottering off to the woods and having picnics.'

'That's what we *like*, Dad,' I said.

'You bet,' Robbie added. 'So long as it's at the sand-pit.'

'Well, why don't we try going somewhere a little more *exciting*?' said Dad. 'It's very peaceful in the woods, I grant you.'

'Peaceful?' I said, thinking of the constant fiddling and barking and mooing and sneezing and singing yesterday.

'Almost too peaceful. I always seem to doze off and time goes haywire. The day just disappears. Your whole holiday is slipping by and it seems such a waste. I wanted you to have a really brilliant time.'

'We are, Dad, we are.'

'I didn't fix up for you to go on any holiday courses or do any special activities because I wanted us all to have fun together.'

'We *are* having fun, Dad,' I said.

'I know we can't comfortably all fit in the car together, but we could always leave the others to hang out here and go off just us three. We could go to the seaside – or up to London? No, *I* know, how about if we went to the zoo? You used to like going to the zoo when you were little, Robbie.'

Robbie wavered. I knew how much he'd like to go to the zoo *now*. He loved seeing all those animals so much. But there was one small monkey-type creature he wanted to see more – especially as it was his turn to make a wish.

'I love the zoo, Dad, but I'd really sooner go and have a picnic in Oxshott woods,' he said.

'You're a funny little tyke,' said Dad. He patted Robbie on the shoulder. 'I wish I saw more of you, son. I don't think it's necessarily good for you growing up without your old dad. You're such a little worry-guts at times. All this fussing about silly stuff like going on the tube! You should have grown out of that years ago. I think maybe your mum's too soft with you.'

'Robbie's fine, Dad,' I said. 'Mostly.'

'Let Robbie speak for himself, Ros. You're always sticking up for him, doing his talking for him. I know you mean well and it's very sweet, but he's got to stand on his own two feet. You're a little man, Robbie – remember that! And as for you, Rosy-Posy . . .'

Oh dear. Now it was my turn.

'You're such an earnest old-fashioned head-in-a-book girly,' said Dad, pulling one of my plaits. 'I think maybe Mum's keeping you a little *too* young. Maybe it's time you had a few fancy up-to-the-minute outfits.'

He plucked at my T-shirt shoulder and tutted at my torn jeans.

'Perhaps you could go shopping with Alice. She's got

223

a real eye for clothes, great fashion sense. She'd help you choose some stuff.'

'I *like* my old T-shirt and jeans,' I said. 'I don't really want to go shopping.'

I'd have loved new clothes, of course. I sighed enviously whenever I looked at the clothes in Smash's wardrobe. But I couldn't bear the thought of shopping anywhere with Alice. She sometimes looked me up and down with one eyebrow raised. She never *said* anything, but she didn't need to. That look was enough.

Dad sighed at both of us, as if we'd failed an exam.

'Well, we'll go on yet another picnic to ye olde Oxshott woods,' he said. 'But mind you tell your mum I offered to take you anywhere you wanted, money no object. I don't want her to think I'm a cheapskate, not prepared to make a fuss of you.'

Robbie and I murmured and smiled and wriggled away. Robbie sloped off to his room and collected his favourite animals and let them roam in the soft dusty terrain underneath Maudie's bed.

I went to my bedroom and hunched up with *The Railway Children*. I couldn't help envying Bobbie and Peter and Phyllis, whose father was totally out of the picture until the very last chapter.

Smash came kicking her way into the bedroom, playing football with her velvet bomber jacket.

'You shouldn't scrunch it up like that – and you're getting it all dusty,' I said.

'Who cares?' said Smash.

'You care,' I said. 'That's your best jacket. Didn't your dad buy it for you when he was in the States?'

'Yeah, well, I don't care much about *him* any more,' said Smash. 'I sent him this ever so long funny email, reams and reams of it, and do you know how he replied? *Hey kid, Have fun, Love Dad.* Six words. And I asked him all sorts of questions and he's just ignored everything. He didn't even respond when I moaned about Mum and he normally *loves* it when I do that. He's obviously way too busy with his new little wifie to give a stuff about me. Are you *sure* you don't want to think up some brilliant anti-dad wish for the Psammead?'

'No, though I agree it's tempting. But it's *Robbie's* turn for a wish, you know that.'

'Well, have a word with him, see what he wants to wish. He's such a little weirdo, goodness knows what he'll come up with.'

'He is *not* a weirdo,' I said fiercely.

'Hey, calm down, I'm just realizing we haven't got *that* many wishes left till you guys go home and if you don't mind my saying so, *my* wish has been the best of the lot so far, and ultra unselfish too, because we all enjoyed being rich and famous,' said Smash.

I wandered off to see what Robbie was up to. He was under the bed now, mumbling to his creatures.

'Hey there, Robs,' I said, kneeling right down and peering at him.

Maudie's night-time potty was under there too. I hoped he wasn't playing that his animals were at a waterhole.

'It's your turn for a wish! Have you thought what you're going to ask for?'

'Yep,' said Robbie.

I waited.

'Well? What's it going to be?'

'I don't have to tell you first,' said Robbie.

I blinked at him. Robbie usually told me everything. I felt a little foolish, kneeling there with my bottom stuck in the air.

'Do come out, Robbie.'

'I don't have to do what you say,' said Robbie. 'Dad said.'

'I sighed heavily.

'Okay, okay. Stay there. Stay there forever if you like, though you're getting dust all over yourself – and Alice will be doing the picnic soon and I expect she'd have let you make some more cakes.'

Robbie pondered. Then he rolled out from under the bed.

'You'd better have a good wash and change your clothes. Look at you!' I said.

'I don't want to,' said Robbie. 'You can't boss me about.'

'Okay, don't then. But I'm *not* bossy. I'm trying to be helpful. I just want to talk over your wish, in case anything might go wrong.'

'*You* were the one who made the wish by mistake and got trapped in the past, not me,' Robbie pointed out unkindly.

He felt for his animals under the bed, stuffed a handful down his T-shirt and took them off to the bathroom with him. I heard him thumping about making gorilla noises, and then roaring and trumpeting.

'I give up,' I said, and went downstairs to help Alice myself.

She'd decided on bacon, lettuce and tomato sandwiches this time. Smash grilled the bacon and I washed and shredded the lettuce and chopped tomatoes. There were also little sausage rolls. Robbie had emerged, reasonably clean, so Alice let him roll the pastry. Then she made individual gooseberry fools in little pots with lids and washed a punnet of big strawberries and a pound of cherries. Best of all, she made fairy cakes, letting us all have a turn at mixing – *and* licking out the bowl afterwards. When the cakes were in the oven she made some icing and then let us decorate the cakes when they'd cooled down.

'You're ever so good at making picnics, Alice,' I said – but then I felt disloyal to Mum. *Her* picnics weren't anywhere near as elaborate. They were usually cheese-spread sandwiches and an apple each.

'Why are you sucking up to my mum?' Smash hissed.

'I'm not. I'm just stating a fact,' I said.

'She's mad. She makes all this food yet, you watch,

she hardly eats anything herself, just because she wants to keep thin as a pin,' said Smash. 'When I'm grown up, I'm going to eat whatever I want, all the time.'

'Well, you'll look pretty weird wearing those skimpy stage costumes. But I don't suppose it'll matter too much just so long as you can sing okay,' I said.

'Yeah, I want to do another concert at the O2. Hey, Robbie, can you wish that we're all doing a concert? You can sing too. You could be like a little mini version of Robbie Williams – that would be cool, eh?'

'I'm not wishing that. I've got my own wish,' said Robbie.

We had to wait till we were in the woods to find out what it was.

'Hey diddle diddle?' Maudie sang hopefully, looking around – but mercifully the nursery-rhyme people had all disappeared.

We scrabbled in the sandpit, Maudie chanting 'Monkey, Monkey, Monkey!'

The Psammead surfaced reluctantly.

'You again?' it said. 'I only seem to snooze for ten minutes and then you're back disturbing me.'

'Funny Monkey,' said Maudie, stroking it.

It quivered at her touch but let her continue.

'Please try not to wish for anything too *noisy* today,' it said. 'Those creatures parading up and down yesterday had very strident voices and the livestock sounded utterly out of control.'

'Don't worry, I don't want any more nursery rhymes,' said Robbie. 'I know exactly what I do want, though.'

He stood his zoo animals in the sand: his favourite lion, an elephant, a gorilla, a monkey, a giraffe, a zebra and a camel.

'I wish all my animals could come alive,' said Robbie.

The Psammead twitched in alarm.

'*More* livestock – and savage ones into the bargain? *Silly* boy,' it said, but it puffed itself up hugely and then scrambled hastily back down under the sand. We stared at the little plastic animals, knocked off their tiny hooves by the burrowing Psammead.

Then the lion yawned and stretched and kneaded its paws in the sand. The elephant moved its head from side to side, its tiny trunk waving in the air. The gorilla stood up on its hind legs, its hands nearly touching the ground. The black-and-white monkey scampered away from the gorilla, making an anxious little barking noise. The giraffe stretched its long neck, its little ears twitching either side of its horns. The zebra struggled to get as far away from the lion as it could, darting this way and that. The camel stepped out with its two-toed feet, totally at home in the sand.

'Oh!' Robbie whispered, awestruck. 'Look, just look! My animals! They really are real!'

'They're so *sweet*,' said Smash. She picked up the lion – and it batted at her with its front paw and stuck its teeth into the padded flesh of her little finger.

'Ow! The little monster!' she said, dropping it and examining her finger. 'Teethmarks! I'm *bleeding*!'

'It's a *lion*, Smash. And watch out. Maybe it remembers when you tried to bite its head off,' said Robbie.

'Better watch out for that zebra then, Robs. We don't want the lion to start nibbling it,' I said. I picked it up and it stood quivering in the palm of my hand. 'Oh, it's gorgeous. I love its little stripes.'

'Monkey! *Weeny* monkey!' said Maudie.

'*Gently*, Maudie. Very, very gently,' said Robbie as she picked it up to examine it properly.

The monkey gave its tiny bark, ran up Maudie's arm and then ducked under her sleeve.

'It tickles!' said Maudie, giggling.

The monkey nestled inside her T-shirt sleeve, using it as a cuddle blanket.

'I'll have the big monkey then,' said Smash. 'Come here, monkey-monkey.' She poked the gorilla in the stomach. It reared up and beat its chest, showing his miniature teeth. 'Hey, don't you dare bite me too!' she said, flicking him over in the sand.

'Stop it, Smash! Leave my animals *alone*. You've got to treat them with respect. They're little wild animals.'

'Oh, oh, is it going to eat me then?' said Smash.

'My gorilla is entirely vegetarian, so it would think you taste disgusting – but it's ever so strong. I bet it could tear your finger right off if it wanted,' said Robbie.

'Keep it right away from Maudie then,' I said.

The elephant trumpeted and raised its tail. Several little balls of elephant dung dropped in the sand.

We all stared – and then rocked with laughter.

The camel looked down its nose at us and spat contemptuously, which made us laugh more.

'Oh, Robbie, this is such a brilliant wish,' I said.

'See!' said Robbie triumphantly.

'Only it's just as well the Psammead didn't make them life-size or we'd all be savaged to death by now,' I said.

'Some of us are,' said Smash, examining her finger. 'If I get rabies, I shall make sure I bite you back, Robbie.'

The lion roared, and the zebra jumped right out of my hand and started running swiftly out of the sandpit.

'Quick, catch him, or we'll lose him!' said Robbie. 'I'll have to make them some sort of pen. Well, separate pens for the lion and the zebra!'

I caught the poor little zebra and tried to calm it, stroking its tufty mane and scratching it very gently between its ears. Then I caught the giraffe, who knelt down on my other hand, its head looking all around nervously on the end of its long neck. Robbie held his lion in one hand, the gorilla in the other. The lion stopped roaring and lay down submissively and the gorilla curled up as if Robbie's hand was a little nest.

Smash held the elephant and the camel. 'But no pooing or spitting,' she said, wagging her head at them.

Maudie was still in charge of the monkey. It darted

out of her T-shirt and perched on the lobe of her ear, holding on tight to her silky hair with its tiny paws.

'Okay, let me think. The camel's fine staying in the sandpit. We'll just make a big ridge across it so that he can't climb up and out – simple!' said Robbie. 'Here, little guy, you have a nap in my pocket.' He very gently tucked the gorilla away and then scooped the sand around, making his big ridge.

'Put him down in his little desert then, Smash,' said Robbie. 'There you are, camel. Good camel, you're back in all that lovely sand.'

The camel seemed mildly appreciative, fluttering its double row of minute eyelashes and smiling as it started plodding.

'Now find a home for this elephant, quick, before it does another poo,' said Smash.

'He'll like some grass,' said Robbie. He climbed out of the sandpit to the grassy bank. He made a fence with several big logs and then gently took the elephant and set it down on the soft mossy grass. The elephant waved its trunk.

'See, he likes it. And this is your home too, lion, you like grassland – and you as well, giraffe. Pop him down, Ros,' said Robbie.

'Next to the lion? No fear!'

'He can look after himself, honestly. If my lion tries to bite him, he'll kick him hard and butt him with his head,' said Robbie. 'But we'll make a completely separate pen for the zebra, because they're what lions like to eat most.'

'Can the little zebra have a pen right the other side of the sandpit then, just in case?' I said.

The zebra was definitely my favourite. I helped construct its own private grassland in a safe little valley, and put it down to graze.

'There!' said Robbie. 'Now, my gorilla and the Colobus monkey like the forest, so they can live in those ferns there. Out you come, gorilla.' He took it carefully out of his pocket. The gorilla had found an old Smartie and was biting into it like a biscuit.

'I don't think that's very good for you,' said Robbie. 'But I suppose it makes a change from all those green leaves. I get sick of eating salad too. There you are, good boy. Here's your lovely new forest. Maudie, put the monkey here too.'

'No, *I* want monkey,' said Maudie. 'He tickles me.'

'Well, *I'll* tickle you if you let your monkey have a scamper in the ferns. I think he'll really like it there,' said Robbie.

Maudie reluctantly detached the little monkey from her ear and put it in the ferny shade. It chattered happily, ran right up a fern and then swung itself to the next one.

'There! He's better at climbing trees than you or me, Smash,' said Robbie.

He sat cross-legged, watching over his little zoo,

utterly absorbed. I hovered over the zebra a little anxiously, keeping an eye on the lion. Maudie sat right in the ferns so that every so often the monkey jumped down and ran across her.

Smash tickled the elephant and the giraffe with a blade of grass. She was sensibly wary of the lion. But after half an hour she started yawning and fidgeting.

'This is all very sweet and lovely, and they look cute, but this wish is getting a bit boring now,' she said.

'Don't be so stupid, Smash. It's the most amazing wish ever,' said Robbie.

'But nothing's happening,' she complained.

'Just watch the animals! It's so interesting seeing them adapting to their new habitat,' said Robbie.

'Yeah, well, *I'm* not adapting to this habitat. I want my computer and my Xbox. I want to go home now,' said Smash.

'Oh, Smash, that's not fair. Let him play with his animals a bit longer,' I said.

'He can take his little animals home with him and make them a brand-new zoo in Maudie's room,' said Smash.

'It won't be anywhere near as nice for them, though, not like being in the wild,' said Robbie. 'Still, I have made a sort of zoo under Maudie's bed. Oh!' He sat up suddenly and started nibbling his lip anxiously. 'Rosalind?' he said. 'You heard me make my wish to the Psammead?'

'Yes, of course I did.'

'Well, what exactly did I say? Did I say "I wish these animals could come alive"?'

'Yes.'

'*Or* did I say "I wish *all* my animals could come alive"?'

'We don't know,' said Smash. 'It was your wish, not ours. Why, what difference does it make?'

'Well, these ones here, my lion and my elephant and my zebra and my monkey and my gorilla and my camel, they're not *all* my animals. I couldn't get the whole lot into my pockets, you see. I just took my African mammals out with me because I collected them first and they're my favourites. But I've also got my Indian mammals. I left them under my bed. And, you see, I was just wondering – could the Psammead's wish have affected them too?'

'Mmm, yes, I see what you mean,' I said. 'Well, it won't really matter, will it?'

'Yes, it will. There's a tiger and a leopard and a wild boar. They'll all have a terrible fight – and there's a rhino who'll keep charging everything,' Robbie said anxiously, near tears.

'Calm down, Robs, it's okay. I'm sure they'll be fine. Though maybe we'd better go home just to be sure. You can make them all a new zoo in Maudie's room. It'll be fun. You can use her building blocks to make proper pens,' I said.

'I'll need to take home lots of sand for the camel, and

grass and greenery for all the others,' said Robbie. 'How am I going to carry it all, *and* the animals?'

'I know!' I said. I ran over to Dad and Alice. Dad was doing *The Times* crossword and Alice was flicking through *Grazia* magazine. They both smiled at me peacefully.

'Still playing your funny sandpit game?' said Dad indulgently. He peered over at the others. He could obviously see Maudie and Robbie and Smash – but not the little animals scuttling here and there, making tiny roars and trumpets and barks and whinnies.

'Yes, but actually we'd like to pack up soon and go back home. I think Maudie and Robbie are a bit tired,' I said. 'Shall I help gather up the remains of the picnic?'

'That's very helpful of you, Rosalind,' said Alice.

I grabbed the big picnic cool bag.

'Yes, I'll put the leftover sandwiches in. Oh, hang on a minute, I think Robbie's got sand in his eyes,' I said. I charged over to the sandpit with the cool-bag strap over my shoulder, and seized hold of Robbie.

'What are you *doing*?' he said, wriggling, as I pulled his eyelid open.

'I'm just pretending you've got sand in your eye.'

'But I haven't!'

'I *know*. It's a subterfuge.'

'A subwhat?'

'We're going to bung some sand and stuff in the picnic bag and the animals can all squeeze in there too, only

236

I'll hang on to the zebra just in case. I don't trust your lion. There are sandwiches in there if they're hungry. The carnivores can eat the bacon and the vegetarians can snack on the lettuce.'

We packed up the portable zoo and shut the cool bag, hoping the animals would settle down and go to sleep. It was quite a long walk back and Robbie usually dragged his feet and whined, but he stepped out smartly now, eager to see if there were any more live creatures at the house.

'Don't worry so, Robbie. If they *are* alive, they'll just be rootling around in Maudie's room. And, even if they've got out, Dad and Alice won't be able to see they're real.'

Dad and Alice couldn't see them – but other people *could*. As we trooped through the garden gate of 52 Acacia Avenue the front door opened and a stout middle-aged lady came rushing out, handbag in one hand, a J-cloth still clutched in the other. She was screaming hysterically.

'I wonder what's up with Bridget? She's my mum's cleaning lady,' said Smash.

'Bridget! Goodness, what's happened? What's frightened you?' said Alice, rushing to her.

'Is it burglars?' said Dad, reaching for his mobile.

'No, no, it's *rats*!' Bridget sobbed. 'Terrible snarling rats, *lots* of them. I went to hoover under Maudie's bed and there they were, all trying to bite me. I'm not going back in the house, not for a million pounds. Terrible rats! You'll have to call in Rentokil.'

'*Rats!*' said Alice, and she clutched Maudie and started screaming too.

'Oh lord, *rats*?' said Dad, going white. 'Right, Alice and you children, stay outside, out of harm's way. In fact we might be better if we *all* stand clear, while I phone the experts.'

But Robbie dived through the open door without a second thought.

'Robbie? Robbie, come back! Don't be foolish, son, rats can bite. Robbie, please!' Dad yelled.

Robbie hurtled down the hall and up the stairs, taking no notice.

'I'll have to go after him,' said Dad. 'You stay here.'

Dad hurried up the stairs while we waited, breathless. Alice retreated to the garden gate with Maudie in her arms.

'Keep *back*, kids. David might chase the rats *out*. Oh dear lord, how terrible!'

'Calm *down*, Mum. I'm sure there aren't *really* any rats. I bet Bridget made a mistake,' said Smash. 'I bet Dad won't find even a teeny little mouse.'

And at that moment Dad came back, still chalk white, but grinning all over his face. He had his arm right round Robbie.

'It's okay, folks. Panic over! Bridget made a mistake. Poor woman, you'll have to phone her, Alice, just to make sure she's all right,' said Dad.

'But she said she saw *lots* of rats.'

'She went to hoover under Maudie's bed and saw Robbie's little toy animals. She got such a shock she thought they were rats!' Dad said, laughing shakily. 'Look, show Alice, Robbie.'

Robbie held out his hands. He had a leopard in one palm, a tiger in the other. They were both snarling and showing their teeth – but Dad and Alice were still affected by the Psammead wish and couldn't see them move.

'Just little lumps of plastic!' said Dad.

'Oh, thank goodness!' said Alice.

'Nice weeny pussy cats!' said Maudie, reaching out to stroke one.

'Careful, Maudie, they might bite,' said Smash.

Alice and Dad laughed as if she were joking.

'You kids and your pretend games!' said Dad. 'Mind you, Robbie, you couldn't have known there weren't *real* rats in the house. It was incredibly brave of you to go dashing in like that, especially when I know you can't stand rats either. You had those awful nightmares after listening to that Marvel O'Kaye and his lurid stories. I'm really proud of you, son.'

'Well, I was pretty sure there weren't *really* any rats,' said Robbie truthfully.

'Don't be so modest, lad. Well done!'

'You're both one hundred per cent certain there aren't any rats at all?' said Alice, still fearful.

'Come in and see for yourself,' said Dad.

So we all trooped upstairs. Dad and Alice saw little

plastic toys scattered about the carpet, utterly motionless. But Robbie and Smash and Maudie and I saw a weeny wild boar savagely disembowelling one of Maudie's fluffy teddies, a golden jackal gnawing one of her bedroom slippers and a furious rhino charging at her potty.

12

'Hey, Ros, wake up,' said Smash. 'I've just had a brilliant idea.'

I was in the middle of a lovely dream where Anthea and Jane and I were all playing with our dolls. Mine was exceptionally beautiful, with big blue eyes and long golden hair and a cream dress patterned with tiny daisies. I didn't *want* to wake up.

'Come *on*, sleepyhead!' Smash bounced out of her bed and sat on mine, tugging at my duvet.

'Stop it! I'm asleep,' I groaned. I looked at my alarm clock with one eye. 'It's only six o'clock. Are you crazy?'

'*Listen!* Maudie will be waking up any minute and Alice always gets up ever so early to give her a drink of milk. Well, let's ask if we can *all* have breakfast – a breakfast *picnic* at the sandpit. That way we'll really be able to make the most of our wish all day long. It's *my* turn – and I'm going to ask that I can fly. I had this dream last night, you see. I was flying right up above Mum and David and they couldn't reach me, though they kept leaping up and down, trying. It was such fun. Then I was flying over to see my dad in the Seychelles and he was whirling round with me and it was so cool, but then *she* started flying too, you know, Tessa, my new stepmother. She was just like Tinkerbell, and actually she *is*. Isn't it weird when dreams do that? And she swooped off with my dad in a swirl of fairy dust and I was left, just kind of hovering in mid-air. The dream went downhill after that – but the flying part was truly great.'

I must have been looking doubtful because she gave my shoulders a little shake.

'I'll wish that you can fly too, silly. And Robbie and Maudie, though she might be a bit little.'

'You want us all to fly to the Seychelles to see your dad?' I said.

'Well, I thought at first I did. I mean, I don't even need to do the flying part. I could just wish me there. But I got to thinking in my head how it would *really* be. Tinkerbell would make a fuss, for a start – and my dad would think I'd stowed away on an aeroplane or something and get in a right state. And – and if he *really* wanted me there he'd have asked me along too.'

'No child gets asked along on a honeymoon, Smash,'

I said gently. 'But if you just want to *fly* then I think that's a fabulous wish. Anthea wished for wings and their wish was *wonderful* – until they landed on the top of a tall tower and fell asleep and their wings disappeared after sunset and they couldn't get down.'

'Okay. Flying it is – and we'll avoid all towers. Let's go and wake Maudie and get *her* to ask for the breakfast picnic. Then we can fly all day long. We could fly abroad, *not* as far as the Seychelles, but we could go to Paris and circle right round the Eiffel Tower – or the Leaning Tower of Pisa in Italy – or – or some other European tower. I don't know, I've always been rubbish at geography.'

'You're great at ideas, though,' I said.

She grinned at me. 'Yes, I am, aren't I?' she said.

We crept into the next bedroom to wake Robbie and Maudie. Robbie was curled up, clutching his lion. When we woke him up, he looked at the little lump of moulded plastic so wistfully I wanted to cry.

'We've thought of a great wish for today, Robbie!' I said quickly. 'It's *flying*!'

'*I* thought of it,' said Smash. 'And we're going to try for a breakfast picnic at the sandpit – so wake up, little Maudie! That's the girl, wake up, darling, we need you!' Smash tickled Maudie gently. She wriggled and stretched and then wound her arms round Smash's neck.

'My Smash-Smash,' she said.

I struggled to feel pleased for Smash that Maudie

243

clearly liked her the most. I had Robbie after all. Though Robbie seemed in a sad grumpy mood just now.

'I don't want a picnic at breakfast-time – it's too early,' he grumbled, and hunched back down under his duvet.

'You want to go flying, though, don't you?' I said, trying to coax him out.

'Not especially. I bet I'm useless at it. Or I'll get travel sick or something. You'll see, something will go wrong. It always does,' said Robbie.

'You loved your animal wish, Robs, and that didn't go wrong, did it?' I said. Maudie's teddy and slippers would never be quite the same again, but she didn't seem to mind.

'Yes, but I can't ever have that wish again, even though it was the best wish ever,' Robbie said mournfully.

'Oh, put his head in a bucket, will you?' said Smash impatiently. 'Now, Maudie, you run in to Mum and Dad, okay, and take your little dolly's plate and cup and saucer. We'll put it in your little straw basket – they'll think that's really cute – and then you tell them you want to go on a breakfast picnic. They'll play pretending a picnic, but you must say you want a *real* breakfast picnic. Beg for us to go on one, all of us. Can you do that, Maudie?'

'Picnic!' said Maudie happily, and she threw half her tea set into her basket and padded off in her pyjamas.

Smash and I nipped back to our room. We heard Dad and Alice murmur sleepily. Then they laughed a little.

They clinked the china, obviously playing at picnics. Then they gently said no. They said no again. They argued for quite a while. Then they sighed. They got out of bed. We heard Maudie chuckle.

Dad knocked and poked his head round the door.

'Are you awake, girls? Guess what? We're going to have a breakfast picnic.'

Smash and I did a high five when he'd gone to the bathroom.

'Good old Maudie,' said Smash. 'We'll do the same next time, and the time after that, and –'

'There isn't going to be one – a time after next time. Robbie and I go home the day after tomorrow,' I said sadly.

'Oh rats! I'm staying another two weeks!'

'Mum finishes her Summer School on Saturday,' I said.

'Yes, but can't you stay on anyway?'

'Well, not really, because Mum's taking us to visit our gran.'

'Oh, that's not fair! I don't want to be stuck here by myself!' said Smash.

'You'll be able to have some more Psammead wishes all to yourself,' I said.

'Yes, but it won't be such fun, not without you,' said Smash. 'It's funny, when we used to meet up I thought you were awful, this little nerdy bookworm –'

'Thanks,' I said.

'But I didn't get to know you properly. Or Robbie – thought I do still think *he's* nerdy. I'm glad I've got you for my stepsister.'

'I'm glad I've got you for *my* stepsister,' I said. I was surprised to find out I really meant it. Smash could still be a royal pain at times, and she'd always be an awful show-off – but she was brave and resourceful and fun.

When we were washed and dressed, we went downstairs to help Alice make the breakfast picnic.

'I wonder what you eat for a breakfast picnic?' said Smash. 'Cornflake sandwiches?'

Alice had been given no warning, but she rose to the occasion wonderfully. She made toasted bacon sandwiches (storing them in special little bags to keep them warm) and sliced bananas in soft white rolls. She popped six Greek yoghurts in the cool bag with a carton of orange juice, made up a thermos of coffee and took a kilner jar of her home-made apricot compote.

'Yum yum! You're really inventive when it comes to picnics, Alice,' I said. It felt strange praising her when she was the scheming blonde who had stolen Dad away from our mum, but I was getting more used to her now.

I was surprised when she went bright pink.

'I like making picnics for all the family,' she said. She paused. 'It's been fun, all of us together,' she added.

'Watch out, Mum. You're going to be lumbered just with me next week,' said Smash. 'And I'll be five times as irritating without Ros and Robbie to play with.'

'Well, I'll just have to be brave and cope somehow,' Alice joked, but she reached out and ruffled Smash's mop of dark hair.

It was almost a relief when Dad tripped over two of Robbie's animals on the stairs – the African and Indian elephants were on a vast mountain trek. Dad yelled at Robs impatiently and Robbie went into a sulk. It had been so weird, everyone being sweet and kind to each other. I wondered about choosing this – that everyone be sweet and kind – for the last wish tomorrow, but it would be rather a strain – and not necessarily *fun*.

Oxshott woods were surprisingly busy early in the morning, with people walking their dogs and earnest runners hurtling through the trees. They all smiled when they saw our picnic baskets. Maudie skipped along with her own tiny straw basket, rattling her cup and saucer and plate. When we were sitting in our usual place beside the sandpit, Alice served her a miniature meal on her own crockery: a square of bacon sandwich and half a banana roll, with juice in her weeny cup.

'I've never had a breakfast picnic before. It's actually a great idea,' said Dad. He held up his mug of coffee and toasted Maudie. 'Well done, little Maudie!'

Smash and I rolled our eyes at each other. Robbie was still a little sulky, hunched up with his back to us so no one could see he was pretend-feeding his lion with strips of bacon. He made little roaring noises of appreciation, forced to pretend his animals were alive now.

We finished our breakfast picnic enthusiastically, then ran over to the sandpit, still chewing.

Smash scrabbled with her hands in the sand. Robbie and I joined in. We searched till our fingers were sore, our arms like rotary diggers, but we couldn't seem to find the Psammead.

'Oh no, maybe Anthea and the others have wished him back to the past and now he's stayed there,' I said.

'He's not silly enough to wish himself back to the past, unlike *some* people,' said Smash.

'He doesn't seem to like it now in the present,' I said. 'He thinks modern children are very bad-mannered. I wonder why?'

Smash chuckled, and waggled her sandy finger in the air, miming chalking up a point.

'You try searching for the Psammead, Maudie. I bet you can magic it up easy-peasy,' Smash said.

Maudie patted the sand hopefully.

'Monkey? Come here, nice Monkey!' she said. But even Maudie didn't seem to be able to summon him up today.

'Oh no, he *can't* have disappeared today, not when I've got us here extra early with the breakfast picnic,' said Smash.

'And I did think flying was a particularly *good* wish,' I said.

'Not as good as mine yesterday,' said Robbie. He laid himself flat in the pit and spoke into it, in danger of getting sand up his nose and in his mouth. 'It was the best wish *ever*, dear Psammead, and I never got a chance to thank you properly.'

There was a little movement in the sand. Then two eye stalks observed the prostrate Robbie. The rest of the Psammead's head pushed out, followed by his furry arms. He rested his chin on his paws.

'Well, here's your chance, child!' it said, right in Robbie's ear. 'Thank me properly!'

'Oh, Psammead, thank you, thank you, thank you! It was so *wonderful* when my animals were alive. It was just the best thing *ever*. I'll never forget yesterday as long as I live. You are the kindest and most clever magical creature ever,' said Robbie.

The Psammead stuck its head in the air, looking superior. It seemed in the mood for yet more praise, so I joined in.

'We're the luckiest children ever, having you grant our wishes,' I said.

'Especially if you grant our wish today, because I've got an absolute corker,' said Smash.

'Nice Monkey! Kind Monkey!' said Maudie. 'Where your legs?'

The Psammead hopped right out of its burrow, shaking the sand from its fur and giving itself a good stretch.

'Here they are,' it said fondly to Maudie, waving first one hind paw and then the other at her.

'And where your *tail*?' said Maudie, remembering that most monkeys have long tails swinging in the air.

'The Psammead's not really a monkey. It's never *had* a tail,' I said.

'Indeed I *did*, long ago,' said the Psammead. 'It was a most elegant appendage, very long and fully furred. It was my most distinguishing feature, and much admired. I was very proud of my fine tail, I'll have you know. But once, when I was all puffed up, summoning a juicy megatherium for a cave-family Sunday dinner, a *Tyrannosaurus rex* lumbered past and thought I'd make an extra tasty canapé before his own dinner. I was so immersed in puffing myself up that I wasn't even aware it was there until I saw its horrifying head hurtling down towards me, jaws gaping. I rolled away from it as fast as I could, but I didn't have time to tuck my tail about me. Those jaws snapped – and I lost my tail.'

'Oh, how terrible!' I said.

'It was indeed,' said the Psammead. 'I still feel a sharp pain in my rear when I dwell upon it. But I have endeavoured to accept my new blunt-ended appearance over the years. I am still a rather handsome creature, even though I say so myself.'

The Psammead preened itself. I didn't dare look at Smash or Robbie. The Psammead was utterly wonderful, but looks-wise it did seem quite one of the most unfortunate creatures ever, with its big fat furry body, its heavily wrinkled face, its little bat ears, and its eyes wavering on those weird pink stalks.

'Yes, you are exceptionally handsome,' I said, trying hard to keep a straight face.

The Psammead smiled at me benevolently.

'You would like a wish today then, children?' it said.

'Yes, please. It's my turn and I'd very much like to wish that we could all fly. Please. If you're feeling particularly obliging. I jolly well hope you are,' said Smash.

'Certainly,' said the Psammead, and it started puffing itself up. And up and up and up until it seemed ready to split in two. Then it collapsed abruptly, gave us a little nod and dug itself into the sand.

At the same time I felt a strange itching, burning feeling on my back. Smash felt behind her, Robbie started scratching his own back and Maudie peered over her shoulder, startled.

'What is it?' said Smash. 'What's happening?'

The strange feeling grew stronger, so that my shoulder blades prickled fiercely, as if they were being pushed right through my skin. I could actually feel them poking through the thin material of my T-shirt. I twisted round worriedly, and felt something sharp and then soft, like a feather sticking out of a pillow. A *feather*!

'Oh goodness, I think we're growing wings!' I gasped.

There were two points protruding through my T-shirt now, and once they were free they pushed harder, growing with amazing speed. At first they were tightly rolled up like furled umbrellas, but as they grew I experienced a dragging, aching feeling that made me brace my shoulders, and all at once the long, dark, pointy wings opened wide. I flapped them in the air, creating great gusts of wind all around me. I craned my neck in awe at the sight of my feathery new wings. They were a beautiful sky blue shading to soft navy at the tips.

'Look at my wonderful wings!' I cried.

'No, look at *mine*!' Smash shouted, whirling round and round, stretching her own wings out like a great cape. Hers were scarlet edged with gold, so bright you could barely look at her.

'I've got wings too!' Robbie yelled. 'Mine are like *animal* wings!' They were a beautiful deep yellow-sandy colour spotted all over with brown – leopard wings.

'*My* wings, *my* wings!' Maudie sang, jumping up and down, flapping her own little wings in the air. They were snowy white with a layer of pink underneath, beautiful baby wings. 'Maudie fly!' she said, and she jumped higher . . . and then *hovered* an inch or two above the ground, flapping so hard her face went as pink as her under-feathers.

'Look at Maudie!' I said. 'She really *is* flying. Careful, darling, don't go too high!'

I waved my own wings and felt a strange lifting sensation in my arms and legs, but I couldn't seem to get properly off the ground.

'I can't do it!' said Robbie, standing on tiptoe and flapping his arms as well as his wings. 'Look, I'm trying and trying, but I can't do it, I *knew* I wouldn't be able to!'

'Watch me,' said Smash, leaping upwards wildly, flapping her own wings so hard she nearly blew us both over – but even she fell down again with a thud.

'Ouch!' she said. 'Maudie, hey, how do you *do* it?'

Maudie giggled and rose upwards, paddling with her legs, until she was up by our heads. She tried to circle round us but went head over heels instead, over and over, squealing with laughter.

'Having fun, Maudie?' Alice called happily, not reacting at all to the sight of her precious daughter tumbling about in thin air.

'Maybe *that's* the way,' said Smash, and she threw herself in the air. Just for a moment she seemed to hang there, suspended, but when she flapped her wings hard she hurtled down again, landing in a heap a second time, ruffling all her new feathers.

'Ouch *again*! I can't believe the Psammead could be so mean. It's given us wings and yet they're totally useless – we can't fly at all.'

'They're very pretty, though,' I said, reaching round and giving my wings a stroke.

'I told you,' said Robbie, wriggling his shoulders. 'I knew our wings wouldn't work.'

A flock of birds flew out of a tree, squawking, as if they were mocking us.

'They're green parakeets,' said Robbie, craning his neck to look at them. He ran along the ground on his skinny stick legs, wings flapping. He wasn't looking where he was going and tripped over a tree root.

I ran to him.

'Are you all right, Robs? Please don't have hurt yourself! Are your legs all right? And your arms?'

'It's more my bottom! I landed with a bump,' said Robbie. 'Did I fly just a little bit?'

'Not really!' I said gently.

'How come Maudie can do it and not us?' Smash demanded. 'Look, mine still aren't *working*.' She flapped her wings furiously.

'Maybe – maybe we're trying too hard?' I said. 'I just don't think we've got the knack yet. It's like swimming or riding a bike. You can't do it at all at first, and then suddenly you realize you're doing it after all – Oh!' I gasped as I suddenly stepped up in the air. I was only a very little way up, so that I could still touch the tops of the ferns, but I wasn't on the ground at all – I wasn't walking, I was flying, really truly flying.

'Look! Look, I'm *flying*!' I said, reaching up to hold Maudie's little hand above me.

'Well, tell us how you *do* it!' Smash shouted.

'I don't *know* how!' I moved my arms and legs experimentally and flapped hard with my beautiful blue wings. The moment I concentrated it felt strange and awkward and I slid down into the ferns, tumbling over on to my back, though I managed to snap my wings shut quickly so I wouldn't crumple them.

'Don't stop now, Ros. You were doing great!' said Robbie.

'Show *me*!' said Smash, pressing her lips together and straining every muscle to get airborne.

'I'm sure you're trying too hard,' I said. 'It doesn't work if you do. The moment I tried to think how I was doing it I felt so strange and silly I couldn't do it any more. It's like when you try to work out exactly how you walk. Your legs go stiff immediately and your arms won't swing the right way. Don't *think* about it too much.'

'That's an idiotic thing to say. How can I *help* thinking about it?' said Smash. 'It's my wish and it's being completely wasted. It's extremely annoying that you can fly, Ros, yet I can't. And look at little Maudie – she's absolutely ace at it.' Smash's expression softened as she peered up at Maudie, watching her bob up and down comically. Then suddenly her own knees bent, her arms wavered, her scarlet wings flapped – and she rose up too, right beside Maudie.

'Oh joy! Oh wonder! Oh glory!' Smash shrieked.

'Oh woe! Oh horror! Oh despair!' Robbie wailed. 'Now I truly *am* the only one who can't do it.'

'Hold my hands, Robs,' I said. 'Now, stop thinking about flying altogether. Think about . . . your animals. Imagine little yellow wings on your lion. And your tiger would have orange wings with black stripes, and your giraffe would have very delicate spotty wings and, oh

255

my goodness, your two elephants would have to have very strong grey leathery wings to haul them upwards.'

Robbie stared at me, starting to laugh in spite of himself – not actually noticing that we were both rising upwards, above the grass, over the ferns, higher this time, up as high as Smash and Maudie.

'Reach out and hold Smash's hand, Robs. I'll hold Maudie's and we'll make a flying circle!' I said.

We joined hands, Robbie squealing with excitement, and played an aerial game of Ring a Ring o' Roses. Maudie went 'Atishoo atishoo!' with such emphasis she tumbled over again, flying with her head hanging down and her fat little legs waggling in the air. Smash and I tried to pull her upright and found ourselves plummeting down to earth, with Maudie bouncing first on my chest and then Smash's. Robbie stayed suspended in the air, looking down on us, a great grin spreading from ear to ear.

'I'm flying!' he said. 'I'm the *only one* flying!'

Now he was up there he wouldn't come down. He flew round and round and round, going 'Whoo-whoo-whoo!' triumphantly. He was so proud of himself he flew over Dad and Alice, hovering above them like a human helicopter.

'Look at *me*, Dad!' he said.

Dad sat serenely underneath him, totally unaware that Robbie was right up above his head.

'*Dad!*' Robbie shrieked.

Dad looked round vaguely. 'Are you having fun, Robbie?' he called.

'You bet, Dad!' Robbie said.

Maudie bounced up into the air again as if she were on a trampoline, clearly having fun herself. Smash and I took a little longer to get the knack back again. It was so difficult not to tense up and try too hard.

'Let's climb a tree,' said Smash. 'Then we'll be up there already and all we need do is step out into the air.'

'And maybe plummet down head first,' I said.

Smash tried anyway, swinging herself up a tree like a monkey, going right up to the tiny branches at the top which wouldn't usually bear her weight – and then she went *on* climbing in the air, her wings unfurling. There she was, flying right up above all of us.

'Come on, let's go exploring!' she cried.

'No! Wait for me! Robbie, Maudie, stay there!' I shouted, reaching up and trying to catch them by the ankles.

Then that strange light tingling feeling started and I was suddenly up there with them, flapping my wings, *flying*.

'Let's all hold hands so we can't lose each other,' I said.

'What, like babies?' said Smash scornfully.

'Maudie *is* a baby and we need to look after her,' I said.

'Okay, come and hold *my* hand, Maudie,' said Smash.

'Can't catch me, Smash-Smash!' Maudie giggled, bobbing about just out of reach.

It didn't work when we *were* all holding hands. It was like trying to hold hands when you're running. We jerked up and down, pulling each other all over the place.

'All right, it isn't working,' I panted. 'We don't need to hold hands, but stay together, *please*.'

We let go and flew upwards, above the trees. It was a little breezy there and we found we didn't need to flap our wings at all. We could just swoop and swirl where the breeze took us. It felt so good we all cried out joyfully – and a woman walking her dog looked up at us and screamed.

'Oh no! I think it's the *same* woman who saw the nursery-rhyme people. The poor thing, she'll think she's hallucinating!' I said.

'Let's go higher then, where people can't see us,' said Smash. 'I want to see just how high I can go.'

'Don't fly *too* high, Smash!' I said – but of course she didn't listen to me.

13

Smash soared up and up and up until she was just a little black dot in the sky. My heart started thudding, scared she would disappear altogether. But then she suddenly started tumbling down again, going a little too fast.

'Quick, Robs! We have to catch her,' I cried, flying swiftly sideways.

Smash hurtled down head first and I *just* managed to throw my arms round her. Robbie hung on to her feet and I held her under her arms. Her head lolled on my chest a moment, showing the whites of her eyes, and I shook her in terror. Then she started gasping and panting and struggling.

'Smash, what is it, what's happened?' I said.

We flew her down to the ground and laid her on the grass. Maudie flew down too and patted Smash's pale face anxiously.

'Smash-Smash?' she said. 'Get better!'

Smash opened her eyes and sat up shakily, still gasping for breath.

'There! I'm okay now, Maudie. Don't look so worried,' she said.

'Breathe deeply, in and out,' I said. 'You're still ever so white. What went *wrong*?'

'I don't know. I was feeling absolutely great, rocketing up and up, and then I started to feel a bit sick and dizzy, in fact I puked a bit in the air. I hope it didn't land on any of you lot. Then I think I fainted, though I've never fainted in my life before. Do you think I'm ill?'

'Perhaps you can get flying sick? I often get carsick,' said Robbie.

'You would, you little wimp,' said Smash. 'But *I* don't. I've never felt like that before.'

'You've never flown right up in the sky before, silly. You were higher than the highest mountain. Oh, *I* know! Simple! You ran out of oxygen. That happens to mountaineers – they get altitude sickness.'

'You're such a know-it-all, Rosalind,' said Smash. 'You're really irritating sometimes. I bet you're forever waving your hand in class, bursting with the right answer. I'm sure everyone sighs and goes "Oh no, there's Rosalind Hartlepool showing off again."'

I felt myself going crimson. 'Why do you always have to be so mean and hateful to everyone, Smash?' I said.

'Oh, poor little diddums, I was only *teasing*.'

'Yes, but you're really horrible sometimes. I don't know why you still keep picking on Robbie and me. I thought we were all friends now,' I said, dangerously near tears.

'We *are* friends. That's what friends are for. You can tease them all you like,' said Smash.

'Well, I don't think you can have many friends if that's your attitude,' I said.

It was Smash's turn to blush – and I realized I'd hit on the truth. I suddenly felt sorry for her, even though I was furiously angry with her too. I made a supreme effort.

'Anyway, what are we doing, squabbling, wasting our wonderful flying time. Let's have another go,' I said.

We all stood up and this time we managed to take off together. I wanted us to stay very low, practically skimming the ground, but we were still in the woods and it was hard work dodging the tree trunks. We had to weave in and out as if we were doing a complicated country dance.

'Perhaps we ought to go a *little* higher,' I shouted, so we rose up above the treetops.

Maudie laughed excitedly.

'Higher and higher, like Smash-Smash,' she said,

tipping her head back and stretching her white fluffy wings.

'No, no, not that high, Maudie!' Smash said, grabbing hold of her. 'I was very silly going right up high. Didn't you see me fall? Don't you be silly too, my Maudie.'

Smash caught my eye and pulled a little face at me. She wasn't exactly saying sorry, but I could see she *was*.

I reached out and squeezed her hand.

'Come on!' I said. 'Let's fly!'

We flew over Oxshott woods, on and on, catching the breeze again and riding up and down on it. Flocks of birds flew away from us, squawking anxiously, thinking we were great birds of prey.

The sun came out and warmed our wings. I could feel my cheeks glowing, my whole body tingling. I could hear Smash singing at the top of her voice, Robbie yelling 'Look at me!', Maudie laughing – and if the Psammead had grown a pair of furry wings and joined us I'd have wished we could go on flying forever and ever and ever.

We flew over more woods and commons, then a grand ornamental park, then a little town.

'Is that where Dad lives?' Robbie yelled. 'Which is our house?'

'No, we're much further away. I haven't got a clue where we are,' I shouted back – and for once in my life I found I didn't really care.

'*I* know where we are – *look*!' Smash shouted, and she gave a great whoop.

My eyes were watering in the wind. I gave them a quick rub and then saw strange spirals and circles sparkling in the sunlight.

'What's that?' I asked.

'Chessington World of Adventures!' said Smash. 'Come on, let's have a free ride on the biggest roller coaster!'

We flew nearer, until we could see all the rides properly and hear screaming as children swooped up and down. We hovered over a huge ride that spiralled round and round and up and over, and then saw a space in one of the hurtling carriages.

'That one! Now!' said Smash, grabbing Maudie.

I clutched Robbie, and the four of us swooped through thin air and landed with a little thump in the carriage. The two boys in the front screamed their heads off – but everyone was screaming and we were whirling up and down and round about so fast that no one could do anything.

We waited till we edged right up to the very steepest part at the end, and then as the carriage started tip-tip-tipping down we jumped up and flew out into the air. The boys screamed even louder – but they were hurtling down so fast they couldn't let go of the rail to point at us.

'There's animals over there! It's like a little zoo. *Please* let's see the animals!' Robbie begged breathlessly.

'For goodness' sake, we can see animals any old day,' said Smash. 'You can't go down to see the animals, not in the middle of that crowd. They'll all stare at you and say, "Little boy, do you know you've got two great spotty wings sticking out of your back?" and they'll cart you off to a freak show. We'd better beat it, actually, those boys are pointing up at us. Come *on*.'

She flew off, still clutching Maudie, so we had to follow her. Robbie got a bit fed up after that and kept moaning that he was tired and his back ached and he was starting to feel dizzy. I was getting tired too, and my own back ached *and* my shoulders and neck. I just wasn't used to the weight of my beautiful blue wings.

'Smash, we need a *rest*,' I shouted after her.

'Oh, you two are hopeless! Look at Maudie – *she* doesn't want a rest, do you, darling?' Smash said.

Certainly Maudie was still bobbing along merrily, her little white wings flapping like handkerchiefs.

I didn't know what to do. I couldn't go down to earth with Robs to have a ten-minute rest. Smash and Maudie would fly miles away from us and we might never be able to catch them up. Yet I could see Robbie was really struggling now, getting redder and redder, his face creased up with effort.

'Smash!' I called again.

She looked round and saw Robbie.

'Okay, okay,' she said, peering downwards. 'There's a great big park beneath us. We can swoop down and hide among the trees for a bit. Oh! Look! *Animals*, Robbie!'

There was a large herd of fallow deer standing tranquilly below us, flicking their white tails as they nibbled grass.

'There!' said Smash triumphantly, as if she'd conjured them up herself.

We all flew down and landed on the soft grass in front of the deer. They didn't seem at all startled and went on feeding placidly, but a little girl spinning a hula hoop gasped at us and let her hoop clatter to her ankles.

'You've got *wings*!' she cried, her eyes huge.

There wasn't any point denying it, as we were all four flapping frantically, trying to get the knack of folding our wings up neatly, feathers dovetailed into place.

'Where's your mum?' I asked the little girl.

'Back there, in the trees,' said the little girl. 'I came out here to do my hooping.'

'Well, hoop away then,' said Smash.

'You really do have wings,' said the little girl, and she stepped out of her hoop and edged right up to me. She reached out and touched the very tip of my wing with one trembling finger. '*Real* wings,' she repeated. 'So, are you . . . are you *fairies*?'

Smash snorted with laughter.

'That's right! We're definitely fairies. Aren't we pretty?' she said, striking a silly pose and batting her eyelids.

'I've always, always wanted to see a real fairy,' said the little girl earnestly. 'I've got all the Rainbow Fairies books *and* the Flower Fairies with the pretty pictures.'

'I'm not a fairy!' said Robbie indignantly.

'Oh yes, you are,' I said firmly. 'We're *all* fairies, but you mustn't tell anyone about us, even your mum, or we'll disappear in a puff of smoke. You won't tell, will you?'

'No, I absolutely won't,' said the little girl, shaking her head vigorously. 'But why are you all so *big*?'

'That one's little,' said Smash, pointing to Maudie.

'Yes, but she's still *quite* big – and you're *ever* so big,' the little girl said tactlessly.

'All the better to give you a thump if you're cheeky,' said Smash, flapping her wings.

'Oooh! They're so beautiful!' said the little girl.

'We're a new breed of big fairies,' I said.

'Can you grant wishes?' asked the little girl.

'Well, it depends,' I said cautiously.

'Can you make *me* a fairy too?'

'No, I'm afraid you're not quite magic enough, but I tell you what – would you like to fly up in the air with us, just a little way off the ground?' I offered.

'Oh yes, *yes*!'

'Okay! Smash, you take one of her hands. Robbie – Robbie, come over here!' I said.

Robbie was crouching by the deer, making little murmuring sounds of encouragement to them.

'Don't shout, you'll startle them,' he hissed, but he came over reluctantly.

'We're going to help this little girl to fly and we all need to pull her up and get her airborne,' I said.

'And me help too,' said Maudie.

'Yes, we'll all help,' I said.

'I thought we came down to have a *rest*,' said Robbie, but he held out his hands.

We stood in a circle, the little girl giggling excitedly.

'Okay, one two three – fly!' I said.

We all knew how to let ourselves go now and just drift upwards, but it was much harder dragging the small wingless girl up with us. Smash and I had to haul hard, flying lopsided, but we just about managed to get her off the ground.

'Oh! Oh, I really am flying!' she cried. 'Mummy, look!'

'Sh! It's a secret! You mustn't tell your mum, remember. She won't believe you anyway, she'll think you're just telling stories,' I panted. 'I think we're going to have to set you down soon, it's ever so tiring.'

We managed to whirl her round in a circle for a minute or so and then we all collapsed back on the grass.

'Can we do it again?' she asked eagerly.

'No, we're too tired. Run away and play now,' said Smash. She tried to lie flat on her back, but her wings got in the way, even when she folded them up tight. She had to roll over on to her tummy, groaning. '*Go!*' she barked at the little girl, who was staring.

The little girl ran off, clutching her hula hoop.

'Don't be mean to her. Imagine how exciting it would be to go to the park and discover four fully grown fairies,' I said.

'I wish you'd stop calling me a fairy,' said Robbie. 'I ache all over. How do birds sleep? They're meant to put their heads under their wings but it's impossibly uncomfy,' he said, experimenting.

Maudie was the only one of us who didn't seem at all tired. She ran around in the grass, hopping and skipping right up in the air, singing her favourite mad nursery rhyme.

'Hey diddle diddle,
Jack and Jill went up the hill
Atishoo atishoo,
We'll all have tea.'

'I'd like some tea,' said Smash. 'In fact I'd like some *lunch*. It seems *ages* since our breakfast picnic.'

We suddenly realized we were all very hungry and thirsty indeed.

'There's bound to be a park cafe somewhere. I'll treat us,' said Smash, fishing her fat purse out of her jeans pocket.

'Yes, but how are we going to stand in a queue with our wings?' I said. 'We'll have a huge crowd round us in no time.'

'Mmm,' said Smash. 'Leave it to me.'

We flopped uncomfortably on the ground a little longer and then flew up into the air, seeking out a cafe.

'There's a little food van in the car park, that'll do,' said Smash. 'We'll fly down behind the trees and walk over. Just act dead casual, as if wings are simply the latest fashion.'

We tried to do exactly that, but it wasn't easy. Drivers got out of their cars and stared at us, children pointed, and dogs barked hysterically. The people already queuing at the van stepped backwards, as if they were frightened of us.

'We'd like four big Whippies, please,' said Smash. 'And four bars of chocolate, those ones, oh, and four of those fruit pies, yum, yum. And four cans of Coke.'

'Maudie will get hiccups,' I said.

'Okay, four little fruit juices then,' said Smash. 'That'll please Mum – all the fruit, dead healthy.'

The people surrounding us relaxed a little, because Smash sounded so ordinary, but they still stared at our wings as if bewitched. We tried to keep them tightly furled and as still as possible, but it was a great struggle, and way beyond Maudie, who hopped about flapping her dear little white wings, showing off their pink underside.

The man in the van was also staring, mesmerized. Smash shuffled her feet impatiently.

'I *said*, we'd like four ice creams, all with chocolate

flakes – and four Galaxies and four fruit pies and four fruit juices. Please,' she repeated.

'Do – do you have money?' he whispered.

'Of course I do,' said Smash, waving her purse and getting out a twenty-pound note.

'Well, I wasn't to know. So, what *are* you then, with your fancy wings? You're not . . . ?' He bent forward out of his serving hatch and hissed the word. '*Angels?*'

Smash cracked up laughing.

'Do I truly look like an angel?' she said. 'No, we're in a *film*. We're playing these children who get lots of wishes and in this scene they wish they can fly.'

'But where are all the film crew and the cameras and everything?' the man asked, starting to gather everything together and make our Whippy ices.

'They're over there,' said Smash, pointing vaguely. 'They've got their own food canteen but we wanted ice creams, didn't we?' she said to Robbie and me. We nodded very hard, trying to act equally convincingly.

'But your wings look so real,' said a woman in the queue, and she reached out and touched Smash's scarlet feathers. 'Oh my God, they're *warm*,' she said. 'Feel!'

'Hey, get off! Watch out or you'll break them and then the special effects crew will do their nuts,' said Smash. 'They're great, aren't they? Dead convincing. There's a kid back there, she seriously thought we were fairies. Sweet, eh?'

'What are they made of?' someone said, marvelling.

Smash shrugged, making the feathers on her wings flutter.

'Feathers!' she said. 'Duh!'

'Yes, but – how do they move?'

'That's the complicated bit. We have these little electronic devices stuck to our shoulder blades, very sensitive, so that every time we move our wings do too,' said Smash.

'But can you really fly with them?' said the ice-cream man.

Smash rolled her eyes.

'Of course not. It'll all be computer-generated images on screen,' she said.

'Yes, of course,' he nodded as he finished making the last Whippy. He embellished it with rainbow sprinkles, raspberry sauce and an extra flake, and handed it to Maudie, who nearly fainted with joy. 'Amazing what they can do nowadays. Well, tell the rest of the film crew to come over here for ices and cold drinks.'

He handed us our ice creams and helpfully put the chocolate and pies and juices in a plastic carrier. Smash paid him and we said goodbye to everyone. Then we walked off.

'Fancy thinking they could really fly! You are *stupid*!' someone said behind us.

'Let's tease them,' said Smash, grinning. 'One, two, three – *fly*!'

271

She rose up, fluttering her glorious red and gold wings. There was a great gasp from the crowd round the van.

'After spinning them all that story!' I said to Robbie.

'She's *such* a show-off,' he said. 'I suppose we'll have to follow her now.'

We looked round at Maudie.

'Fly!' I said.

Maudie didn't take off properly because she was so eager to eat her ice cream. She bobbed along, feet trailing in the grass, as she nibbled her chocolate flake, an expression of total bliss on her face. Alice didn't usually let her have ice creams from vans. People were running up to her, arms outstretched, as if they were going to catch hold of her.

'Quick, grab Maudie!' I shouted.

Robbie and I jerked her up in the air. Maudie gave a great wail of despair because we'd jerked the ice cream right out of her cone. It fell on the grass and Maudie kicked and struggled to get back down on the grass too so that she could try to scoop it up.

'No, Maudie! Look, have *my* ice cream,' I said – but mine didn't have sprinkles and sauce and two flakes, and Maudie sobbed bitterly.

We'd made such a spectacle of ourselves now, with people running underneath us and screaming and pointing and take photos of us on their mobiles, that we didn't like to land in a different part of the park to have our lunch. We did our best to eat it while we were still airborne. It was just about possible, Smash flying between us and handing out food and drink at intervals, but it was like trying to eat a three-course meal while running. We all ended up with hiccups. Maudie only had a lick of chocolate and a sip of juice. She was still sobbing softly for the loss of her ice cream. Then she started rubbing her eyes and trying to suck her thumb, clearly tired out and in need of a nap.

We were flying above another town now, with no suitable place to land, so we had to take it in turns to hold Maudie and steer her along while she slept. We were all getting pretty tired again too, though we livened up a little when we flew along a big river. We copied the swans, flying in a bunch, and then swooping down, scraping our toes in the water, flapping hard to stop ourselves sinking.

There were too many boats on the river, though. People kept shouting and staring up at us. Smash played up to the crowd, flying right down to wave to the people on a big pleasure boat. They waved back at her foolishly, looking astounded.

'Smash, *stop* making such a show of yourself,' I begged.

'Why not? It's fun!' she said.

'Yes, but what if someone calls the police or the newspapers or a television crew?' I said.

'That would be brilliant! They'd never be able to catch us,' said Smash.

'They might.'

'You think they'll suddenly produce giant butterfly nets or something?' said Smash.

'The police have got helicopters. They could chase after us in the air.'

'And then what are they going to do? I bet there's no law that says you're not allowed to fly,' said Smash. 'Stop being such an old spoilsport, Rosalind. Come on!'

'Where are we going now? Haven't we flown far enough?' Robbie gasped. He was taking his turn to carry Maudie, but it was a real struggle for him.

'Look, give Maudie back to me,' said Smash. 'There now. Come on, Maudie, it's time you woke up. You don't want to miss all this lovely flying, do you?'

'Ice cream,' Maudie mumbled, but she rubbed her eyes, flapped her wings hard, and started flying along under her own steam.

'That's my girl,' Smash encouraged her. 'We're going to London now. We're going to fly up to Buckingham Palace and peep in the windows and see if we can spot the Queen.'

'No, we're not! London's miles and miles and miles away – and how on earth would we find our way there anyway?' I said.

'Easy-peasy. We just carry on flying upriver,' said Smash. 'The Thames goes right through London, doesn't it, so we just follow it.'

'But it will take *ages* and we're tired out already,' Robbie complained.

'*You're* tired. I'm fine. I'm having the best time in the world,' said Smash. 'Come on, please.'

'Smash, *listen*. It'll take all afternoon to get to London, maybe even longer. Then what are you going to do when our wings disappear at sunset? Dad and Alice will go spare if they snap out of the spell and we're missing for hours all over again.'

'Who cares?' said Smash. 'This is the one day in my whole life that I can fly and I'm jolly well going to make the most of it.'

She flew on determinedly while we hovered in the air, not knowing what to do.

'I want to go *home*,' said Robbie.

'I do too, but we can't just *leave* her,' I said.

'Why not? Look, she's left *us*,' said Robbie.

Smash was already a tiny little bird shape in the distance. She was circling a tower block, peering in the penthouse windows, doubtless pulling faces – and then suddenly she was gone.

'Smash? Smash, what's happened? Where *are* you?' I shouted, though she was much too far away to hear me.

'Can you see where Smash is?' I said urgently.

'Over there, somewhere,' said Robbie, pointing vaguely.

'Yes, but *where*?'

'I can't quite see her at the moment.'

'Maudie, can you see Smash-Smash?'

'Smash-Smash?' said Maudie.

'She was way over there, by those big flats, peeping in the windows. Then she just vanished!' I said.

'Well, she'll have flown further on,' said Robbie.

'No, I was *watching*. I'm sure she didn't. Come on, we've got to find her,' I said. 'And all keep together, okay?'

We flew in a little V-formation towards the tower block: me first, then Robbie to the left of me, Maudie to the right. I kept hoping I was wrong, that I'd somehow taken my eye off Smash and that she was simply way ahead of us – but though I scanned the horizon I couldn't spot her. I looked anxiously downwards too, remembering how she'd suddenly plummeted when she'd flown too high. There was no sign of her, but if she'd fallen into the river the weight of her wings might have sucked her under straight away.

'Oh, Smash, please be all right!' I whispered, flying frantically. I mostly thought my stepsister maddening, but I found I loved her too. I couldn't bear the thought that something had happened to her.

We were getting near the tower block now. I flew towards the penthouse. There was a little rooftop garden with a lounge deckchair, and a drink on the fancy marble table. There was no one there – but when I got really close up I saw red feathers scattered across the concrete paving.

'Smash! Smash, where *are* you?' I yelled.

'Here! Here, but be careful. This lunatic's tied me up!' Smash screamed from somewhere inside.

'Robbie, keep Maudie safe, whatever you do,' I said.

'No, no, *you* keep her. I'll rescue Smash. I'm the boy,' said Robbie, struggling to get hold of me.

Maudie took no notice of either of us. She flew ahead and landed lightly on the tips of her toes and ran right through the open glass door of the penthouse flat. We charged after her, not folding our wings quickly enough, so that we jostled each other, briefly entwined.

'Smash-Smash!' Maudie cried.

I hurtled forward in a flurry of feathers. Smash was tethered to a table leg by a dressing-gown cord, about to throw a huge glass vase at a man cowering in a corner.

'Smash! Stop it! You'll kill him!' I shouted. 'And don't get glass all over the floor – Maudie's got bare feet!'

'He tried to kill *me*!' said Smash, outraged. 'I was just having a peep at him, tapping away on his laptop on his lounger, and then he looked up and saw me and I practically wet myself, the expression on his face was so funny – but then he took aim and chucked his wretched laptop at me. Look, I'm still *bleeding*!' Smash pointed to her forehead. 'I was so stunned – *literally* – that I just sort of flopped forward and he grabbed hold of me, and pulled me in here, and tied me up with his horrible dressing gown and then you'll never ever guess what he did, the total *creep*.'

'What? What did he do?'

'He went and phoned a newspaper! He's *selling* me

for thousands of pounds!' Smash shouted, aiming the vase again.

'No! Don't! That's a Lalique vase, for God's sake. Listen, I don't want to harm you – any of you. I can't *believe* this! What the hell *are* you, some kind of aliens? I just want to keep you safe. You're *mine*, I saw you first.'

'Of course we're not *yours*, you stupid man!' I said, rushing to Smash and trying to undo the dressing-gown cord.

'Leave her! You're staying, all of you. You're my story!' said the man. He seized hold of me and tried to push me to the ground.

'Don't you *dare* touch my sister!' Robbie shouted, and he punched the man in the chest. He was trying to be fierce, but his fist was small and made no impression at all.

'Hit him where it *hurts*!' Smash yelled.

I tried to scratch the man's face but he grabbed hold of my hand, bending all the fingers back, making me scream. Robbie twisted round and kicked him hard between the legs. I don't know if he was deliberately aiming there or whether it was sheer luck, but the man doubled up, making a weird *Ooomph* noise.

'Quick, quick!' I said, struggling with the cord again. 'Let's all get *out* of here.'

I gave one last frantic tug and then the knot loosened. Smash jumped up, gave the man another kick herself, and grabbed Maudie. Robbie and I clutched hands and then we all ran out of the room, back on to the balcony.

'Noooo!' the man wailed behind us.

'*Yes!*' we shouted, and then we stepped up into the air, spread our wings and flew away.

We flew *back* along the river. Even Smash had lost her taste for further adventures now. Her wings had lost a lot of feathers in her struggle with the horrible man, and some were crumpled and sticking out at painful angles. Maudie was tired now, so we had to take turns carrying her again. My fingers were hurting a lot and I still felt sick with shock. Robbie was the only one of us who had suddenly got his second wind.

'Did you see the way I kicked the man, *wham, bash, bonk*? He just dropped like a stone. I overpowered him totally, didn't I, even though he was much bigger than me. I saved you, Ros, and you, Smash, and Maudie too. I saved you all!'

I let him exaggerate for a while, but by the time we were halfway home we were all heartily sick of his boasting. And then it started to rain. We discovered that you get much wetter up in the air than you do down on the ground. It's bad enough being soaked to the skin, but it's far worse having sopping-wet feathers. Because our wings weighed so much more now, our heads hung down and our shoulders hunched, and it was a terrible effort to fly on doggedly. It was so dark because of the rain that it was difficult to gauge time. I didn't *think* it could possibly be near sunset, but I started to worry all the same. What if our wings suddenly disappeared when we were here in mid-air? Would we plummet downwards?

We tried flying very low, just in case, but this wasn't practical. People kept looking up and spotting us and screaming.

It was easier when we'd passed all the built-up areas and were flying over woods. Very few people were walking there in the pouring rain. There were so *many* woods and commons and wild patches of land. I started to wonder if we'd manage to find our own Oxshott woods ever again. But Smash seemed to have her own inner satellite navigation system hard-wired into her head. She led us back, back, back, until we suddenly saw the yellow of our sandpit underneath us.

'There!' she said, and we flew down and landed in a tangled heap in the sand. All our beautiful wings were crumpled now, hanging like damp curtains from our backs, moulting feathers as we moved.

Dad and Alice saw us and waved vaguely and dreamily, but seemingly couldn't see our wings. It was still pouring with rain, but they sat together under the trees, their hair plastered to their heads, rain running down their noses and dripping on to their chins. Smash stood up wearily, spread her tattered wings, and flew right over to Alice, circling her several times. Alice didn't even blink.

Smash flew back and squatted in the sandpit with us.

'It's like she couldn't even see me,' she mumbled.

'Yes, she's in a kind of trance. It's the Psammead magic – you know that,' I said.

'She's like that even when she's *not* in a trance. Except when she's nagging at me. And so is my dad. It's like *he's* in a trance all the time now he's met this flipping girl. One measly sentence of email, that's all *I* get. It must have taken him a minute at the most.'

'Oh, stop it. Cheer up. Look, we've had the most simply amazing day, flying around, all because of your special wish,' I said.

'Yeah, but I'm getting a bit sick of it now. Let's wake the sleeping beauties and go home,' said Smash.

'We'll have to wait till the wings fall off,' said Robbie. 'I know *they* can't see them, but everyone else can. They'll try to catch us and sell us to the papers, just like that horrible man in the flats.'

'Well, surely it's way past sunset by now. It's raining so hard you can't *see* any sun. Hey, Mr Psammead!' She flopped down with her chin in the sand. 'Are you there? It's me, Smash, the shouty one. I'm soaking wet and I've been bonked on the head and I haven't had any tea at all. I want to go *home*. Can't you make an exception just once and pop out and grant us one more teeny-weeny wish. We just want our wretched wings to fall off.'

'You're not ever going to get it to come out now, not when it's pouring with rain. The Psammead *hates* water. He'll have burrowed way, way down to get away from it,' I told her.

'He'll be giving an Australian boy a wish now,' said Robbie. 'Hey, that's an idea! Maybe we can all wish to go to Australia tomorrow. I'd simply love to see some kangaroos and koala bears.'

'I think they're just in special zoos and play-parks now,' I said. 'And it's *my* wish next. I'm going to try to make it special for all of us, seeing as it's our last wish. Only I don't quite know what it'll be yet. Flying will be hard to beat,' I added politely, for Smash's benefit.

'I'm fed up with flying,' she said. 'Here, Rosalind, give my wings a real tug. Maybe we can just pull them off.'

I tried pulling them as hard as I could. Smash yelled in pain.

'I'm sorry! I didn't mean to hurt you,' I said.

'No, it's okay. Try *harder*,' she said.

It was no use. The wings seemed as much part of her as her arms and legs.

'Perhaps we're stuck with them forever now,' Smash said gloomily, opening and shutting her wings, spraying the rest of us with raindrops. 'How will we ever get clothes that fit over them? And it's going to be a real struggle getting through doors, and we're never going to fit into bed properly. We'll never be able to go out without causing a riot – though that might be quite good fun.'

'You didn't look as if you were having fun tied up to that table. Good job I came along and rescued you,' said Robbie. 'Did you see the way I hit that man and I punched him and I kicked him – *kerpow, bash, bang!*'

'Shut up, Robbie. You've told us too many times already,' I said.

It didn't stop him telling us again, so Smash and I rolled him in the sand to stop him. We started fighting in a silly, giggling, soggy sort of fashion, all of us clumsily weighed down with our wings. Maudie climbed on top of all of us, bouncing about, jumping on us as if we were a human trampoline. Then she tumbled down abruptly and we huddled up in a heap. We were suddenly light and free. Our wings had gone at last!

'Mum, Dave, let's go home!' said Smash.

Dad and Alice stared at us. They plucked at their wet clothes, and then scrambled to their feet. Dad looked at his watch and shook his head, unable to believe the time he saw there. They hurried us home, taking turns to carry Maudie, checking on us three constantly, feeling terrible that they'd kept us out in the rain unfed most of the day without realizing.

When we got home, there were steaming baths and hot chocolate and baked potatoes, and it all felt very cosy. Dad switched on the news on television as we were going up to bed.

'You'll never guess what,' he said, when he came up to say goodnight. 'There have been sightings of four so-called aliens all over Surrey – children with great big wings. You guys didn't see anything like that while we were in the woods? They might have passed right over our heads.'

'It was probably some stupid stunt, Dave,' said Smash.

'Yes, although goodness knows how it was done. Do you know something even weirder? There was some very blurry footage of one of these flying creatures. Someone said they'd caught one for a few minutes but then it escaped. It was screaming and shouting and spitting like anything. It looked a little like you! I couldn't help laughing. I bet *you'd* like to fly, wouldn't you, Smash?'

'Not necessarily,' said Smash. 'In fact I really think it wouldn't be that much fun at all.'

We were too tired to get up early and plead for a breakfast picnic, even though it was our last day together and we wanted to make the most of our wish.

We very nearly didn't get a *lunchtime* picnic, because Dad and Alice tried very hard to take us on a proper day out.

'You *can't* want to go off to that very same sandpit spot *again*,' said Dad. 'We were there all day yesterday.'

'We love it there, Dad. Please, please, let's go back there,' I said.

'Well, what's your mum going to think when you go back home tomorrow and she asks what you've done and you say "Oh, we went to the same boring old woods day after day after day, rain or shine"?'

'We won't say that at all, Dad,' I said. 'We'll say we went to the woods, and we all had fantastic picnics together, and then Robbie and Smash and Maudie and I played in the sandpit and we had the best holiday *ever*.'

'Oh, Rosy-Posy,' said Dad, giving me a hug.

Alice looked pleased too, and tried even harder with our last picnic. She made tiny cream-cheese and smoked-salmon bagels, barbecued chicken wings, and a selection of bite-sized sandwiches: egg mayonnaise with toma-toes, crayfish and rocket, Brie and apricot, and turkey and cranberry sauce. We had a French apple pie with tangy cream, and a big bag of red and yellow cheeses. We drank freshly squeezed orange juice and Dad and Alice had a bottle of lemonade – but it smelt like wine.

'We need something chocolatey too,' said Alice. 'Could you be an angel and make your special chocolate crispy cakes, Robbie?'

While Robbie was happily complying, Smash got me to one side.

'What are you going to wish for?' she asked.

'Well . . . I haven't properly decided yet. I want it to be something we *all* want – and I want it to be something that won't go *wrong*.' I started chewing my thumbnail anxiously. 'Only I can't think *what*, exactly.'

I expected Smash to sigh at me impatiently and tell me I was hopeless, but to my great astonishment she suddenly threw her arms round me. In my shock I bit hard on my own thumb, but I decided not to make a fuss.

'You'll think of something, Ros. You're good at that,' Smash said. 'And even if you *don't* we've had lots of amazing wishes – especially mine – and we've all had a great time together. I agree with you – this has truly been the best holiday ever.'

'Oh, Smash!' I said, hugging her back.

'Right, that's enough mushy stuff,' Smash said quickly. 'Let's go and scrape the leftover chocolate out of Robbie's mixing bowl.'

Maudie had got there before us and was happily licking, chocolate all round her mouth and cheeks and chin.

'Maudie's not really supposed to have chocolate,' said Alice. 'Still, I don't suppose it matters just this once.'

'She's turned into a little chocolate flake herself,' said Smash, picking Maudie up.

'Then me want ice cream!' said Maudie, making us all laugh.

Maudie must have thought of her dropped ice cream yesterday, because she clamoured desperately for a Whippy when she saw an ice-cream van on the way to the woods, but Alice wouldn't hear of it.

We ate our splendid picnic appreciatively.

'Three cheers for Alice and her wonderful picnics,' said Dad, raising his glass.

'Hurray, hurray, hurray,' we said, a little awkwardly.

'And one little cheer for me and my chocolate crispy cakes,' said Robbie.

'May we go and play our game now?' I asked.

'Monkey!' said Maudie, grinning. Alice had wiped all round her face with a damp flannel, but she still managed to have smears of chocolate on her nose, like new little freckles.

'Yes, go and play your funny monkey game,' said Dad fondly.

We walked to the sandpit, Smash and Robbie looking at me expectantly. I kept trying to think of something wonderful — and yet I'd learnt to second-guess the Psammead and knew it had a way of making everything turn out to have a down side.

'Have you decided yet, Ros?' asked Smash.

'No!' I wailed, as we started digging.

'Could you perhaps ask the Psammead's advice?' Robbie suggested. He had his lion with him and was making him dig too with his little plastic paws.

'I could try, but I think I read in one of my E. Nesbit books that the Psammead never ever gives advice,' I said.

'It's so weird to think it's in those other books. I wish *I* was in a book like Robert,' said Robbie.

'Maybe we will be one day,' said Smash. She looked at me. 'You turned out to be a children's writer when we were rich and famous so *you'd* better write the book, Rosalind.'

'I could never *really* write a whole book,' I said, but my heart started thumping at the thought. It was also thumping with *effort*. We'd dug quite deep into the sandpit now, but without uncovering a furry paw or a bat ear.

'Where *are* you, Psammead?' said Smash, digging energetically.

'Monkey, Monkey?' said Maudie, scrabbling in the sand.

We dug and dug and dug without any luck.

'We really will be in Australia at this rate,' Robbie panted.

'You don't think he's actually *gone*, do you?' I said, sitting back on my heels.

'To *Australia*?'

'To anywhere. Or someone else might have dug him up and taken him. Because he's never been this far down before.'

'Oh, I do *hope* he's still here,' said Robbie. 'It would be awful if we can't say goodbye.' He lay down in the big hole we'd dug. 'Please come and see us one last time, Psammead!' he called.

'We'd just like *one* more wish!' said Smash. 'Though if you could manage a few more for me next week that would be good too.'

'Dear Psammead, please, please come and see us, even if it's just to say goodbye,' I said.

'Monkey! Monkey, Monkey, Monkey!' Maudie called.

There was a sudden little eruption deep down in the

sand. An eye stalk peeped out and regarded us crossly –
then another.

'Oh, Psammead, it's *you*!' I said.

The Psammead's wrinkled little face emerged, its ears
quivering.

'Of course it's me. Who *else* would it be? I am the
sole resident of this sandpit. Woe betide any rabbits
or rodents who attempt to burrow in beside me,' said
the Psammead, easing its whole self out of the sand.
It stretched and yawned enormously, its eyes twitching
on their delicate stalks. 'Oh dear, I'm still so *sleepy*. Why
did you come digging at my door so insistently? Have
I to perform yet another wish? Wish-wish-wish-wish.
You're never satisfied.'

'We're very nearly satisfied, dear Psammead. You've
been tremendously kind and obliging. I know it's a bit
of a cheek, but we were wondering if we could have just
one last wish,' I said.

'Well, so long as it's just the one,' said the Psammead.
'Then I think I'll hibernate for a while. I had to dig far
down yesterday to avoid that loathsome torrential rain.
Excuse me, my whiskers are quivering at the thought. I
very nearly got a drenching. But when I was eventually
enveloped in wondrous dry sand an unusual lassitude
came over me. I'm worn out with all this daily wishing.
I need to rest and recuperate.'

'Yes, we quite understand, dear Mr Psammead,' said
Robbie, giving it a sympathetic stroke.

'Just *one* more wish then?' said Smash. 'Dear, kind, sweet, extra-generous Mr Psammead.'

The Psammead rocked backwards and forwards on its back paws, idly scratching its furry tummy. Its eyes swivelled round, taking us all in.

'Just one *last* wish,' it said eventually.

'Hurray!' Smash cried, making the Psammead jump and flap its ears in protest.

'Will you kindly stop shouting right in my ear? I have very superior sensitive hearing and it is therefore extremely painful.'

'I'm sorry!' Smash whispered. She nudged me. 'Hurry up and wish, Rosalind.'

'Yes, go on, Ros,' said Robbie.

'Wish, wish, wish,' said Maudie.

They all looked at me. The Psammead drummed its fingers on its fur impatiently.

I swallowed, struggling. 'I – I wondered – it seems incredibly greedy, but could we . . . ?'

'Spit it *out*, Ros!' said Smash.

'Would it be possible for us each to have our heart's desire?' I said.

'You what?' said Smash.

'I know it sounds a weird wish. I found it in a book of fairy stories,' I said.

'Oh, typical,' said Smash. 'How is that going to work if it's part of a flipping *fairy* story?'

'Would you mind holding your tongue, Miss Shouty

Person,' said the Psammead. 'I think fairy stories are eminently suitable, as I am indeed a sand-*fairy*. I think it's an admirable wish, Rosalind.'

'But what *is* our heart's desire?' said Smash.

'I thought the Psammead could maybe work it out itself, as it's so magic and all-powerful,' I said.

'Exactly,' said the Psammead, preening.

Then it hopped nimbly right up to me and put its strange monkey fingers on my temples. Its ancient eyes focused on me, staring directly into mine. I felt as if it was looking right inside my head and learning what was there. Then it backed away and did the same to Robbie. The Psammead moved on to Smash reluctantly. She giggled and fidgeted as it took hold of her.

'Be still!' it commanded, and she sat suddenly rigid, biting her lip.

I wondered for an awful moment if the Psammead was cursing her, turning her into a statue to teach her a terrible lesson, but when it backed away from her she blinked and rubbed her eyes. The Psammead hopped over to Maudie, inspecting her carefully first to make sure she wasn't too damp or sticky. It put its wrinkled face close to hers and gently laid its paws on her forehead. Maudie wasn't the slightest bit overawed, like us. She pursed her lips and gave it a big kiss, hugging it enthusiastically.

'Lovely Monkey!' she said.

The Psammead wriggled and squirmed.

'You're quite a lovely small child,' it muttered, and then it backed away from her, wiping its paws.

It stood contemplating us for a few seconds, its little eyes very dark and beady on the end of their strange stalks. Then it started puffing itself up.

We watched as it got fatter and fatter and fatter, larger than we'd ever seen it before. Its eyes twitched, its ears pulled taut, its paws extended at full stretch. It stood there, swaying with effort, a pulsating puffball. Then it suddenly collapsed down into a small shrunken creature, still quivering with effort. It crawled to the centre of the sandpit and started digging. It paused, halfway into the sand.

'Goodbye,' it said, in a tremulous voice.

'Goodbye, dear Psammead,' I said. 'And thank you so, so much.'

'We will see you again, won't we?' Robbie asked anxiously. 'After you've hibernated yourself back to full health?'

The Psammead mumbled something, but it was scrabbling so hard we couldn't quite hear what it said. It gave one last scrabble and disappeared entirely.

'Was that a yes?' said Smash.

'It might have been,' I said.

'I do *hope* it was a yes,' said Robbie.

'Monkey gone!' said Maudie, holding out her arms as if she were trying to snatch him back.

We all looked at the empty sand. Then we looked at each other. We waited. And nothing at all happened.

'Well?' said Smash. 'Is that *it*?'

'I – I suppose so,' I said.

'But where's the magic?' said Robbie.

'Where *Monkey*?' said Maudie.

'Monkey's gone now, darling. Look, all gone,' said Smash, patting the sand. 'And it looks like all the magic has gone with him!'

'But we saw him puff up like crazy,' said Robbie. 'He really was wishing for us.'

'Wishing *what*?' said Smash.

'Whatever our heart's desire is,' I said.

'Well, it hasn't worked, has it, because you all know *I* want to be rich and famous, and so that's my heart's desire. Yet there's no sign of that bodyguard and the limo and all those crowds of fans,' said Smash. She took a deep breath and sang, 'I'm just an angry girl.' Her voice sounded thin and reedy.

'No sign of any voice either,' said Robbie unkindly.

'What about you, Tree Boy? Go on, have a go at climbing. That's your heart's desire, isn't it?'

'I'm not sure now,' said Robbie, but he stood up and went to the nearest tree. He stared up at its length and spat on his hands.

'Careful, Robbie!' I said.

He leapt for the first branch – and missed.

'Whoops,' said Smash. 'And what about you, Rosalind?' She scrabbled in my jacket pocket for my book. 'Is this your own first novel?'

I couldn't help looking at it with mad hopefulness – but it was my crumpled dog-eared copy of *Five Children and It*. I flicked open the pages and found a drawing of Anthea, Jane, Cyril, Robert and the Lamb. I stroked Anthea's hair as if I were brushing it.

'Maybe the Psammead thinks my heart's desire is to meet Anthea again?' I said. 'Perhaps she'll come back to our time?'

We all looked around but there was no sign of any of the book children.

'They've all gone away,' Maudie sang softly.

'Oh no, *please* don't have wished those nursery-rhyme nutters back! That would really do my head in,' said Smash.

We looked around us again, but couldn't see any of them, not a cat or a sneezing child or a black-and-white girl clutching a kettle.

'What a waste of a wish,' said Smash.

'Monkey, Monkey,' said Maudie.

'Maybe that's it!' I said. 'Maybe *that's* what we all desired? To see the Psammead again!'

'I bet that's right,' said Robbie. 'Oh, clever Ros! So next time we come and stay with Dad and Alice we can see it all over again and have lots more wishes.'

'Well, we could have done with *one* more right this minute,' said Smash. 'What are we going to do *now*?'

'Play Monkey!' said Maudie.

So we invented as many monkey games as we could

295

think of. We played Catch the Monkey, which was just an ordinary chasing game, with all of us taking turns to catch Maudie the Monkey, and tickle her each time. Then we played Monkey Goes Round the Sandpit, which is self-explanatory and made us all very hot and dizzy. Then we played pretending to *be* a monkey. We scratched ourselves and jumped about making ooh-ooh-ooh monkey noises. Then we sat down exhausted and played I Went Along the Road and Saw a Monkey.

'I went along the road and saw a monkey and a little kitten,' I said, and pointed at Robbie to go next.

'I went along the road and saw a monkey and a little kitten and a big roaring lion,' said Robbie, pointing to Smash.

'I went along the road and saw a monkey and a little kitten and a big roaring lion and a rock star playing a guitar,' said Smash. She pointed at Maudie. We all had to help her, chanting it along with her.

'I went along the road and saw a monkey and a little kitten and a big roaring lion and a rock star playing a guitar – and an ice cream!' said Maudie.

We carried on and on and on until the list was ridiculously long and Maudie and Robbie had long ago dropped out, but Smash and I wouldn't give up, gabbling great long lists of nonsense until we dissolved into giggles.

'I won!' said Smash.

'Rubbish, *I* won!' I said.

So we started *another* game of I Went Along the Road and Saw a Monkey, laughing helplessly. Smash invented a rude version of the game which made us laugh even more.

'This is weird,' said Smash breathlessly. 'We're having almost as much fun as if we'd had a proper wish.'

'Maybe that's the wish then? Our heart's desire is for us all to play together and have fun,' I said, trying not to be too disappointed. 'That's the way it would work out at the end of a Victorian storybook. The children would all be taught a moral lesson and learn to like each other and make their own amusements.'

'Those Victorian storybooks sound horribly preachy and dull,' said Smash. 'And if that's the case it's a bit of a waste of a wish, because we do that anyway. Play and like each other and have fun.'

'You don't like me very much,' said Robbie.

'Oh, you're okay – in small doses. In fact I could honestly say you might even be my favourite brother,' said Smash, tickling him.

She didn't *have* any other brothers, but Robbie still seemed delighted with the compliment and squealed happily. Then we all had a tickling contest. It was most fun tickling Maudie because she went into peal after peal of laughter if you tickled her, rolling around helplessly, bright red in the face. I got a little anxious about her, but when I made the others stop she cried, 'More! More tickle! More, more, more!'

'It sounds like you guys are having great fun,' Dad called.

'Watch out for Maudie, though. She'll wet herself if you're not careful!' said Alice.

They were clearly not in their usual trance – and when a lot of black clouds clustered above us they started gathering up the picnic things.

'Come on, you lot, it looks like it's going to pour again. We don't want to get soaked to the skin like yesterday. Let's go home,' said Dad.

I paused by the sandpit. I patted it smooth and tidy with the palm of my hand. Then I wrote with a twig:

THANK YOU SO MUCH FOR EVERYTHING.
R. I. P.

'Who's Rip?' said Robbie.

'It's what people put on gravestones. The Psammead's not *dead*, Rosalind,' said Smash.

'Yes, I know, it's just resting, and R. I. P. means Rest in Peace, and that's what I want it to do,' I said. I gave the sand another little pat, as if I were stroking the Psammead itself.

Then we walked back through the woods together. There was an ice-cream van tinkling away at the end of the road. Maudie jumped up and down and went 'Please! Please! Please!'

'No, Maudie, don't be silly. You don't want a nasty cold

ice cream full of chemicals,' said Alice, which was silly of
her, because it was clear Maudie wanted one desperately.

'Please, Mum, let her have one. She was so upset when
she dropped hers yesterday and I think it was maybe
my fault,' said Smash, without thinking.

'Maudie had an ice cream yesterday?' said Alice.

'Well, *no*, that's the point. Look, let me buy one for
her. Let me buy *all* of you an ice cream,' said Smash as
a diversionary tactic.

Alice looked like she still wanted to argue, but Dad
said quickly, 'I think that's a brilliant idea, Smash. How
kind of you.'

So we all had an ice cream as we walked home. Smash
made sure Maudie's was the biggest ice cream of all,
with raspberry sauce and rainbow sprinkles. Maudie
nuzzled into it, her eyes shining. She got tired of it long
before it was finished, but it gave her a good ten minutes
of exquisite pleasure.

'Do you think ice cream was maybe Maudie's heart's
desire?' Smash asked me.

'Maybe,' I said.

'Well, lucky her, because she's had it now and it can't
get taken away from her after sunset, unless she's sick,
and I don't think the Psammead would be that mean,
not to Maudie,' said Smash. 'I think it might be *very*
mean to me, though. It doesn't like me at all.'

'Yes, it does. I don't know why you always say that. It
just doesn't like you shouting,' I said.

'Anyway, I can't see how it would ever give me my heart's desire, seeing as I've already had it. You can't get better than a gig at the O2 arena,' said Smash.

'You were truly great that day,' I said loyally.

'Yes, I was, wasn't I?' said Smash. 'I wish everyone could have seen me.'

'You had *thousands* of people seeing you, silly.'

'Yes, but not people like . . . like my dad. Or my mum. Or even *your* dad,' said Smash. She paused. 'He doesn't like me either.'

'Yes, he does.'

'No, he doesn't. I catch him looking at me sometimes, and it's as if he's wondering how his lovely little Alice could possibly have such a dreadful difficult daughter,' said Smash. 'What am I going to *do* next week when you and Robbie are gone?'

'You can play with Maudie. Don't you dare say *she* doesn't like you, because you know perfectly well you're her favourite,' I said. 'She loves her Smash-Smash.'

'Smash-Smash!' said Maudie, and she ran to hold Smash's hand. Maudie was still covered in ice cream and very sticky indeed, but Smash picked her up and gave her a piggyback all the way home.

'You kids had better start packing,' said Dad. 'You don't want to leave it all to the morning – we'll be in a bit of a rush. Can you phone your mum, Rosalind, and tell her I'm aiming to get you home about lunchtime tomorrow?'

I phoned Mum. She didn't answer for ages and then

when she *did*, there was so much noise her end we could hardly hear each other.

'Where are you *now*, Mum?'

'Oh, we're all in this pub, celebrating the end of our course,' said Mum.

'You're in a pub in the *afternoon*?' I said.

Mum giggled. 'Don't sound so disapproving, darling.'

'I'm not, it's just I'd have thought you'd go out celebrating this evening.'

'Oh, we've got a party this evening. It's going to be great fun,' said Mum.

'So you've liked your course, Mum?' I asked.

'I've had the best time ever,' said Mum. Then she paused. 'I mean, the best time I could ever have without you two. But you said you were having a good time at Dad's this holiday?'

'Yes, the best ever,' I said.

'I'm so glad. And Robbie's okay too? Can I have a little word with him?'

I called Robbie to the phone. I could hear Mum asking him what he'd done this holiday.

'We had lots and lots of picnics – really super picnics with heaps of different yummy things to eat, not just sandwiches,' said Robbie.

Alice was busy washing Maudie's face and hands, but I think she heard because she went pink and smiled.

Mum was asking Robbie what else he'd done.

'Oh, heaps and heaps,' he said. 'I climbed some trees

and I looked after all my animals and I did lots of cooking. Alice lets me make my chocolate crispy cakes. She says they're her favourites.'

He wasn't being tactful.

'Better tell Mum you miss her,' I mouthed at him.

'Oh, I *do* miss you, Mum,' said Robbie. 'Alice is very nice but she's not one bit as lovely as *you*, Mum.'

I think Alice heard, but she didn't seem to mind. 'You can make more chocolate crispy cakes for our tea, Robbie,' she said. 'And maybe we could make some biscuits? How would you like to make a gingerbread man?'

'Could I possibly make a gingerbread lion?' asked Robbie.

'Well, we'll have a go,' said Alice. She nodded at Smash and me. 'Come on, you girls. Let's all make gingerbread animals.'

Dad said he had some shopping to do so he went out, while we all baked. Alice didn't have special animal-shaped cutters, so our gingerbread lions and elephants and gorillas and giraffes spread into strange new species with bloated bodies – though they tasted very good. Maudie joined in too, making a round blob with paws sticking out of its sides. It had funny little stick-on eyes and a big raisin smile.

'Oh, darling, that's so lovely,' said Alice. 'What is it?'

'Monkey!' said Maudie proudly.

Alice took photographs of all our lumpy gingerbread animals. She took photos of us too. She took several more of Smash playing with Maudie. Smash groaned and pulled silly faces.

'Stop messing about, Smash. Smile properly,' said Alice.

'What are you taking a photo of *me* for, Mum? Just take Maudie. I'll only spoil it.'

'No, you won't. I want a photo of my two girls,' said Alice. 'I'll take one of you two together, then one of all four of you, and then one of you just by yourself. You can download it on to your computer and send it to your dad.'

'As if he cares,' said Smash – but she stopped pulling faces and gave Maudie a hug as Alice snapped away. Before Alice took the last photo, Smash quickly ran her hands through her hair and sucked in her stomach and smiled earnestly at the camera.

'There, you look great, Smash, see,' said Alice, showing her the little Smash image in the camera.

'No, I don't. I look awful!' Smash protested, but she looked pleased even so.

She went to get her computer.

'I'm going to download them all. I want to keep them,' said Smash. 'I'm not going to bother sending any to Dad. He's clearly not fussed about me. He hasn't sent an email for days and days and . . . ooh!'

'What?'

'He has, he has! He's sent me an email – oh my God, it's a whole *page*.' She read it all the way through, her eyes shining.

'Happy now?' said Alice.

'He says he's having a great time – but he's missing me,' said Smash.

'Well, of course he is,' said Alice. '*I* miss you terribly when you're not here.'

Smash stared at her.

'You are such a dreadful fibber, Mum,' she said, pretending to punch Alice on the arm.

'I'm *not* fibbing,' said Alice, putting her arm round Smash.

For a split second they leant against each other and hugged. Then Smash wrinkled her nose and said, 'Yuck, Mum, do you *have* to wear that rosy perfume? It gets right up my nose.'

Alice tucked Smash's hair behind her ears appraisingly and said, 'I do wish you'd let me have your hair styled properly – you look such a mophead.'

They looked at each other and laughed. Smash went off to write an immensely long email back to her dad, Robbie lined up all his animals for a grand race across the carpet and Maudie snuggled up to Alice for a storytelling session. Alice patiently read *The Tiger Who Came to Tea* five times in a row, and Robbie lent Maudie his tiger so she could act it out.

I wandered off and flicked through all my books, but I couldn't seem to settle to any of them. I loved Anthea and Jane, especially now, and I also liked Bobbie and Phyllis; I cared about Pauline, Petrova and Posy; I admired Sara Crewe; I felt sorry for Mary Lennox; I felt like a fifth sister to Meg, Jo, Beth and Amy – but for once I didn't feel like immersing myself in their lives. My *own* life had become just as dramatic and exciting as any storybook.

I heard the car draw up outside the house. It was Dad coming back from his shopping trip.

'Kids? Come and see what I've got,' he called.

I thought he'd just gone to Sainsbury's for the weekend food shopping, but when I went downstairs I saw he was holding a big *cage* in his hands.

'Robbie? Where are you, son?' Dad called, setting the cage down in the living room.

Robbie came running in, a plastic animal in each hand – and then stood still. He dropped his lion and elephant on the carpet where they lay, paws in the air, forgotten. Robbie stepped towards the cage cautiously, trembling with excitement.

'I know your mum has a No Pet policy, and I understand. You can't have a dog cooped up in your little flat, and it wouldn't be fair to it anyway when you're out all day – but I thought this little chappie wouldn't cause too much trouble.'

Robbie knelt down in front of the cage, his eyes huge. He peered through the bars. Two beady brown eyes peered back at him.

'It's a hamster!' Robbie whispered. 'Oh, can I get him out, Dad, just so I can say hello to him properly?'

'Yes, if you're careful,' said Dad.

'Very, very careful!' said Alice nervously.

Robbie undid the side of the cage and slipped his hand in slowly. He stroked the hamster on the tip of its golden head, down its little wriggly body, and then gently picked it up. The hamster scrabbled for a moment.

'Watch him!' said Alice.

Robbie held it cupped in his hands, whispering to it reassuringly. The hamster looked up at him as if it understood straight away that it was safe and protected.

'Do you like him, son?' Dad asked.

'Oh, Dad, I *love* him.'

'Look at you! You've got a real knack with animals, I can see that. So what are you going to call him?'

'His name's Giant,' said Robbie, stroking the tiny creature.

'He's so sweet. Look at his little nose twitching!' I said. 'Oh, Robs, you're so lucky.'

'You can share him if you like,' said Robbie. 'You can come and stroke him whenever I'm busy.'

'Can *I* have a stroke, Robbie?' said Smash. 'Oh, Dave, can't I have a hamster too?'

'No!' said Alice. 'Absolutely not.'

'You can share him with Robbie and me if you like, Smash,' I said.

'Yeah, but you're going home tomorrow!'

'Well, we could send you bulletins about him, and photos, and you can maybe come and visit him.'

'Can I?' said Smash.

'Only you have to be extra quiet and gentle and never ever shout or he'll panic,' said Robbie.

'Am I ever anything else?' said Smash, which made us all laugh.

'I've got *you* a little present, Smash,' said Dad, fumbling in a carrier. He brought out a little folded black thing. Smash took it uncertainly. She shook it out.

'What is it? A swimming costume?' she said.

'It's a leotard. You know, girls wear them when they're doing gymnastics. I know you said you weren't interested, but when I saw my mate Tim in the gym he was still talking about you. He's still running his gym courses and I wondered if you'd find it fun after all. You could start on Monday.' Dad paused. 'Of course, you don't *have* to go. In fact maybe it was a stupid idea.'

'No, no, it's a great idea,' said Smash. She was very red in the face. 'Thanks, Dave,' she said awkwardly. 'Hey, will that boy who beat me at Shipwreck be there too? I hope so. I'm *so* going to beat him back.'

'What's in your other carrier, David?' Alice asked.

'I nipped into a bookshop. I picked this up for Maudie, seeing as she liked that nursery-rhyme puppet show so much. It looks kind of familiar, all these funny pictures. Did I give you the same book when you were little, Rosy-Posy?'

'Oh, Dad, yes, the exact same one. Look, Maudie!' I flipped through the book. 'Who's that?' I said.

'Hey diddle diddle, the cat and the fiddle!' Maudie shouted, stabbing at the page delightedly.

'And these two?' I said, turning the pages.

'Jack and Jill, Jack and Jill!' Maudie cried.

'Good heavens, how does she know that?' said Alice. 'She's not *reading*, is she?'

Maudie chuckled. I found her the Ring-o'-roses page. She circled her finger round the dancing children and then went, 'Atishoo atishoo!'

'My goodness, that's right!' said Dad.

'I bet she knows this one too,' I said, flipping backwards and forwards through the book. 'There! Who are *they*, Maudie?'

'Polly and Sukey and the kettle!' said Maudie. 'Oh dear, they've all gone away.'

'We've got a child genius!' said Dad. He was fishing in his carrier bag. 'I wanted to find a book for you too, Rosy-Posy, but it's so difficult, you've read so many. So in the end I plumped for this.' He handed me a big fat blue book with a lovely swirly marbled cover. I took hold of it and opened it at the first page. It was empty.

'It's a notebook. I thought you might like to write your own stories in it,' said Dad.

'Oh, Dad, that's a really fantastic present!' I said.

'You can write all about this holiday,' said Smash.

'All the sandpit part,' said Robbie meaningfully.

'And then you can get it published and end up with a whole long queue of people at a book-signing!' said Smash.

I stroked the blank pages – and then wrote the very first sentence in my best handwriting. Dad and Alice started preparing tea together. Smash changed into her leotard and did a few practice handstands. Robbie started training his hamster to run on the little wheel inside his cage. Maudie sat with the nursery-rhyme book in her lap, singing to all her favourites.

'I think the Psammead *did* work its magic after all,' I said. 'Robbie's got a real live animal to love and I might just write a proper story and Smash has suddenly got everyone liking her. The Psammead looked into all our hearts and saw what we *really* wanted.'

'What about Maudie?' said Smash. 'Do you think it really was that ice cream?'

I went and knelt down beside Maudie.

'Maudie, listen a minute.'

'Hey diddle diddle,' sang Maudie, pointing to the right page.

'Yes, it's a lovely book.'

'Jack and Jill went up the hill.'

'Maudie, concentrate a minute. When we were all by the sandpit and the Psammead – you know, the monkey, when it was looking right at you, remember?'

'Atishoo atishoo,' Maudie sneezed.

'What were you thinking about when you were cuddled up with the monkey?'

'They've all gone away,' Maudie sang, shaking her head. 'Monkey gone away.'

'Yes, I know.'

'But Monkey come *back*,' said Maudie.

'Do you think so? Is that what you were hoping?' Smash asked.

'Yes, my Monkey. See Monkey more,' said Maudie.

'We all hope so,' said Smash. 'Oh, you clever little thing, Maudie. I bet that *was* your heart's desire, to see Monkey again and again and again.'

'But hang on,' said Robbie, looking stricken. 'If it's a Psammead wish it will stop happening as soon as it's sunset. Oh no, I can't bear it if Giant disappears!'

But when we went to bed that night, long after dark, Giant was still happily squeaking in his cage, and Smash's dad had sent her another email. And my notebook still had its first sentence:

'What's that you're reading?' said Smash, grabbing the book out of my hand.

'I adore E. Nesbit's books' – Jacqueline Wilson

FIVE CHILDREN and IT

E. Nesbit

I do hope you read Edith Nesbit's wonderful story Five Children and It. It's not only one of Rosalind's favourite books – I love it too. I read it over and over again as a child and wondered what I would wish for if I ever discovered a Psammead.

Why not try one of E. Nesbit's other stories too? She wrote two more books about Anthea, Cyril, Robert and Jane: The Story of the Amulet and The Phoenix and the Carpet. The Story of the Treasure Seekers is also one of my favourites – and perhaps her most perfect book is The Railway Children. The mother in that book is a writer who always has buns for tea if she sells a story. I like to do that too!

When I read a biography of E. Nesbit, I discovered that she also had a new silver bangle to celebrate the publication of each book – whereas I always choose a special silver ring. If the Psammead really would grant me a wish, I'd love to go back in time and meet E. Nesbit. I hope we'd discuss writing and children, and maybe she'd swap one of her silver bangles for one of my rings.

Read on for an extract from

Five Children and It

The children dug and they dug and they dug, and their hands got sandy and hot and red, and their faces got damp and shiny. The Lamb had tried to eat the sand, and had cried so hard when he found that it was not, as he had supposed, brown sugar, that he was now tired out, and was lying asleep in a warm fat bunch in the middle of the half-finished castle. This left his brothers and sisters free to work really hard, and the hole that was to come out in Australia soon grew so deep that Jane, who was called 'Pussy' for short, begged the others to stop.

'Suppose the bottom of the hole gave way suddenly,' she said, 'and you tumbled out among the little Australians, all the sand would get in their eyes.'

'Yes,' said Robert; 'and they would hate us, and throw stones at us, and not let us see the kangaroos, or opossums, or blue-gums, or Emu Brand birds, or anything.'

Cyril and Anthea knew that Australia was not quite so near as all that, but they agreed to stop using the spades and go on with their hands. This was quite easy, because the sand at the bottom of the hole was very soft and fine and dry, like sea-sand. And there were little shells in it.

'Fancy it having been wet sea here once, all sloppy and shiny,' said Jane, 'with fishes and conger-eels and coral and mermaids.'

'And masts of ships and wrecked Spanish treasure. I wish we could find a gold doubloon, or something,' Cyril said.

'How did the sea get carried away?' Robert asked.

'Not in a pail, silly,' said his brother. 'Father says the earth got too hot underneath, like you do in bed sometimes, so it just hunched up its shoulders, and the sea had to slip off, like the blankets do off us, and the shoulder was left sticking out, and turned into dry land. Let's go and look for shells; I think that little cave looks likely, and I see something sticking out there like a bit of wrecked ship's anchor, and it's beastly hot in the Australian hole.'

The others agreed, but Anthea went on digging. She always liked to finish a thing when she had once begun it. She felt it would be a disgrace to leave that hole without getting through to Australia.

The cave was disappointing, because there were no shells, and the wrecked ship's anchor turned out to be only the broken end of a pickaxe handle, and the cave party were just making up their minds that the sand makes you thirstier when it is not by the seaside, and someone had suggested going home for lemonade, when Anthea suddenly screamed:

'Cyril! Come here! Oh, come quick! It's alive! It'll get away! Quick!'